ARACHNE'S WEB

ELIZABETH CORRIGAN

*To the Towson Science Fiction and
Fantasy Writers Group that was
Without you, this book would not exist.*

PART I

CHAPTER 1

Present Day

ROSLYN TURIN SANK INTO THE plush white chair in her psychologist's office. "I think I'm losing my mind."

Dr. Tanner set her datapad on her streamlined silver desk. She was younger than Roslyn had expected a doctor to be, in her late twenties at most, and prettier, with shiny brown hair, tanned skin, and long-lashed brown eyes. "And what causes these thoughts?"

Roslyn stared out the panoramic window behind her therapist. At that hour of the evening, the planet Orpheus hung large in the purple sky, and the crescent moon of Daedalus glimmered in the background. "It all started with the tests for university. You're from off-world, so maybe you don't know. All graduating students on Ariadne, even the servers, are required to take them, even though only the most talented and brilliant students will perform well enough to get scholarships."

Her eyes darted back to her therapist as she folded her hands together then separated them again. "I knew I had no chance of getting in. I mean, I'm good enough at school but nothing special. And I'm not rich like my friend Bliss. My parents are dead, but they were born servers. This was my only chance to do something else—my only chance to be free."

Dr. Tanner pushed a button on her datapad, and it made a small chirping noise as it lit up. "And you were disappointed you didn't get in."

"No, that's the thing." The faux-leather cushion squeaked as Roslyn moved forward in her chair. "I *did* get in. I tested off the charts in art history and archaeology, though I've never studied either subject. I've always been good at drawing but not enough to do it professionally. When I saw all these paintings I'd never seen before in my life, I suddenly knew which of the old masters had painted them and in what style—Monet, Picasso, Aderfell, Ciorelli, Inoue."

She gestured furiously with her hands. "And archaeology! Most of those techniques are totally outdated now since we're light-years away from the ancient civilizations on Earth. But I knew about the techniques of digging artifacts and authenticating them as well as more recent methods of data analysis. It was like I had held objects from hundreds of years ago in my hands and appraised them."

Roslyn caught a glimpse of her reflection in the window. She looked as crazy as she sounded, her normally pale face flushed with excitement, strands of straight brown hair hanging loose from her messy bun. Even her hazel eyes held a glint of the demonic in them. "And that's not even the craziest part."

Dr. Tanner didn't look as if what she had heard so far perturbed her at all. If anything, she seemed mildly interested, as if Roslyn had described a new restaurant, not an experience that defied all reason. "And what is, as you say, the craziest part?"

Roslyn raised a helpless hand then dropped it to the armrest. "I have these dreams—dreams where I'm someone else."

Dr. Tanner reached out and straightened the holographic photo emitter on her desk. It displayed her standing next to a handsome blond man with his arms wrapped around a child who had her brown hair and his blue eyes. "And who do you think you are in these dreams?"

"Somebody else. Somebody rich. Somebody confident." Roslyn picked at the hangnail on her thumb. "It's stupid. I mean, that's not my life. I know it's not. I was born a server on Ariadne, and when that happens, you *stay* a server on Ariadne. Really, I should be grateful for that, because I get all kinds of benefits people on Orpheus or the other moons don't have. I get everything I need to live on and two weeks' vacation every year to one of the local resorts. Crime on Ariadne is lower than anywhere else. I get full health care benefits. If I were a factory worker on Daedalus who needed to see a therapist, I wouldn't be able to."

"That's not—"

"And I know I haven't always been grateful for this." Roslyn pulled harder at the loose piece of skin. "I used to get all up in arms about how we should be free. I blame my best friend, Bliss. I mean, really, I'm her personal server, but her parents let us play together when we were little, and she's more like a sister than anything else. That's always given me a fair degree of privilege. Like, she gives me all her old clothes when she replaces her wardrobe every season. Which means my clothes are always a year out of date, but they're a lot nicer than what I could afford on my clothing stipend, and I can save that money instead. Apparently, it gave me the idea I was as good as the Bhanushalis, and I know that's wrong."

"I know you think—"

"My dad died less than a year ago, and I've had to grow up a lot since then." Roslyn yanked, and her hangnail came free. "I have to learn to take care of myself. Even with my savings, I'm never going to have the opportunity to go somewhere else, and even if I did, what would I do? Bliss is off at university, which means that while she's gone, I spend all my time taking care of her dog. What kind of future would

I have anywhere else?" She realized her cuticle was oozing blood and stuck her thumb in her mouth, finally giving Dr. Tanner the opportunity to speak.

"Roslyn." Her voice was firm but not unkind. "I want to hear all about your life, and I will need a proper history from you, but first, in order for me to help you, I need you to tell me about your dreams."

Roslyn sucked on her thumb for a few seconds then removed it from her mouth. "Right. The dreams." She examined her cuticle. It throbbed, pulsing white and red, but it had stopped bleeding. "I'm this other woman. I mean, she looks like me, and she sounds like me, and she has my name, but... her whole life, it's like nothing I've experienced."

Dr. Tanner picked up a stylus and made notes on her datapad. "What is her life like?"

"She's... an antiques dealer, I think. She appraises art and all kinds of old computers and things. Just like..." Roslyn ran her finger along her thumb where the hangnail used to be, looking for remaining bits of loose skin.

"Just like you did in your tests." Dr. Tanner tapped her stylus against her lips. "If you did well enough on those tests to get a scholarship, why aren't you at university?"

Roslyn dropped her hands in her lap and flopped back in her chair. "Because Dr. Sienko didn't believe me. He's the head of our school board. He's friends with the Bhanushalis and has always looked down on me because he thinks I'm an upstart server girl. So when he saw my name come up on the scholarship list, he investigated it very closely. Since I never took any classes in art history, he accused me of cheating—which I didn't, unless stealing answers from a past life is against the rules."

Dr. Tanner frowned. "Is that what you think these dreams are? Memories of a past life?"

Roslyn scanned the knickknacks on the silver end table to her left. The odd symbols on a spherical metal ball at the end of the table caught her attention, but she couldn't quite place why. *Probably some ancient language that came with the rest of my archaeology knowledge.* "I don't know. If they are, they must be from a recent life. That Roslyn girl had a shop in Rhodes, and the town was only built twenty or so years ago. Besides, she looks exactly the same as me and has the same name. That wouldn't happen with reincarnation."

She picked up a red cube with black diamonds on the side and studied it. "But the thing is, I know everything about her. She has a journalist brother named Will who lives on Orpheus. She lives with her boyfriend, Gavin. He's a doctor, a celebrated surgeon. Her whole life is perfect, yet she's missing something."

"I think that's very important." Dr. Tanner's datapad made a few more blipping noises.

"It is?" Roslyn put down the cube and ran her fingers over the stones in the small, rectangular Zen garden.

"Yes. Don't you see, Roslyn?" Dr. Tanner's voice remained calm. "You're unhappy with your life. You know you're quite fortunate, but you still feel something is missing. You create this world where you have everything you imagine you want, and you still feel the same emptiness. I think this feeling of isolation is what we need to work on. We can find ways to fill it together. What do you think?"

Roslyn lifted the small rake and combed the sand. "You could be right. But it doesn't explain how I know about art. And it doesn't explain the other dreams."

"Other dreams?"

Focusing on creating straight lines in the grains around the rocks, Roslyn nodded. "They come after the ones about Other Roslyn. They're... darker, scarier. I'm in a dimly lit room, and a deep male voice speaks to me in a language I don't recognize. As he speaks, strange runes made of blue light flash in front of me, but I don't recognize them from anything the other Roslyn has studied. I can't understand his words, but I know the voice is telling me, *ordering* me, to read these symbols."

She cocked her head to the side as her gaze fell back on the metal sphere near the far end of the table. *Now I know where I've seen them.* "They look like this!" She whipped her head around to look at Dr. Tanner. "I've never seen these symbols anywhere but inside my head. Where did you get this?"

"I'm not sure." Dr. Tanner stood up and walked around her desk, her stiletto heels making small ripping noises as they snagged the burgundy carpet. Leaning over and peering at the sphere, she said, "Oh, that. I got it from some bric-a-brac dealer back on Orpheus. He tried to sell it as an alien device I could unlock if I found the proper code." She laughed as if she didn't believe such a thing were possible. "I figured it was either a relic from some forgotten civilization or a prop from a science fiction movie. Either way, I liked it, and it was cheap, so I bought it for my office."

"Do you know what this means?" Roslyn's heart beat faster. "This is the first evidence I've had my dreams are real!"

Dr. Tanner tsked and leaned back against her desk. "Now, Roslyn. I would not be doing you any favors if I encouraged these thoughts you have that your dreams are somehow memories. Most likely, you have simply seen an object similar to this and have incorporated the symbols into your dream. What we must do is figure out why your unconscious is creating these dreams and what the images mean to you. But first I need you to understand and accept the false nature of these visions. And to that end, I have a homework assignment for you."

Setting the sphere back on the table, Roslyn said, "Okay."

Dr. Tanner smiled. "Every time you have one of these dreams or every time you find yourself believing they might be real, I want you to repeat to yourself that they are manifestations of your discontentment. After that, you should remind yourself of all the positive things in your life."

Roslyn sank back in her chair. "I can do that, I guess.

But wouldn't it be better to investigate? To see if I can find any evidence of those dreams being real?"

"No, Roslyn. Our goal is to make you more content with yourself and your life. Attempting to reinforce your fantasies won't help with that." Dr. Tanner picked up her datapad and made a note. "Investigating the veracity of your dreams will only make you focus on them more."

Roslyn glanced at the sphere. She wanted to argue, but she didn't think Dr. Tanner would listen. *I'll just have to look into the other Roslyn's life on my own. When I find out she really existed, Dr. Tanner will realize I'm telling the truth.*

CHAPTER 2

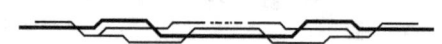

Present Day

"TRAINS IN SPACE. THERE'S JUST something fundamentally wrong with that." Jack Zhao stared at the metallic wall where a window would be on a *real* train and slumped back in his seat. "I mean, how do they even work?"

Cobalt's nose was buried so deeply in his datapad that his only visible feature was his shiny black hair. "Must we have this conversation again? The stations orbit the moons—and Orpheus, of course—and the tracks rotate to keep the route constant. The hull is made of inurdium, which is light and sturdy enough to withstand the pressure. You know all this."

Jack did know. He'd sat through the same science classes as Cobalt—and that was a lot of science classes because Daedalus had been the center of engineering for the system since the human race started mining inurdium there generations ago. He'd stayed awake through enough history classes to know humans had developed the technology to travel to Orpheus after destroying their own planet, Earth, yet a central part of him couldn't shake the awe he felt at humans traveling between the stars.

And what kind of word is inurdium, anyway?

He kicked Cobalt, and that time, his brother looked up. Jack suspected the creases at the corners of Cobalt's almond-shaped dark eyes and the set of his frown matched Jack's in the way only an identical twin's could. He waved his hand at the datapad. "What's so much more interesting than me, anyway?"

"At the moment? Just about everything."

And he's back to ignoring me. Jack wondered how his twin could be so *stolid.* He wouldn't be able to go five minutes without telling Cobalt what he was upset about. After kicking the base of Cobalt's seat a few times, he reached over and grabbed the datapad out of his hand.

"Wha—?" Cobalt's eyebrows went up, but before Jack had flipped the device to face him, Cobalt had crossed his arms and sat back in his seat.

Jack flicked his finger across the datapad to get the title of Cobalt's choice in literature. "The technical manual for the Wingspan-553E?" *Technical manuals indeed. Why does my brother have to be so* boring? *But at least he's got good taste. Wait a minute...*

"Hey, is this what you're going to get with your share of the loot?"

Cobalt's voice dropped to a whisper. "No, I'm not going to get anything with my share of the loot, because we're going to be in jail."

"You worry too much. We're not going to jail. We've done this dozens of times." Jack glanced down at the diagram of the personal spacecraft still visible on Cobalt's datapad. "Hey, does this use a Cleophite engine? Because I'm seriously reconsidering my opinion of it as a tier-1 vessel if it does."

Cobalt snatched his device out of Jack's hand. "Shoplifting from Imri's store and hotwiring a few piloters is not the same as robbing a train." He darted a glance at the door to their private compartment.

"I know. This is going to be so much better. Ten million units in diamond bars. We're going to be rich."

"Why, Jack? Why do we need to do this? We had a good

thing going for us on Daedalus. Mom and Dad's ship repair business was thriving, and we had steady jobs ahead of us."

Jack had to admire Cobalt's last-ditch effort to talk him out of it. *But how can I make him understand? He would be content to repair other people's engines for all eternity.* "I had to get out, Blue."

Cobalt shook his head. "You could have gone to Orpheus, to university. You scored higher than anyone on Daedalus on your tests, though you haven't paid attention to a single lesson since Ms. Aerlin brought a tarantula to class in the third form. You could have gotten a job working on any of the spacecraft that came through the shop. You could have traveled anywhere. Why was grand larceny your only option?"

"I..." *I don't know how to explain it. It's all over my skin any time I think about the future. It's happening right now. It's like electricity—or ants. Like electric ants crawling in my skin, demanding I do something extraordinary, something insane, something no one else would do.* "You don't have to do it. You can sit here while I go do it. You'll have plausible deniability."

Cobalt's frown eased up a bit. "And would you do the tech work or distract the guards?"

"Both. I'll make a plan. I could... I could..."

"Besides, to have plausible deniability, I would have to not know everything I know." Cobalt sighed. "It's fine. I'm in. You know I'm in. I just wish I understood why."

Does he mean why I want to do this or why he's in? "It'll be amazing. You'll see."

"It'll be something." Cobalt glanced down at his datapad. "And of course I'm going to replace the engine on the Wingspan. What do you take me for?"

Jack sauntered down the aisle, admiring the smooth motion of the train and also feeling like trains should rattle more. He focused his senses as he approached his destination. Some raucous laughter emerged from one of the train compartments, and passengers had their noses buried in datapads in another. Since the train's official time matched that of the destination—the moon Ariadne—most compartments were dark, their occupants snoozing through their travel time.

I know they need to fit a lot of people on these trains, but do there have to be so many cars? The Intermoon Express between Daedalus and Ariadne had one hundred twelve cars, so even though his compartment was relatively close to the front, he still had to walk through thirty cars to get to the engine room. *You have to travel nearly the distance to the moon to get to the end. Car, car, car, blah, blah, blah. And poor Cobalt has to walk all the way to the other end.*

At last, his quarry came into sight, and his gut twisted when he saw that a woman was manning—if that was even the right word—the controls. He knew his job was to manipulate her, but pretending to be interested in a woman felt like a betrayal of *her. Maybe just pretending to be interested in the train is enough.*

He hoped the empty swallow going down his throat didn't catch anyone's attention as he smiled for all he was worth and knocked on the empty doorframe leading into the control room.

The woman at the helm turned. Her rosy face was pretty, even if her cheeks were a little too full, and the headband barely holding her curls out of her face was a decade out of style. "Can I help you?"

"I'm so sorry." Jack gave her an innocent look. "I just... I was looking for the dining car and must have gotten turned around. This is the engine room, isn't it?"

"Yep." The engineer's tone had a bite to it. "That's what they call it. The engine's on the other side of that wall, though. This is the control room for the computer, though the AIs mostly run themselves."

Aha. Not annoyed with me. Bored. I can definitely work with that. "Really?" He glanced around the room. "Where are the computers?"

She raised a black datapad. "Everything's on here."

"Would you show me? I'd love to get to know how the train works."

The woman pulled a stool out from under the desk, and Jack took it.

"I'm Jack." He held out his hand.

She shook it. "Chora."

"Like the university?"

She gave him a self-mocking smile. "And the city it's in. My parents are professors. They wanted me to be one, too, but I couldn't imagine being stuck scurrying between a classroom and a research lab all my life. So the first chance I got, I ran away to the stars and haven't looked back. Except for holidays—Dad does the best roast. Sometimes these long trips with nothing to do aren't quite what I signed on for, though."

"I get that." And he did, because that was exactly how he felt. He studied the way Chora bit her lip and wondered if she could be *her*, the girl he was waiting for, the one he had to remain faithful to, and the one he loved. *She can't be. I mean, if she were, I would* know.

Every time Jack decided a girl couldn't be the one he was looking for, Cobalt pointed out it was ridiculous to expect to recognize a girl he couldn't name or describe and whom he had, in fact, never met. But Cobalt was also an aromantic asexual who had a hard time grasping the finer points of love.

"The train pretty much runs itself, all preprogrammed with AIs and stuff." Chora glanced at him out of the corner of her eye. "But of course I have to be here if anything goes wrong."

"Does anything go wrong on the average Daedalus-to-Ariadne jump?"

"Well..." Chora bit her lip and looked out the door. The metallic hall remained as empty as it had a moment ago. "This isn't exactly a run-of-the-mill trip. You see, on Ariadne, some of the megacorps are so rich and powerful they trade in diamond bars. But of course, the diamonds are mined and processed on Daedalus, which means that a couple of times a year, they have to ship the diamonds to Ariadne. I'm not supposed to tell anyone, but this season's shipment is on the train right now."

Well, this is going to be easy, Jack thought as his brain confirmed that Chora was definitely not his lost love. *My girl is hopefully at least a little discreet.* "Show me."

Chora ran her finger across the scanpad a few times until Jack could see the outline of a car. The long lines running parallel to the door were plated inurdium, which would take the diamonds housed between them to cut through. The red dots on either side of the car represented the guards standing there.

"Can I see, like, a live picture? I mean, a whole car full of diamond bars." Jack didn't have to pretend to want to see that. He almost wished he were the mechanical genius so he could be the one standing in the room with all that treasure.

"Hm. We've got cameras in there, but it's dark." Chora pinched her lips as she leaned over the datapad. "Maybe..."

Jack leaned forward, brushing the corner of the pad with his arm. "You've got to be able to—"

"Don't touch that!" Chora ripped the datapad away from him.

He reared back. "Cronos, I'm sorry! I hope I didn't mess anything up."

Chora swiped several times on the datapad in quick succession. "I'm sure it's fine. I— Oh, you just turned the airflow to the secondary system for a minute. That's not a huge deal. I can flip that right back and... There!" She breathed a sigh of relief. "All better! But... I think you should probably go."

"You're right. I don't want you to lose your job. Thanks for the tour." He gave her a half smile and walked out. His step was just a hair springier than it had been on his approach. *Let's see if Cobalt can do his part.*

Four guards on this side of the treasury car. Probably four on the other too. Cobalt eyed the insignia on the blacker-than-black uniforms. *ZimmerCorp.* Zimmer Investments Corporation paid enough to have their pick of graduates from Bellerophon. The moon was dedicated to turning out warriors for the greatest army humanity had ever seen, but since humanity's sole military force had no one to go to war with, most warriors ended up selling out to the corporations rather than keeping the peace.

"It's all leading up to a big war between the megacorps. Mark my words." Cobalt rolled his eyes at the paranoid rants he'd always heard in his head when he thought about Bellerophon. He must have known some rabble-rouser in his past, but all the Daedalytes he could remember were a steadier lot. It must have been one of his parents' regular clients when he was a kid. A lot of pirates came to the shop a few times, then got themselves blown up on a misguided crusade and never came back.

Cobalt took shallow breaths and watched the image of the guards on his datapad. He had crept up the side of the last few cars—kept empty to protect the cargo—careful to keep out of sight of the guard's infrared detectors. He had his coolant suit on to fool them, but the hood was hard to see through, so he didn't want to keep it on any longer than necessary.

How did I let Jack talk me into this? he thought, but his question didn't hold the exasperation it implied. He already knew the answer. It was because he could never say no to Jack. He told himself he feared what Jack would do on his own, but he knew he was more afraid of what he would do without Jack. Sometimes he felt like he and Jack had been twins for longer than their nineteen years. The universe had decreed that Jack and Cobalt were two sides of the same coin, and Cobalt couldn't defy the universe—or Jack.

The upper half of Cobalt's datapad flashed a dull orange once, but it was enough for him to know Jack had activated the neutralizer. The gas should make the guards foggy and unaware of their surroundings but not enough that they were aware it was happening. If Cobalt had measured the dosage right—and of course he had—he should have just enough time to do what he needed to.

He hustled over to the door of the next car, not daring to breathe. Though he knew he had measured the medicine correctly and that his screen would not have flashed if Jack hadn't deployed the gas, he was human enough to know that there was always room for error—or in that case, calculated risk. A small percentage of people reacted badly to the gas and became violent in their confusion, though they usually had a grace period before the punching started.

Cobalt tiptoed up to the door as silently as he could in his bulky coolant suit. When the guards didn't move, he reached past them to open the power console for the next car. With all the skill he wished were being put to use fixing piloters in his parents' shop, he inserted a device that would cut all power to the car for ten minutes.

Content that most interior defenses would rely on the car's inherent power, Cobalt got to work on the lock. He disabled it with laughable ease and inched open the door, checking every step of the way for a trap or alarm, but he found none.

A cursory look over the room indicated no security systems still operational, and Cobalt had to push down a stab of disappointment that the heist wouldn't be a bit more of a challenge. He pushed a button on his scanpad, the one that would summon the drone he had keeping pace with the train. He had calculated the exact speed and timing to get the drone to land in the right place on the train, and he wasn't surprised when the drone drilled exactly where he'd expected.

While the drone created a circular hole in the ceiling, Cobalt opened a case of diamonds. Jack had wanted to steal the entire car's worth, but Cobalt had talked him down. One case of diamonds was plenty to make them rich, and one missing case might not be noticed as quickly. Besides, they couldn't hide a drone that could hold that many diamonds. Cobalt suspected the last bit was the only thing that had convinced Jack.

Cobalt hesitated before lifting the diamonds into the drone. *This is it. I am really stealing ZimmerCorp diamonds.* He considered putting them back and walking away before he could get into any more trouble, but it was too late for that. He had already drugged the guards, cut the power, and drilled a hole in the ceiling of the train. Leaving the diamonds would not save him from jail time. He loaded them into the drone and pushed the button that made it deploy a portable force field over the hole in the ceiling then fly off to its preprogrammed coordinates.

He looked at the time on his datapad. His ten minutes were almost up. He slid back out the door and made his way back to his seat, stopping in one of the empty cars to dispose of his coolant suit.

Well, that went smoothly. I don't know if Jack will be pleased or disappointed by the lack of drama. Probably both.

CHAPTER 3

Present Day

"LET'S HEAR IT FOR YOUR champion, Gavin Ibori!"

Gavin stared into the blinking red light of the camera and tried to smile. People had always told him he had the most exuberant smile they had ever seen, full of bright-white teeth standing out against his dark-brown skin. His brown eyes lit up, they said, and they felt peace that almost made them believe in a higher power. Gavin suspected his current expression reflected none of that. He was pleased, he reminded himself. *Who wouldn't be pleased to win their region's title in the Bellerophon games?*

Games. He could hear the scoffing sound in his brain. The competition involved battles of every sort, from hand-to-hand fighting, to swords, to chases with laser pistols and small space vessels. That people considered that kind of warmongering a game disgusted him, though he wasn't sure why. He had been raised to it.

"Tell us, Gavin! Who was the greatest influence on your victory?"

Gavin felt like he should know his interviewer's name. The man was on the news all the time, flaunting his civilian status with his lack of uniform and nonregulation bushy mustache. Gavin had mixed feelings about nonmilitary people who chose to live on Bellerophon. On the one hand, he envied them because they could leave. On the other, he resented them for staying.

As he answered the question, Gavin felt his jaw clench. "My parents, of course. General and Colonel Ibori are true children of Bellerophon. They have instructed me since birth that the most noble of all pursuits is glorious combat for one's nation."

He hated lying, not that his words, strictly speaking, were untrue. His parents *were* believers in the Bellerophon party line, and they had done their best to instill the same values in their son. That they had failed was not a comment on their diligence but on Gavin's intransigence.

From the way his father, General Elliot Ibori, smiled and clapped in the crowd, Gavin knew he believed winning the games had made him understand the glory of battle. In fact, all it had done was make him grateful that war only existed in tales of humanity's past.

"I would also like to thank my friend Archon, whom you're going to interview next. Archon has trained with me since we were children, and I am proud that his performance gained him the wildcard slot in the final games."

Gavin glanced at the side of the crowd where a blond man in a cadet's uniform stood at attention. Only someone who knew him well would see the gleam in his eye and the upward quirk of his lip indicating his excitement.

Archon. Always the perfect soldier. Like everyone thinks I am.

"Finally, I would like to thank my girlfriend, Windla, without whose tireless support I could never have made it this far."

The brown-haired girl standing next to Gavin's parents blushed and looked down when he mentioned her name. Gavin almost regretted thanking her. Windla never sought the spotlight, which was one of the things he loved about her. He knew that if he managed to escape the life of glory his father had planned for him, Windla would still be by his side.

"How do you plan to win the final competition?" the interviewer asked.

Win? I'm just hoping to survive it. Gavin was not looking forward to the weeks-long survival challenge, which would be broadcast for all of Orpheus and its moons to see. Competitors weren't supposed to die in the games, but accidents had happened.

"I've participated in many survival challenges and battle-training exercises throughout my education. I expect the finals to be the biggest challenge yet, but if I remember what my wise instructors have taught me, I should be able to perform well."

Never say "but." Always say "and." It changes the whole meaning of the sentence for the better, the soft voice advised Gavin in his head, but he couldn't remember who had spoken those words to him or when.

"Well, there you have it, folks! Gavin Ibori, victor from our lovely home of Calliope! Over the next week before the final competition, we'll be digging deeper into his life, and you'll know more than you ever wanted to know about him!"

Gavin called upon every ounce of his training not to blanch at the words. He didn't want reporters digging around in his life, even if he had nothing to find.

And Calliope was *not* lovely. The scientists there constantly tested chemical weapons they claimed were safe but weren't—and left the sector smelling like rancid gas.

Gavin moved over to where his parents and girlfriend were standing. His mother, Colonel Reyna Ibori, hugged him, and the general shook his hand to the tune of a hundred camera clicks and flashes. Windla stood on tiptoe and kissed Gavin's cheek. He clasped her hands to his chest as she pulled away.

"Shouldn't you be on your way to university?" he asked. He was proud of Windla for scoring high enough on the literature exam to gain admission to Chora, even if it seemed as though no one else on Bellerophon was going. He only wished his parents had allowed him to take the exam. Surely if he had won a scholarship, they couldn't have prevented him from going. *Which is probably why they didn't let me take it.*

"I couldn't miss your big day!" Her blue eyes stared into his brown ones, and for a moment, he forgot the cameras. "I'm catching a train this afternoon. Although maybe I shouldn't."

"What?" Gavin squeezed her hands harder. "Why shouldn't you? Studying literature is your dream!"

"I know," she said. "But what kind of life can we have together if I go? You're going to be a great general, and Bellerophon doesn't hire literature professors."

Gavin knew he should feel conflicted. He loved Windla, so he should want her to stay, yet every fiber of his being wanted her to do whatever made her happy, whether she was near him or far away. Something deep inside him believed love required sacrificing his happiness for hers.

His father sniffed. "You should do your alleged best friend the honor of listening to his interview. He listened to yours."

Gavin's stomach tightened. *He's right, though he just wants to stop me from changing my mind and convincing Windla to stay.* His father thought Gavin could do better than a woman who always had her head in a book, but Gavin didn't think he could do better than an intelligent woman who would do an excellent job helping raise their children.

Every time he had that thought, though, a deep voice in his head told him he was forbidden from having children. He assumed he had over-internalized his father's lecture about the mission being the most important thing, but his father's tenor did not match the timbre of the command. Realizing he still wasn't listening to his friend's speech, Gavin turned his attention to Archon.

"Well, of course Gavin beat me this time," his friend said. "That's because I'm saving everything for the finals." Archon gave the camera a big wink and smile, so all the viewers across the system would know he was jesting.

"Well, there you have it, folks! The champions from Calliope!" The interviewer focused on the camera, making it clear that Archon was dismissed.

Archon was making his way through the crowd, presumably heading toward his parents, when Gavin's father stopped him. "A fine performance you made in the games," he said. "You certainly gave my son a run for his money."

Gavin's friend stopped and saluted. "Thank you, General. Your son has been an inspiration to me for many years, and I look forward to serving with him in the years to come."

After Gavin's father returned the salute and gestured to dismiss him, Archon continued through the crowd. His father looked as though he wanted to talk to Gavin, but Gavin turned to Windla.

"Go to Chora," he said. "You'll always regret it if you don't. If we're meant to be together, we'll find a way."

"That sounds like crazy mystical talk. No one believes in that kind of stuff anymore." Windla smiled, her eyes brimming with tears. She understood she needed to go.

And Gavin understood that he needed to compete in the accursed final—and if he ever wanted to please his father, he needed to win.

CHAPTER 4

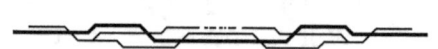

Present Day

"**S**O IS EVERYTHING IN CHORA made of light and glory?"
Bliss Bhanushali looked around her utilitarian dorm room, which was half the size of the room she'd had to herself at home, then turned back to Roslyn's face on the viewscreen and laughed. "Hardly. From what I've seen, I can't tell why anyone would live on Orpheus. The entire planet is one big, dirty city. They must have brought giant fans to clear the smoke from the campus commons in the publicity shots. I would rather be on Ariadne."

"Most people can't afford to live on Ariadne, and most of the people who live here are servers. No one wants to be a server."

"Don't say that!" Bliss hated when Roslyn acted like being a server was some kind of huge oppression. She'd always thought of Roslyn as a sister, not her server, and she felt a pang inside every time Roslyn treated her as her oppressor.

Roslyn sighed. "Fine. I'll just think it."

Twisting a lock of her wavy black hair around her finger, Bliss asked, "So how did the visit with the therapist go?"

"Apparently, I'm not crazy, just overexcitable and unhappy... or something."

Bliss raised her eyebrows at Roslyn and blinked a few times.

Roslyn groaned. "Okay, fine. I need to keep telling myself my dreams aren't real and remind myself how awesome my life is. Then we can figure out what my dreams really mean."

Nodding, Bliss said, "Good plan."

"Though I don't see why past lives are considered mumbo-jumbo, but it's completely believable for my dreams to have secret meanings."

Bliss bit her lip. She didn't want to believe Roslyn had cheated on her university entrance exams, but she couldn't see any other alternative and hoped seeing the therapist would help Roslyn see how fortunate she was.

With a bang, the door to Bliss's room opened and slammed against the wall, and a dark-skinned girl in a bright-pink top burst into the room. She took one look at Bliss's frilly white blouse and made straight for Bliss's closet. "You are not wearing that to the party tonight."

"What's going on over there?" Roslyn asked.

"My roommate, Lexi."

"She sounds like a piece of work."

Bliss felt heat rise to her face as she looked up to see if Lexi had heard the comment. Her roommate, however, seemed oblivious, though she did toss Bliss's favorite gray pencil skirt into the trash.

"She's all right, really."

"You think everyone is 'all right, really.'"

Even you, Bliss thought then chastised herself for being uncharitable.

Lexi held up the orange beaded halter top Bliss's aunt Ruby had given her for her birthday then tossed it on her own bed.

"I've got to go," Bliss said to Roslyn. "My wardrobe needs my help."

"It's fine. I've got to take Her Royal Dogginess out for a walk, anyway."

"Aw! Tell Snookems I said hi!"

"I will never forgive you for giving the name Snookems to a dog I have to introduce to people." Roslyn pushed a button on her datapad, and Bliss's screen went black.

Bliss rolled onto her back and propped herself up on her elbows. "What are you doing, Lexi? That shirt's mine. And what's this about a party?"

"It'll look better on me than you. Your skin's too light."

Bliss looked down at her brown hands. She had never thought of herself as light-skinned before, but she supposed compared to Lexi, she was.

Lexi shoved a sparkly blue top and a lacy white skirt at Bliss. "Here, put that on. I got us invited to a party the engineers are throwing. They're total nerds, but rumor has it they serve the best booze on campus. They make it themselves."

"I'm not going to a party full of..." Bliss paused, searching for the right word. "*Moonshine* the day before classes start."

Lexi pulled her shirt off. She didn't have a bra on, so Bliss looked away, missing, she was sure, her putting on the orange halter. "What's moonshine?"

"An Old Earth word for homemade liquor." Bliss tapped her finger on her datapad. She couldn't remember where she'd heard the word before.

"Well, aren't you quaint." Lexi looked herself over in the mirror and gave her reflection a wicked grin. "And you are going to this party, because I'm not going alone."

I suppose the halter does look better on her, Bliss thought, though she would never have chosen to wear it with bright-blue slacks, as Lexi had done.

"You won't be alone. If the booze really is the best on campus, hundreds, if not thousands, of people will be there."

Bliss cringed at the thought. Funneling every student from a planet and its three moons into one university had its virtues, but it also made for unmanageable crowds.

Lexi tossed a pair of blue-beaded platform sandals at

Bliss and hit her leg hard enough to leave a mark. "Get dressed. You're going."

An hour later, Bliss was ready to go home. Her head was throbbing in time with the pounding dance music no one was dancing to, and her mouth still held the taste of what she was never again going to describe as moonshine. The glows of Orpheus's moons—green Ariadne, red Daedalus, and brown Bellerophon—were all beautiful in their own ways, and the bitter-and-sour concoction Bliss had drunk resembled none of them.

Lexi had ditched Bliss before they even walked in the door, at which point Bliss had considered leaving. But she figured since she was already at the party, she might as well try to have a good time. When she failed, she decided she should inform Lexi of her departure. If the police raided the party or the side-room fire-and-chemical entertainment exploded, Bliss didn't want Lexi to worry. Though after spending only two days in Lexi's company, she suspected Lexi took care of herself and expected everyone else to do the same.

Bliss did her best to walk around the globs of congregated people locked in drunken conversation. She scanned each group, looking for her roommate's beaded braids, and the second time someone pinched her butt, she was ready to give up the situation as hopeless. Then she spotted them.

The room fell away as Bliss looked at the man Lexi was talking to. *He's beautiful.* He had dark-brown hair and eyes that she could tell even from that distance were a piercing gray. His frame was thin but muscular, and the pleats in his pants were a few years out of style.

Bliss trusted her instincts when it came to people. Even at three years old, she had felt drawn to Roslyn, and when she'd met Lexi, she had felt the same tug. The feeling she got as she approached the man was less of a gentle pull and more of a full-on yank. Then he looked at Lexi with an expression of pure adoration, and Bliss remembered she was in the middle of a party she didn't want to attend.

She hoped none of the partygoers had noticed her gawking, and a quick glance around indicated that no one cared what she did. Bliss made her way across the room, knowing that even in her platforms, she moved with a grace Roslyn envied. She kept hoping beyond hope that the man would look at her, but his gaze remained focused on Lexi.

Lexi gave Bliss an irritated look when she reached her roommate's side. "Where have you been? I wanted to introduce you to people, but you disappeared."

Bliss recalled her walking away, saying, "Catch you later," as soon as they had arrived, but she'd obviously misunderstood.

"I was just telling Will here about my music career." Lexi gestured to the man, who tore his gaze away from her long enough to smile at Bliss.

"Don't you mean your *future* music career?" Bliss instantly regretted the catty words. "I mean, you have to be accomplished to be admitted to Chora to study music, but surely you've still got a lot to learn."

Lexi bared her teeth in a feral grin. "My fame is inevitable. I've got the talent, the courage, and the grit, and I've got the willingness to fight dirty. I'm going to be a household name soon. Just you wait and see."

Will laughed. "Don't you think it would be more rewarding to have a small following of people you knew personally?" he asked.

Lexi snorted, and if Bliss hoped the undignified noise would lessen the adoration in Will's eyes, she was disappointed.

"Do you want to write articles only five people read?" Lexi asked.

"Actually, I think working for a small-town vidcast would be quite rewarding," he answered. "Or some fringe network that investigated things that are really going on, rather than the watered-down news you get from the megacorps."

"Megacorp news is not watered-down," Bliss said. "Just last week, IlmerComm released the entire schedule of the Bellerophon Games, and that's supposed to be classified."

Will raised his eyebrows. "A megacorp defender, I see." Bliss had expected him to sound disappointed, but she could better describe his tone as puzzled.

"How could I not be?" she asked, certain her face was mirroring his wrinkled brow and pursed lips. "Megacorps provide a livelihood for most people in the system! That's food, shelter, medical treatment, and everything else!"

"Megacorps make sure everyone is so dependent on them that they don't even notice all they're doing is making more money for the richest people in the galaxy!" Will's passion for the subject manifested in the quiver of his hands and the glint in his eyes.

"Those rich people take care of everyone who works for them!"

"Because of heavy regulation! Do you really think if there were no laws requiring stipulations to workers, the corporations would give anything to their employees? Take a good look at the human history of laissez-faire politics."

"I suppose you're one of those believers in the virtue of small businesses, then? You know small businesses can't take care of their employees the way megacorps can. They can't afford to."

"It's capitalism that's the problem." He slammed the heel of his hand against his other palm. "The megacorp CEOs think they're better than us, living in their fancy houses on Ariadne, with servers waiting on them hand and—"

"Servers' lives are a lot better than the lives of the poor on Daedalus. If they would rather have that life, they're welcome to leave!"

Will's gray eyes stared right through her as she found herself out of breath. "You know better, Bliss."

Bliss's heart skipped a beat. *Did he just call me by my*

name? She was sure she hadn't introduced herself. "What did you say?"

He laughed. "I said, 'You know better.' But maybe you don't."

Bliss exhaled. She must have imagined it. He couldn't know her name. They'd never met.

"I know all I want to know." She held out her hand. "I'm Bliss Bhanushali. My father is CFO of ZimmerCorp. I'm studying business with the hopes of following in his footsteps."

"I'm Will." As he shook her hand, he looked straight into her eyes for the first time. Again, she felt that jolt of something between recognition and destiny. "Journalism student. My father is long dead, but I suspect he wouldn't be pleased to have a conspiracy-nut son."

Lexi stomped her foot. "Ugh, this party blows!"

Bliss had forgotten about Lexi in her fervor, but Will clearly hadn't. He immediately held out his hand to her. "Wanna dance?" he asked. "I bet if we start, other people will join in."

A smile lit up Lexi's face. "Why, yes, I do."

Will took her hand and led her toward the center of the room without a by-your-leave. Lexi turned back to Bliss with a smug expression.

"I bet you're a great dancer." Bliss could barely hear Will's voice over the din.

"You'd better believe it." Lexi's words, on the other hand, seemed directed at Bliss.

Bliss turned her head away. She didn't really want to watch Lexi and Will all over each other, but she couldn't pinpoint why she should feel that way. The man was clearly an anarchist. Her father would not approve. *She* did not approve. So what if she felt some kind of unnatural connection to him in the pit of her stomach? Her stomach was stupid. She didn't believe in destiny, and she was going home.

CHAPTER 5

Present Day

*B*LIP.

Detrick jumped.

I shouldn't jump. It's stupid to jump. It goes off fifty times a day. He had set it up to ping every time a story that might involve one of his targets appeared in the classified or unclassified datasphere. That was a lot of stories. He got dozens of hits every day. But he jumped every time.

Detrick pressed a few keys to bring up the triggering case. It was a vid. He hated vids because he couldn't skim them and had to watch the whole stupid thing.

He pushed Play. A newscast from Bellerophon appeared on his screen—Calliope, judging from the yellow haze in the air. He hoped it wasn't a true hit. Tegan would kill him if he sent her to Bellerophon. Well, not actually kill him—probably. It wasn't like he wouldn't come back. But she would be angry and maybe refuse to bring him that LaserForce 985 he needed, the one she could only get from the arms dealers at Eurydice. He didn't want to have to go get the LaserForce himself. The arms dealers made him nervous. They were the only people he knew who had more guns than he did.

Besides, he would have to leave the apartment. He hated leaving the apartment. Everything was right there—his computers, his bed, his food. Outside was a ton of stuff he didn't need, like dogs, like guns that weren't his, and like people who weren't him or Tegan.

Or Will or Bliss. But he wasn't supposed to think that. Will and Bliss weren't his friends anymore. Tegan had said so.

Besides, his apartment was so nice. It smelled like the disinfectant he used to clean every surface. His bed was made so well he could bounce a rock on the white sheets. His kitchen and refrigerator were clean of the food that plagued so many other people's living spaces. And behind the white panels of his walls and ceiling were his guns. He loved his guns more than just about anything, possibly more than Tegan.

The newscaster on the vid was blathering on about the Bellerophon Games. He hadn't caught the reporter's name. It must have flashed on the bottom of the screen, but he had missed it. He hated missing things. He considered rewinding to find out the name but decided against it. Not knowing was his punishment for not paying attention.

He had almost reconciled himself to his ignorance when Gavin Ibori walked onto the screen.

Maybe it's not really him. Maybe it's someone who looks like him. It's been a while since I've seen him.

The name "Gavin Ibori" flashed across the bottom of the screen.

"Shit."

Tegan was going to kill him. He pulled up her contact information on his datapad and, after a few deep breaths, pushed the button to call her.

His datapad buzzed as it tried to reach her. The sound always made him envision a cloud of insects in the datasphere. Sometimes when he slept, he dreamt of a swarm of yellow jackets coming out of his datapad and stinging him to death. Insects were another reason not to leave the apartment. Sometimes an insect got into the apartment. It never ended well for the insect.

A clean-cut blond woman with sharp features appeared on the screen. "Hi, this is Tegan. I'm not available right now, but leave a message, or just some heavy breathing if you're Detrick, and I'll get back to you."

Detrick's breath came faster. He never knew what to do at such times. He was supposed to leave a message, but messages were permanent. He might say the wrong thing. After a moment, the datapad beeped three times, and Tegan disappeared.

Blip.

Detrick jumped. *Another trigger?* They didn't usually come so close together.

It wasn't a video that time, and it wasn't on Bellerophon. That boded well. He skipped the transcript of the conversation between ZimmerCorp employees. Someone had robbed a crate of diamonds they were shipping from Daedalus to Ariadne. Detrick only knew two people with the technical know-how to pull off a heist that big. *Not that it couldn't be someone I don't know.*

He pulled up the passenger manifest for the train in question and scrolled to the bottom.

Zhao, Cobalt.

Zhao, Jack.

Again, he pulled up Tegan's contact information on his scanpad and pressed the button. Her face appeared more quickly that time.

"What is it, Detrick? I'm a little busy, you know. I told you I would be there in two days with your stupid gun."

"I found them."

Tegan blanched. "What? All of them? Even Will?"

Detrick shook his head once. "No. Not all. Jack. Cobalt. Gavin."

Tegan nodded. "They're not all together, are they?"

31

"Cobalt and Jack are. They're on a train bound for Ariadne. They stole some diamonds. I'll send you the information."

"Great. Where's Gavin?"

Detrick mumbled an answer.

"Speak up."

"Calliope. Bellerophon."

"Fabulous."

Detrick breathed a sigh of relief. "Oh, good. I thought you would be mad."

"I *am* mad, you idiot. I was being sarcastic."

Detrick didn't say anything.

"Look, I'm going after Jack and Cobalt first. They committed a crime, so it should be easy enough to get them transferred to my custody. We'll worry about Gavin later."

"I'm not going to get my gun in two days, am I?"

"You don't need another gun, anyway. Where would you even put it?"

"I have a spot—"

"Focus on finding Bliss. She always ends up near the others. Maybe you'll get lucky and find Lexi."

"I thought you wanted me to find Bliss."

"Find Bliss, and you'll find Lexi. Find Lexi, and you'll find Will. This is basic transitive-property stuff. I thought you were some kind of math genius."

Detrick had always excelled at mathematics, but everything got more complicated when someone threw people into the equation. "Bliss equals Lexi equals Will. Got it."

Tegan rolled her eyes. "Close enough. Get on it." Her face disappeared.

Detrick pulled up his search program and started retooling it to focus on Bliss. *You would think I could get a break now.* He had no idea what he would do with a break, but it was something he was supposed to want. *After all, I found three of them. And Tegan's said over and over she only needs blood from three bodies.* Shrugging, he returned to the code. He liked having something to focus on, anyway.

CHAPTER 6

Twenty Years Ago

THE SOUNDS OF MURMURING VOICES and clinking crystal met Roslyn's ear, and the lingering tang of champagne rested on her tongue. She looked down at the pale-gold liquid in the quarter-filled flute in her hand then at the red heels on her feet, which matched her dress so well they must have been custom-made.

I must be dreaming. She didn't have anything so nice in her real life. *Also, either this dress is itchy, or Old Roslyn is as allergic to rich people as I am.*

What? Old Roslyn? New Roslyn? I'm just Roslyn, one-time archaeologist, now minor peddler of antiques to the few people rich enough to afford them.

As she moved through the gathering of elegantly dressed individuals, Roslyn kept the small smile affixed to her face. She suspected Senator Gillis's wife's dress, a beautiful Grecian number draped over her generous form, itched less than hers did, but she couldn't bring herself to envy Lady Gillis. The senator cheated on his wife with any woman who caught his eye, yet they looked down on Roslyn. They didn't know how much more Roslyn could be if she really wanted, if she didn't care about the rules governing the Transients.

"You hate it here," someone at Roslyn's side said, and

she turned to see a tall, dark-skinned man with kind brown eyes and a fashionable hat over his close-shaven head.

"Don't you? This party is for you, the celebrated surgeon Gavin Ibori, who saved the life of the ZimmerCorp CEO's infant son. Yet you'd rather be in the slums of Daedalus or the battlefields of Bellerophon."

Gavin smiled, his white teeth a glorious contrast to his dark lips. "You would hate either of those places even more than Ariadne."

"Well, there's not much work for an antiquities dealer in either place. But you're getting too famous here. We need to leave. Maybe we should compromise and move to Orpheus. It's more cosmopolitan. I could set up a shop there, and you could still help the underprivileged." *Or else you could just leave me.*

"Oh, no." Gavin's smile fell, and he shook his head. "I know that look. I'm not leaving you."

"I don't understand why. You know I don't deserve you."

Gavin's warm hand came up to cup her cheek. "*Deserve* has nothing to do with it. I love you, Roslyn. I want to be with you for as long as I can."

Roslyn leaned into his hand and closed her eyes. *That's what I want too,* she told herself, though she knew it wasn't true. She didn't want to stay and be a shopkeeper anywhere. She wanted exploration and adventure.

When she opened her eyes, she saw someone in her peripheral vision. *It can't be. It can't.* She focused her attention back on Gavin. "We'll go to Orpheus. We can start planning tomorrow. It'll be an adventure."

It wouldn't be an adventure. She'd been to Orpheus when the planet had just been discovered, and *that* had been exciting, and she had been on the original scouting team for each of the moons as well.

Now that humanity's happily settled here, there's no adventure left. Once upon a time, the government had considered reinvesting in the discovery of new worlds, for when they destroyed Orpheus as surely as they had destroyed Earth. With the conservatives in power, that wasn't likely to happen anytime soon, though. If the closest Roslyn could get to adventure was exploring a new city, she was going to do it.

As she forced a smile, a bell rang, and the master of ceremonies announced dinner. Roslyn took Gavin's arm and walked with him to the seat of honor next to Gerald and Elaine Zimmer. Course after delectable course of peppered greens, roasted quail, and chocolate cake with the most exquisite ganache appeared in front of her. She savored every bite, knowing she would not eat such delicacies again for a long time.

The Zimmers were delightful conversationalists, asking about Roslyn's business and Gavin's practice without the slightest hint of disdain in their tones. Nonetheless, Roslyn couldn't help but feel their regard was as fleeting as the sorbet that cleansed her palate between courses. For the moment, Gavin was the hero who had saved their son's life. The next day, they would be beneath recognition once again.

If she had said as much to Gavin, he would say she was being unfair, that the Zimmers valued their son's life above material possessions, and they would likely bear some gratitude toward him for the rest of their days. As for her, well, Roslyn had seen the looks the Zimmers exchanged when she and Gavin admitted they were not even engaged, and she couldn't help but think they had dismissed her as Gavin's woman of the hour.

After the toasts—*quite lengthy,* Roslyn thought, *considering the people had never* met *Gavin*—Roslyn went outside for a breath of fresh air. Rain earlier in the day had forced the party inside, and Roslyn appreciated the opportunity to walk the grounds alone.

The air was almost fluid, smelling of wet dirt and autumn leaves. She moved slowly along the cobblestone walkway, careful not to turn her heel or slip on the foliage covering the rocks, but she had wandered only a few yards away from the party when she questioned the wisdom of her sojourn.

As she reconciled herself to a few more hours of boring small talk, the tree above her shook, spilling droplets of water on her silk dress. She looked up, and her eyes followed a figure as he dropped from the tree and landed on the ground without a care for the slippery surface.

A man with honey-colored skin, black hair, and almond-shaped brown eyes smiled at her. "Hi, Rosie."

"Jack!" Roslyn's one word held a plethora of emotion—surprise, anger, fear, and delight—and she was hard-pressed to say which sprang most readily to the surface.

"Miss me?" His grin widened as he stepped closer.

"No," she lied. She had missed the way he laughed at her stupid jokes, the way he always smelled like gunpowder and adventure, and the way his arms felt around her.

But she wasn't going back to him, not again. She was tired of him ditching her when he got bored with her or, worse yet, when he was happy to have her stay as long as she didn't mind the parade of women she had to share him with.

"Liar." He took another step closer, and she caught that gunpowder smell that should have been unpleasant but somehow ignited her blood as if it were made of the same stuff.

She intended to take a step back, put some distance between them, and tell him to go away. Instead, her heel slipped on a leaf, and Jack had to reach out and yank her closer to prevent her fall. He pulled her hands against his chest, and she could feel his heartbeat. Or maybe it was her heartbeat, or maybe both of theirs, beating in unison. She stared into his brown eyes and knew that if she didn't do something quickly, she would stand in his arms until he saw fit to let her go. *And he always does let me go.*

"I'm with Gavin." Her voice sounded breathy, so she

closed her eyes, took a deep breath, and repeated herself. "I'm with Gavin."

Roslyn pulled her hands out of Jack's, and he let her go. She backed away more slowly that time, making sure of her footing before each step. "I'm with Gavin. He loves me, and we have a whole life together. We're happy."

"You're not happy." Jack dismissed her statement with his tone and a wave of his hand. "You're never happy with Gavin. You don't love him."

You love me, he didn't say, and Roslyn wasn't sure if she was saddened or relieved by the omission. He spoke about her feelings with such certainty and accuracy, which made her all the angrier. She hated that he knew her emotions so well, because he never acted like he cared about them.

"I do love Gavin, in a way." *And either way, I am not having this conversation with you, of all people.* "Anyway, he knows how I feel. I told you. We're happy."

Roslyn expected Jack to argue, and part of her—the stupid part—was disappointed when he didn't. She turned to walk back inside.

"They found a new moon," Jack said.

She froze. *A new moon?* She spun back around, by some miracle not falling flat on her face. "Who did? The government?" *Are they starting up the space exploration program again?*

"Naw, some drunk guy taking a joyride around the system in his space yacht. He nearly crashed into this moon that wasn't on anyone's records. He wanted to make it his own private moon, but his wife convinced him to report it to the OSA. I happened to see their records—"

"You hacked into their system, you mean."

Jack shrugged. "To-may-to, to-mah-to. Either way, the planet Orpheus has a for-real moon that no one has explored before. And I could perhaps use my... let's call them 'unique skills' to get anyone I wanted on the first exploration team."

Roslyn stopped breathing, and a tingle ran its way from

her toes to her scalp. It was the adventure she had been waiting for, an entire new moon to explore, at the behest of the Orpheus Space Agency. *And I could be with Jack again.* The trip was what she wanted more than anything in the system.

She took a deep breath. "No."

"No?"

"No, I'm not going with you to this new moon."

"They named it Arachne."

"Fine. I'm not going with you to *Arachne*. Take Blueboy with you."

Jack rolled his eyes. "Of course Cobalt's coming. Who would fix my stuff if I didn't have him? But you're coming too."

"No, I'm not. I'm going to Orpheus. Gavin and I are going to Orpheus." Maybe they would go to the underwater city of Triton. They hadn't been there in at least a few hundred years.

Jack took a step closer. "Rosie, of course you're coming. No way would you miss this."

She made the mistake of meeting his eyes. They held that same glow and passion for adventure that drove her, and they reminded her why she loved him.

I promised myself I was never going to fall into his trap again, no matter what. Gavin deserves better than that.

You didn't know there would be a new moon.

No. Matter. What.

"I *am* going to miss it. I'm staying here. Or going to Orpheus. One of those. I have a nice, stable life." *I hate nice. I hate stable.* "I'm not giving that up for some empty rock."

Jack grinned again, and Roslyn tried very hard not to let the dimple in his left cheek be her undoing. "I didn't tell you everything yet. It's not just some empty rock. They found symbols—symbols that look like this."

He held up his datapad for her to see. Depicted there was a black rock with curved symbols. They resembled an ancient pictograph language, but no primitive cultures could make their sigils glow blue like that.

Roslyn gasped. "Jack! *Those are Demitrius's symbols!*"

"I thought you'd like that." Jack's smirk said, *I know you better than anyone, Rosie. Don't pretend I don't.* "This moon might hold the secrets of where we came from, and since Demitrius has told you more than he's told anyone else about them, I can't think of anyone more qualified to figure them out."

A mysterious new moon. A language that might be our native tongue. In a big-enough quantity that I could learn it. Jack.

She tried to take a deep breath, but it came out ragged. She wanted to go—more than anything.

No matter what.

"I'm sorry, Jack. I know we would all like to know where we came from, but you'll have to do it without me. If you figure it out, let me know." She turned and walked back into the party.

Present Day

Roslyn shot up straight in bed. Her heart pounded as she replayed the scene she had witnessed.

Witnessed? Or experienced? She got up and went to the bathroom for a glass of water, waiting for the dream to fade. Even five minutes later, the vision was as crystal clear as the cool liquid she was drinking.

Gavin and Jack. She felt like she knew them, and she found herself as drawn to the Jack character as the Roslyn in her dream. *But Dream Roslyn walked away from him. How could she do that? She loves him.*

Roslyn put the glass down and rubbed her eyes. *I really am losing my mind.* "She loves him" sounded suspiciously like "I love him," and Roslyn had no intention of falling in love with some guy she had met in a dream, especially one who didn't seem to return Dream Roslyn's affection. She shook her head then went back to her room and grabbed her dream journal off her nightstand.

CHAPTER 7

Present Day

COBALT SHOOK JACK. FOR SOMEONE so full of energy, his brother sure could sleep like the dead. Cobalt was annoyed enough to wish that the nonexistent girl Jack was always yammering on about would show up right then, just so she could see the line of drool coming out of Jack's mouth. That would be sure to end any relationship before it started.

"Come on. Get up. We're at Ariadne."

"Five more minutes."

"Nope. Now." Cobalt grabbed Jack's hands and pulled him into a sitting position. When Jack started to slink back down, he grabbed him under the arms and pulled him up. "We do not want to be the last people on this train."

Jack mumbled something under his breath, but he did seem to be more awake. "All right, all right. You win. But I've told you over and over—we have nothing to worry about, unless you made a mistake on your end that you didn't tell me about."

Cobalt hefted his bag—lighter than before since it didn't contain his coolant suit—onto his shoulder. "I don't make mistakes. Now, come on."

He waited as Jack searched his bench for his datapad, though how he could have lost something half the size of his pillow was beyond Cobalt. Jack eventually found it under the seat and shoved it into his rucksack. Cobalt eyed Jack's pillow and blanket, left in disarray on the cushion, then looked at his own neatly folded set. He considered chastising his brother, but he really did want to get off the train. The train personnel would probably have to unfold them to wash them, anyway, and chastising Jack got him nothing but a headache.

Despite being asleep only moments before, Jack had a spring in his step as they made their way off the train. Cobalt's steps, on the other hand, made heavy thuds on the metallic floor, every step in time with the throbbing in his head. He had slept terribly, both because he missed his own bed and because odds were good he would be sleeping on even less comfortable surfaces than a train bench for years to come.

They stepped off the air-conditioned car and into the Ariadne summer air, and Cobalt's skin soaked up the heat like a proverbial sponge, though he hadn't even realized he was cold until he felt the glorious warmth on his arms. He loved that feeling of traveling from one temperature extreme to another.

The train station was bustling with people. A man in a business suit hustled toward a train about to depart for Orpheus, jostling Jack's elbow on the way. Outside the same train, a dark-skinned set of parents had tears in their eyes as they sent a girl who was likely their daughter off to university for the first time.

But those weren't the people who concerned Cobalt. He kept glancing at the line of uniformed police officers who filled the station. They made a beeline for one of the coaches, and Cobalt did the math to determine it was the diamond-storage coach.

"They know what we did." Cobalt kept his voice at a low rumble, loud enough for only Jack to hear.

His brother glowered at him anyway. "But they don't

know *we* did it. And they won't know if you keep quiet and look anywhere else."

Jack's right. Focus on the task at hand. Cobalt had arranged for them to work for a small repair shop in the Atropos region while they waited for the heist to cool down, so he studied the vid screens showing the departure times for shuttles to different parts of Ariadne.

While he scanned for the next shuttle to Atropos, a news display caught his eye. He couldn't hear the recording, but the headline flashing along the bottom of the screen indicated the reporter with the idiotic mustache was interviewing the finalists for the Bellerophon Games.

"Hey, Jack." Cobalt pointed toward the dark-skinned interviewee. "Do we know a Gavin Ibori?"

Jack barely glanced at the screen. "He looks like a tool."

Cobalt shoved him. "I'm serious. Look. I swear we know that guy."

He shoved Cobalt back then paid attention to where Cobalt had gestured. "Blue, he's a finalist for the Bellerophon Games. Which means he's been training as a soldier for his entire life. We've never left Daedalus until now. How could we possibly know him?"

"You're right. I just—"

The sound of someone clearing their throat behind him and Jack tore Cobalt's attention away from the screen.

"Act cool," Jack whispered, and Cobalt gave him a sideways look. He was not the twin known for his extremes of emotion. In unpracticed unison, they turned to see a man and a woman in blue Ariadne police uniforms glaring down at them.

"Jack and Cobalt Zhao?" If the male officer was doing the talking, he was probably in charge. That was unfortunate. Jack was much better at charming women.

"Is there a problem, Officers?" Jack gave the police what Cobalt thought of as his most innocent smile. Unfortunately, most other people didn't find it innocent in the slightest.

"My name is Sergeant Hernandez, and this is Officer Jenkins." Hernandez reached out to shake Jack's hand, and Cobalt was surprised the cop didn't take the opportunity to slap a cuff on his brother. "You are wanted for questioning regarding some cargo that went missing from this train."

"Wow, cargo went missing? On our train?" Coming from anyone else, that would have been laying it on a bit thick, but Jack somehow managed to sound the perfect combination of quizzical and curious. "I thought it was just a passenger train. Wait a minute." He snapped his fingers and looked at Cobalt. "Do you think it was that woman in first class with all the rubies?" He tsked. "She shouldn't have gone on about them the way she did."

Cobalt grunted his agreement. He knew better than to open his mouth when Jack got into con-artist mode.

Jenkins looked a little uncertain, but Hernandez didn't seem to buy any of Jack's bullshit.

Or else he's just following orders.

"Our orders are to take you to the station. You can tell your story to the detective there."

Jack shrugged. "I mean, I don't know anything about the old lady's rubies, but I'm happy to help out law enforcement if they think I know something useful."

Cobalt closed his eyes. *This is very, very bad.*

The detective slapped a datapad down on the table in the interrogation room.

Wow, I've been in here, like, two minutes, tops, Jack thought. *Idiot cop doesn't even know how to let someone sweat a little.* He had expected to be staring at the bare gray walls, made all the grayer by the too-bright light, for at least an hour before someone came to question him. *Amateurs.*

"Jack Zhao. Arrested three separate times on Daedalus, twice for shoplifting, once for drunk and disorderly. And that's only in the past year and a half, juvenile records being sealed and all. Charges dropped in all three cases. What? You thought if you didn't go to jail for the little stuff, you would try the big stuff?"

He wished they hadn't separated him and Cobalt. Blue wouldn't rat his brother out, but his stoic demeanor didn't always win cops over. Also, he just felt better when his brother was around.

"Detective—and you'll have to excuse me, because you clearly know my name, though I don't know yours—I really have no idea what you're talking about."

Jack wondered where the camera was in the room. He knew there had to be one, but he couldn't see it anywhere. *This is Ariadne. They could have that new hyperstealth tech that makes things invisible.* Jack was dying to see that technology in action, if only to find out if he could see through it.

"Zhao, we have a very reliable tip that you and your brother were involved in the crime, and your record speaks for itself."

"I told your officers when I got off the train—I didn't take the old lady's rubies."

Aha. There. Up in the corner was the shadow of a small square, though nothing was there to create that shadow. He did some mental calculations to determine the angle of the camera then turned to it and waved, not really caring if it made him look guilty. Those people had nothing they could pin on him, and they knew it.

The detective banged the datapad again, and Jack hoped he had gotten one of those ridiculously expensive screen guards or that it was some dummy datapad the cop carried around to scare interrogation subjects with. Because otherwise, the detective was going to break the thing, and that was a waste of government money.

"You know perfectly well this isn't about some lady's rubies," the detective said.

Jack leaned back in his chair and closed his eyes. "In

that case, could you do me a favor and tell me what this is about so I can see if I have any information? If not, can I take a nap or something? I didn't sleep that well on the train."

"The favor was giving you a chance to confess so we could handle this locally. CorpCrime division of the OBI is on its way here, and they're not going to be nearly as friendly as I am."

Jack laid his head down on the table. "Yeah, okay. Whatever. Turn off the lights on your way out."

He hadn't thought the room could get any brighter, but before the detective left, he flipped a switch that dialed up the wattage. *Good thing I'm not actually tired.*

"Now, Cobalt, I know you didn't want to rob the train. You never want to do anything wrong, do you? You want to have a nice, quiet life fixing things." The detective's voice failed to be as soothing as he clearly thought it was, and his trying-to-be-kind brown eyes held a glint of ambition that belied their intent.

And if this cop thinks for one second that I'm going to rat out my brother, he's got another think coming.

"You've got a bit of a rap list."

A bit is right. For one thing, most of Jack's chaotic tendencies were satisfied by truancy and pranking rather than actual crimes. For another, between the two of them, they were usually smart enough not to get caught.

"But nothing so major as stealing from a megacorp. You're in over your head now. You're scared."

Cobalt almost raised an eyebrow at that. He couldn't see his own face, but he didn't feel scared, so he doubted he looked it. He was more curious than anything else. *How did the police manage to identify us as suspects?* But he couldn't ask that without seeming guilty, so he kept his mouth shut.

"I know you're not the instigator here, that your brother

made you do everything. If you tell me what he did, I can protect you."

And there it is. Cobalt wondered how much evidence they had against him and if he should ask for a lawyer. No doubt Jack would scoff at the idea of bringing in outside help. *I mean, I could ask to see some evidence. But no.* He was not the charming twin—or even the smart twin, intelligent though he was. Cobalt was the practical twin, and practicality told him that anything he said could and would be used against him in a court of law.

Practicality also told him to get a lawyer, but he decided to wait and see if he could talk to Jack first. Eventually, the detective would get tired of the nothing he was certain to get out of the twins and put them in a holding cell. *Hopefully the same one.*

"Help me help you, Mr. Zhao."

Cobalt stared straight ahead.

After about two hours of sitting in a brightly lit room, Jack had flipped through his photographic memory to deduce from the size of the shadow on the wall the likely model of the camera he couldn't see. From there, he estimated the tech level of the facility where he was being held, the type of handcuffs they were likely to have, and the best way to pick them. After all that, he was just bored. He hated being bored.

Finally, Officer Hernandez arrived to escort him to a holding cell with a pair of cuffs of a slightly lower grade than Jack had predicted. He couldn't decide whether to be pleased they would be easier to pick or annoyed that he had guessed wrong.

After the cuffs were "secure," Hernandez led Jack out into the hallway, where Cobalt was waiting in a pair of identical cuffs. Jack wished he and Cobalt were the kind of twins who had their own secret language. Instead, they exchanged looks that said they would swap stories when they got to their cell.

As they passed by an open door, Jack heard bits of a conversation.

"Don't see why the OBI needs to get involved. We have things well under control."

Jack recognized Detective I'm-Too-Good-To-Tell-You-My-Name's voice and snickered. The detective had been only too happy to rub the OBI's presence in Jack's face, but neither of them wanted the OBI involved.

"You may think you have things under control, but I assure you, you do not." Jack looked in as the woman spoke, and he saw a short-haired blond woman with intense blue eyes and adorable freckles scattered across her nose. "ZimmerCorp takes theft very seriously, and Jack and Cobalt Zhao are to be considered very dangerous criminals."

The detective made a dismissive noise. "Please. I have met these two. They're petty crooks in over their heads."

"Believe what you want, Detective. The fact is, I have jurisdiction, and I am choosing to exercise..."

As the woman's voice faded, Jack turned to grin at Cobalt. Most people probably wouldn't be thrilled to find a place on the OBI's most wanted list, but Jack wasn't most people. It was more excitement than he had hoped for. Cobalt, however, had grown very pale.

What? Jack thought. *Is he only just now realizing we're in trouble? He's been gloom and doom about jail since Daedalus.*

Cobalt stumbled the rest of the way down to the holding cells, and Jack wondered what was up with his brother. He was normally the cool, calm, collected one. Usually, the only time he flipped out was when he had to lie or give a speech, so judging by his bugged-out eyes and staggered steps, Jack thought the prison had required his participation in a public boasting contest.

When Hernandez had raised the force field to secure Jack

and Cobalt in their cell, Jack turned to his brother. "What is *wrong* with you?"

Cobalt ran a hand over his face. "You know how I said we were going to jail?"

"Yeah?"

"I was wrong. We're going to die."

CHAPTER 8

Present Day

JALAPEÑO CHEESE. WELL, I'D BETTER *keep that a secret.*
Gavin's odds of hanging onto the cheese from his military ready-to-eat meal were about as likely as his odds of winning the competition. His father had made him stay up the night before, watching footage of his fellow competitors, and judging by their performance in the preliminaries, Gavin had his work cut out for him. *Assuming I even want to win this.*

"Ugh, I got hot dogs." Archon's face turned a bit green as he contemplated the package in his hand, though not nearly as green as the lush foliage of the Terpischore forest they were standing outside. "What are the chances someone will trade with me? I also have chocolate pudding."

Gavin had eaten his share of MREs in his life, and "pudding" was a generous term for what would result from the powder in Archon's packet. The dessert was also infinitely superior to the hot dogs his buddy faced as the last approximation of a real meal he was likely to eat for two weeks.

Unless we get captured, of course. Gavin did not want to imagine the look on his father's face if he didn't make it to the end of the survive-and-escape challenge.

"Here." Gavin took the precious tube of jalapeño cheese and handed it to his friend along with his noodles. "Someone will trade you for that. Give me the hot dogs."

Archon's face lit up. "Man, you just gave me jalapeño mac and cheese! I don't want to trade with anyone. Are you sure?"

"Yeah, I've eaten worse." Gavin decided his words didn't count as a lie if they spared his friend's feelings.

Around them, the other competitors likewise compared and traded their MREs. The champion from Euterpe—Gavin thought his name was Abe—swapped his beef stew for chili from the Clio representative. Gavin saw a flash of red as Abe put the chili into his box.

"Hey, Archon, give me your pudding."

"But I love this stuff! And you know I need the caffeine!"

"Hey, I gave you my jalapeño cheese—in exchange for hot dogs. You can sacrifice your pudding to get me some Tabasco sauce to put on them."

Archon grumbled but handed over the pudding.

"Hey, Calliope," Abe said as Gavin approached. He looked even more like the poster child for a Bellerophon soldier than Archon did—blond hair in a buzz cut, perfectly tanned square jaw, and innocent-seeming blue eyes. "Saw your performance in the prelim. Talk is you're the one to beat. Too bad they saddled you with the weakest link over there for a battle buddy."

Gavin looked back at Archon. "Weakest link?"

Abe laughed. "Yeah, you know. Didn't actually win a champion spot in his own right."

"According to his scores, he placed higher than the champions from Erato and Urania."

"I mean, sure, if you want to look at it like that." Abe took the red container out of his MRE and tossed it in the air. Apparently, he knew what Gavin had come over for. "The way I see it, Erato and Urania put forth as much effort as they needed to. And your friend over there? He didn't."

Heat rising to his face, Gavin felt guilt washing over him. He wondered, not for the first time, if he should have let Archon win the competition. The general would have been disappointed, but the contest meant so much more to Archon than to Gavin, and hearing his friend belittled shook him more than he cared to admit.

"Look, I came over to see if you'd trade your hot sauce for this pudding," Gavin said. "I got the hot dog package, and you know that's the least edible of all of them."

"You got hot dogs? Or you traded your buddy for them so he didn't have to have them?"

Gavin closed his eyes and took a deep breath before speaking. Apparently, Abe had paid attention to the trades around him the same way Gavin had. "Either way."

Abe put his hands behind his head then stretched back against them. "Tell you what. I'll give you the hot sauce—for free even. No need to steal your friend's dessert."

Looking Abe up and down, Gavin took in his relaxed position and subtle sneer. "I'm sensing a 'but' in there."

"It's a simple condition. All you have to do is admit that the second stringer over there is the weakest link."

Gavin felt his lip curl. He didn't know who Abe thought he was, but Gavin had no intention of giving him anything he wanted. "Forget it." He gave Abe one last glare before trudging away.

"Enjoy those hot dogs!" Abe called after him.

Gavin sat down on the ground next to Archon and tossed the pudding at him.

"No hot sauce?" Archon asked.

"The price was too high."

"What'd he want? The jalapeño cheese?"

Gavin thought back to how Abe had paid attention to his and Archon's conversation from the same distance and had the brief, traitorous thought that Abe might be right about Archon. But no... Archon was just a trusting type who didn't feel the need to spy on other people's discussions. "It doesn't matter."

Archon shrugged and looked about to say something, but before he got any words out, an authoritative voice rang out from an invisible loudspeaker.

"Attention, soldiers!"

Not soldiers yet, Gavin thought, but that didn't stop him from jumping to his feet and standing straight with his hands at his sides along with the other nine competitors. *The glory of a Bellerophon education.*

"You should all know the rules by this point, but I'll repeat them for you, anyway, just to make absolutely sure. The challenge is simple. We will release you into the wilds of Terpischore for two weeks, and your goal is to survive. You've all been given one meal to sustain you, and if you want to eat after that, you'll have to find something with which to feed yourselves. Cameras will track your progress, and your performance will be broadcast throughout the system. Congratulations! You're going to be famous."

Just what I always wanted. The desire to *not* be famous was ingrained pretty deeply in Gavin, probably because of his father's countless lectures about a soldier serving his nation before all else. Fame felt too much like serving himself.

"But we don't want to make this too easy for you." *Of course not.* "After you've been out there a week, we're going to send an elite team of trackers out to find you. They'll watch the cameras for the first week to get a feel for your behaviors. They're going to try to capture you, and let's be honest, they're probably going to succeed. You're welcome to try to escape, of course. The winner will be selected from among those of you who are free at the end of two weeks. If that's none of you, we'll probably pick a winner anyway."

Gavin took a deep breath. He'd been on survival exercises before, both as part of his education and as part of his father's idea of fun family vacations. He knew how to survive and escape in the wilderness. *Two weeks is a long time, though, and they're not sending out some hapless mooks. I've seen the Bellerophon Games in the past. They send out highly trained trackers. Few escape.*

"We have assigned you a battle buddy. You are not to leave your buddy at any time. You will be scored on loyalty to your buddy as much as your other performance."

Gavin remembered what Abe had said about Archon being the weakest link. Abe was wrong, though. He and Archon had the advantage of knowing each other's methods and signals, and he pitied the contestant paired with Abe, who didn't seem loyal to anyone except for himself.

"We've issued you uniforms, which I'm glad to see you're all wearing. We've also given you backpacks you have hopefully filled with useful gear and not your favorite baby blankets."

As Gavin thought about his knapsack, he hoped he had prepared well. He *had* brought a blanket but one designed specifically to regulate temperature to compensate for the unpredictable Terpischore climate, and had also included a fire lighter, a utility knife, and a device that would temporarily short-circuit handcuffs, for when he inevitably got captured. He hoped his gear would keep him alive.

"All right, soldiers. You won't be hearing from me for another two weeks, unless you're stupid enough to get yourself or your battle buddy almost killed, in which case, we'll extract you. The code phrase for extraction is 'The raven is down.' Don't say it unless you're at death's door, because it's an automatic concession of defeat for both you and your battle buddy."

The raven is down. The raven is down. The raven is down. Gavin mentally repeated the phrase. The last thing he wanted was for him or Archon to die because they didn't remember the exact phrase that would save them.

"I think that's everything you need to know, so get your backpacks together. Your survival starts *now.*"

CHAPTER 9

Present Day

*L*ook for opportunity. Take it. *It's yours.* Lexi sometimes wondered if everyone's internal monologue sounded like a self-help vid, but mostly, she was grateful hers did. Every day, she looked in the mirror and knew she was perfect, and people who didn't feel that way about themselves were lesser beings, even if they didn't know it.

The city of Chora had literally hundreds of coffee shops and bars. They were needed to support the university-going population from four different worlds, after all. Lexi knew that by sheer probability, at least one singer who was performing at one of those locales was going to cancel at the last minute, and she simply needed to find that one. So she put her guitar on her back, hopped on her scooter, and drove through the city.

No matter what vehicle she was operating, Lexi absolutely loved to drive. Her daddy only let her have the scooter at school, but at home, she had access to seven cars and three short-range spaceships. Each of them felt a little different to maneuver, and all were wonderful. She'd had so much practice, she was undoubtedly the best driver she knew.

Lexi loved cars best, the way they hovered just off the ground and flashed their head- and taillights to signal their directions. She could drive them around the grounds of her daddy's estate at two hundred miles per hour because she knew every curve.

Sometimes, she felt like something was wrong with the silent, odorless vehicles people used to transport themselves around. They would be so much better, she thought, with loud engines. Maybe that was why she liked to speed around in her scooter. She could always inspire a few yelled swears from the poor schlubs who couldn't move faster than the monotonous crawl of their slowest member. All the dopes in cars were stuck in traffic, moving an inch a minute and never getting where they were going. Lexi's tiny, maneuverable scooter could dart between the cars. She couldn't go as quickly as she could at home, of course, but she was fast enough.

She had to be careful of stoplights, though not out of any sense of obligation to the safety of other drivers. When it came to traffic laws, stoplights were for lesser people who couldn't react quickly enough to avoid crashes. But her daddy had told her if she got one single citation for running a red light, he would take the scooter away, too, and she'd be forced to walk everywhere or, worse, take public transit.

Or she could find some people who would let her borrow their cars—not give her rides to places but let her drive. Her roommate, Bliss, had a car and seemed like a complete pushover, and that guy, Will, she had met the night before would probably let her have his car. They were welcome to come along for the ride, of course, but she needed to be at the wheel of a vehicle as much as she needed to sing.

Thinking of singing reminded her to slow down and start scouting windows. She passed a bar advertising an open mic night for the next day and made a mental note. That would do if she couldn't find anything better. She would stand out from the other so-called musicians who put in an appearance, but she didn't have any interest in performing for fifteen minutes when she could sing for the entire night.

Eventually, she found what she was looking for: a coffee shop with a lit-up poster flashing Canceled. She parked her purple scooter between two cars and pulled off her helmet, which was another insistence of her father's. "I don't want to see my darling girl's head get smashed in," he'd said, deaf to all of Lexi's pleas that she was too skilled a driver to crash and too good-looking to deserve helmet hair. She'd conceded only because wind-blown hair was a slightly worse look for her, and because her father had spent about a thousand credits on a helmet designed not to mess up her hair.

Lexi stepped into the coffee shop and took a look around the spot that would someday claim to have hosted her big break. The old-fashioned place had wood-accented metal chairs. *Well, probably polymer and not wood. Where can you get wood these days? But damn if it's not authentic looking.* Her acoustic guitar would look much better there than somewhere with a more modern techno-metal décor.

Her daddy had offered to buy her hundreds of electric guitars, of course, or the more common synth machines that created accompaniment to go along with vocalizations. "Accompaniment is a dead art," he would tell her. But somehow, she felt better performing with the guitar. It gave her something to do with her hands. *And it adds that something extra. Shows I've got actual talent instead of just the ability to hold a microphone.*

Lexi strode over to the counter of the nigh-empty shop. She would have to change that, obviously. No point singing to an empty room.

"Can I help you?" the barista asked, already reaching to press a button on the automatic coffee machine. Lexi wrinkled her nose at his greasy hair and pimple-covered face. *Can't he afford an acne cure?* Probably not, if he was working at a place like that. *Well, he'll hopefully be getting more tips tonight. Look at me, helping people.*

"I am about to save your little coffee shop from obscurity," she said, shaking out her mane of braids behind her. "Can I talk to your manager?"

The boy's squinty eyes got a little wider, but they would never open enough to make him anything like attractive. *Should probably be wearing enhancers of some kind because he can't afford the surgery. Pathetic. I really am going to save this kid's life.*

"Um. Okay. Paul?" His squeaky voice had barely enough command to summon a slightly older version of him from a tiny office to the side of the bar area.

"What is it, Mitch?" At least the new guy's voice was deep enough to be somewhat attractive, and he was old enough that some of his acne had cleared up. "Did you break the espresso machine again?"

Lexi snickered inside her head. She knew she was right about the Mitch character being incompetent. She could always tell just by looking at someone how much value they would have to her. "No," she said. "I mean, maybe." She looked at the dirty machine. Surely something that looked as if it were about to spout poisonous mold couldn't be functional. "I wouldn't know. I'm here because you need a singer for tonight. Which means you need me."

Mitch's eyes did that widen-almost-enough-to-not-be-squinty thing again. No doubt he expected her to be terrible and didn't want to listen to her all night, but she didn't feel the need to persuade him of her talents. He, like every other non-believer out there, wasn't worth her time.

Paul looked Lexi up and down. "Sure, why not? You have your own equipment?"

Lexi raised an eyebrow at him and gestured to the quite-obvious guitar on her back. She realized she was antagonizing him but didn't really care. *Though I suppose he could change his mind.* "Speaker's on the bike," she said in conciliation.

"Fine, you can start at seven. Be here at six thirty. Shop's open till fourteen. You can have an hour's break whenever you want it. That's not a problem, is it?"

Is he challenging me? Does he seriously expect me to balk at performing for a full quarter of a day? He probably did. *Whatever.* She had six hours' worth of material. Actually, she had three times that, easily. Songs just came to her, as if she had been writing for longer than her nineteen years.

"Not a problem." She offered him a bared-teeth grin. *I should thank him, I suppose. But no. He's going to be thanking me for all the business he's going to get tonight and every other night he hires me.* "See you in a few hours."

Lexi sauntered out of the shop and hit a button on her wristpad. "Call Bliss."

The wristpad made a few buzzing noises, then Lexi heard a voice at the other end. "Hi, this is Bliss. I'm not available right now, but if you leave a message, I'll—"

She pressed another button then ordered her wristpad to call Bliss again, and she had to do so about three times before Bliss finally answered.

"Lexi, are you okay? I'm sorry! I didn't have my datapad with me. What do you need? I can get to your current location in—" Bliss paused, clearly checking Lexi's location. "Twenty-five minutes. Should I call an ambulance?"

"Oh, no. No emergency. I was just super excited and wanted to talk to you now. I have a singing gig here at seven tonight, and I need you to come."

"Oh, that's sweet of you to think of me, but I—"

"Bliss, please! It's my first real performance! You *have* to be here. And bring people! I need them to ask me back."

"Well, I'm kind of new to college. I don't really know anybody yet."

"Aren't you from Ariadne? Aren't like half the people at Chora from Ariadne? You must know some people!" A desperate twinge laced Lexi's voice.

"I suppose I know a few."

"Great! I'll see you tonight, then!" *And if I don't, I am your roommate, and I can make your life very, very miserable.*

"Um. Okay."

Lexi laughed. "Think of it this way. All these people will get to say they saw my first performance ever when I'm an intergalactic superstar. See you then!" Lexi pressed a button on her wristpad, ending the call.

You are forbidden from becoming famous. Do you understand me, Lexi Ibori? Forbidden. You may think you're immortal, but I have ways to end you.

Lexi shuddered as the dark voice came from the back of her mind. She had no idea why her self-doubt manifested in deep, male tones but had long ago decided she wasn't going to listen to it. She was better than her fears.

She jabbed a button on her wristpad harder than she needed to. "Call Will."

Apparently, the designers of this coffee shop thought if they made these chairs as uncomfortable as possible, they would have faster turnover, Bliss thought. She doubted Lexi had considered the comfort of her guests when she picked the locale.

Bliss looked around the old-fashioned coffee shop and comforted herself with the faux wood surrounding her. She didn't know why she found such things soothing. Her parents were height-of-fashion kind of people, and growing up, Bliss had only seen wood—sometimes even *real* wood—at the homes of family friends her parents mocked for poor taste. Her house had always been light-up screens and colored polymers, but wood felt like home.

Quite a crowd had gathered at the shop, no doubt due to Lexi's marketing. Bliss had worried she might disappoint Lexi by only calling five people—only a couple of whom had agreed to come—but she needn't have worried. Lexi had managed to muster quite a crowd, no doubt through sheer force of personality.

Bliss couldn't help but think Lexi was a lot more fragile than she let on. She walked through the world with an air of absolute confidence, but she wondered how Lexi would hold up if something truly threatened her. *What if she hadn't found a coffee shop to perform in? What if the audience boos her off the backless stool that the poor acne-ridden barista put out for her? Cronos, what if she gets a cramp in her back from sitting for seven hours on that stool?*

Somehow, Bliss doubted that the world ever contradicted Lexi, though, and it wasn't just a privilege thing. Bliss had been born with everything, and the universe gainsaid her all the time. *And it hurts. Every time Roslyn acts like I'm some kind of princess who can't understand pain, I don't know what to do with it.*

Yet she loved Roslyn and still wanted her around, just like she wanted Will around, even though he was some kind of anti-corp socialist who liked Lexi better than her. He was probably attracted to that confidence of Lexi's.

"This seat taken?"

Bliss looked up to see Will standing across from her. Judging by the warm expression in his gray eyes and the not-at-all-mocking smile on his face, she knew he had positive feelings toward her, despite their argument the night before and his quick abandonment of her for Lexi's petulant demands.

That's not fair. Lexi was a bit childish, but I hadn't been enjoying the party, either, and I'm sure my behavior could have been described as "petulant" as well.

Bliss realized she was staring at Will. "Oh, of course not!" A giggle escaped her mouth, and she strove not to cringe. "Please, sit."

Will's smile widened as he pulled out the chair. "Looking forward to the performance?"

The same giggle permeated the air. "Oh, I suppose. I'm mostly here because Lexi needed moral support. Do you think she's as good as she says she is?"

Will's gaze traveled to Bliss's tall, dark-skinned roommate, who was tuning what had to be a real-wood acoustic guitar, probably from Old Earth. "I couldn't imagine someone having that much confidence and being terrible."

Bliss took a sip of her mocha. She missed the real sugar that was readily available on Ariadne but was deemed too expensive and unhealthy on the less luxurious Orpheus. Approximations of the pure sweetener had improved over the course of even Bliss's life, but they could never quite match the real thing.

"So you study journalism?" *Idiot. He said he did last night. Went on about it in great detail. Did you think he made that up?*

"Yeah," Will said. "A free press is an important component of any democracy."

"Of course."

"You believe in democracy, then?" Will asked. "You don't think the corps should rule us all?"

"Corps and governments serve different purposes in our society," Bliss said. "Both have their places. I'm not some kind of monster, you know."

"I don't think you're a monster. I just think—"

Bliss was never to know what Will "just thought," because at that moment, Lexi sat down on her stool, and Bliss lost Will's attention.

"Hi, I'm Lexi! Prepare to have your temperature-regulated socks knocked off, because you're going to love what you're about to hear." She let loose a smile that made the room proffer slightly more enthusiastic applause than Bliss would have expected from a novice performer. Then she sang.

"I drive too fast.
I have no heart,
I don't give a damn who you are.
I don't cry the pain I feel.
I just hurt till it's not real.
Don't break your heart over me."

Well, at least she's honest, Bliss thought. She glanced over at Will, who was staring at Lexi with rapt attention.

He didn't look as happy as the rest of the crowd, though. Something in the twist of his mouth could best be described as "wistful," as if he knew Lexi were dying, and soon all the glory and glamor would fade away. Or maybe he already had broken his heart over her.

CHAPTER 10

Present Day

I WISH I'D ASKED DETRICK TO *do the hacking.*
Tegan O'Leary pressed a few of the blinking red and gold buttons above her head to end the transmission of her false OBI record. She was a decent hacker, *had* to be, in her line of work, if one could call being the minion of a woman determined to discover her heritage at any cost a line of work. Most people would have a hard time thinking of themselves as a minion, but Tegan had always been a mook through and through. Give her an order, and she would follow it. She sometimes considered allowing herself to be reborn in hopes that she would end up on Bellerophon and could join the army, but with her luck, she would end up in a Daedalus slum or an Ariadne plantation. *Especially if there's such a thing as karma.* For the moment, she would work for Phedre, and maybe she would find out where they came from.

Her current task was to take custody of Jack and Cobalt Zhao from the Ariadne authorities, which meant pretending to be OBI. Making her signal look official was easy enough, but if someone investigated, they would spot it as a fake pretty quickly. Detrick, on the other hand, had almost gotten her arrested once, not because they thought she was hacking their datasphere, but because they believed she was one of their agents. She hadn't followed an order that came in, and they thought she had gone rogue. *Maybe I should have just followed their orders and become OBI for real.*

ZimmerCorp was trusting the arrest of the diamond thieves to the local Ariadne police. *A big mistake, if you ask me.* No doubt they would be sending in their goons once they had any evidence, but by then, Tegan planned to have the twins in her custody and on their way to Arachne.

She powered up the *Transcendent Spirit* and pressed the sequence of buttons to repeat her last call. After the sixth ring—Tegan could imagine her quarry sitting at his desk, waiting as long as possible, just to make her sweat—a dark-haired man with a smug smile on his face appeared on the screen.

"Can I help you, Miss O'Leary?" Detective Polanski asked.

"You will be able to when my ship arrives in about—" Tegan glanced at the *Spirit's* fight plan. She knew full well what time she would arrive, but he wasn't the only one who could make his opposite sweat. "Ten hours. And that's *Agent* O'Leary to you."

"I really don't see why the OBI needs to get involved. We have things under control."

Moron. You're lucky I'm getting involved instead of the actual OBI, or worse, ZimmerCorp security. Well, lucky until you find out you're not actually transferring your prisoners to the OBI. Then you'll probably get fired.

"You may think you have things under control, but I assure you, you do not. ZimmerCorp takes this theft very seriously, and Jack and Cobalt Zhao are to be considered very dangerous criminals." Tegan looked behind Polanski at where people were walking outside the door. *Speak of the devils,* she thought. They were hard to make out, but Tegan would recognize her fellow Transients anywhere.

Jack barely glanced at her, but Cobalt gave a start when he saw her. His skin visibly paled, and he stumbled. *He recognizes me. That is... not good.* If the twins knew she specifically was coming for them, they would try to escape. She had, after all, killed them in their last lives.

The detective made a dismissive noise. "Please. I have met these two. They're petty crooks who have clearly gotten in over their heads."

Tegan turned her attention back to Polanski. *Oh, really? You wouldn't even know they were the ones you were looking for if I hadn't given you the tip. They're running circles around you.*

"Believe what you want, Detective. The fact is, I have jurisdiction, and I'm choosing to exercise it. I'll be there in ten hours."

She hung up and put the *Spirit* into gear. Ten hours was far too long a trip if Cobalt had recognized her. The stupid detective had probably intentionally had the conversation where the two could hear, trying to scare them with OBI intervention. He should have figured out already that Jack, at least, was immune to fear.

As she struggled in the traffic taking off from Orpheus, she wished she had Lexi to pilot for her. That girl could drive any vehicle she put her mind to, and Tegan had seen her maneuver the *Spirit* through that kind of backup faster than any cop who could give her a ticket. Tegan lacked Lexi's precision and knew she would wind up in an accident if she tried any such thing.

A ship skidded in front of her, and Tegan had to slam on the brakes. *Cronos take me. This is going to be a long trip.*

CHAPTER 11

Present Day

ROSLYN STOOD OUTSIDE OLDEN DAYES Antiquities and stared at the gold cursive letters that shone from the vidscreen on the door. Their old-fashioned nature made her think of Old Earth kinds of antiques, but the displays in the window showed pieces of tech from about one hundred years ago—old vidscreens, communicators, and a few of those attempts at thought-to-action devices that had failed to catch on. In short, the store was just like the one she owned in her dreams.

She stood far enough from the automatic door that it did not open, and she hesitated to take a step forward, unsure if she was afraid the store would contradict her dreams or confirm them.

"What do you think, Snookems?" she asked the miniature poodle standing obediently at her feet. "Should we go in?"

A man with yellow hair stared at his datapad as he walked down the automatic sidewalk. As he passed, he jostled her, and his velocity caused her to stumble as he turned to give her a dirty look. She glowered as she stood up, rubbing her shoulder, her thoughts a mix of *Like that was my fault* and *I bet that would never happen to Old Roslyn*. Idealizing the old Roslyn was ridiculous, though. Old Roslyn had been tripping over her heels in her dream the previous night.

Either way, she decided that Old Roslyn would not stand on the sidewalk, terrified of the future. She would step inside and find out who she was. Roslyn picked up Snookems's leash, grateful the well-behaved dog hadn't decided to bolt, and with an outward purpose she didn't quite feel, she strode through the automatic door to the shop.

Olden Dayes Antiquities both was and was not as Roslyn remembered it from her dreams. The building structure was the same—two rooms on the main floor and stairs leading up—but the contents were laid out differently. Old Roslyn had made the store look classy, with each precious artifact given its own space. The current store's merchandise lay jumbled about, the lower-quality pieces displayed to encourage more hands-on browsing.

The current owner probably moves more product but at a lower price to less select clientele. Her profit margins are probably poorer overall. Exact values of the products on display ran through her head. *How do I know that?*

Sounds of modern music burst through the speakers into the room, and Roslyn remembered techno remixes of Old Earth classics like Bach and Mozart. A subtle floral aroma blew through the vents, making her nose wrinkle. She had never been a fan of shops scenting their air, mainly because the smells gave her a headache.

Still, she thought. *None of this means my dreams are real. I could have visited this shop a long time ago when it had a different owner, or Bliss could have dragged me here last year, and I could have redesigned it in my head.* Nonetheless, the similar-yet-different building to the one she had dreamt about shook her.

"I'm sorry. We don't allow dogs in here." A heavyset, gray-haired woman in a long black dress emerged from the second downstairs room. "I'm going to have to ask you to—Roslyn?"

Roslyn looked about the room as if some other Roslyn

with a dog were going to emerge from behind the metal wall art. *You're stalling, Rosie,* she thought. She had never thought of herself as "Rosie" before she heard Jack call her that the night before, but something about the nickname both chastened and comforted her.

She looked back at the woman, who had only the barest grip on a carafe of what Roslyn was pretty sure was tea. *Nora always drank tea,* Roslyn thought. She had no idea where she had pulled the woman's name from, because she felt certain she had never seen her before, or at least, not with gray hair.

"I mean, you can't be," Nora continued. "She died twenty years ago, and if she hadn't, she would be my age. You're just the spitting image of the woman who left me this shop."

"I..." Roslyn felt a lump form in her throat. She wondered if she was dreaming, because if she wasn't, the woman had just confirmed all those other dreams were real. "My mother," she said, spitting out the first excuse that came into her head. "My mother owned this shop before she had me. I wanted to see it."

The old woman's face softened. "Of course, that makes sense. I never knew she had a daughter. I'm Nora, dear. I was a friend of your mother's, once upon a time."

I knew it! Roslyn felt at once satisfied and terrified of having known the woman's name. She pushed the terror down and put on a smile for her "mother's friend." "She mentioned you."

"Did she?" Nora looked surprised. "She must have died just after she had you. She didn't live long after she went to Arachne. It's so nice you have any memories of her at all."

Roslyn wasn't surprised that Old Roslyn had ended up going to Arachne. Her resolve in the previous night's dream had mostly been bravado.

"Oh, I meant she wrote about you in her journals." *Art historians keep journals, right? I mean, I have a personal journal, a dream journal, and a Snookems journal.*

"She did love her journals, didn't she?" Nora smiled, apparently reminiscing. "And she never let anyone read them. I'm glad she left them for you."

Old Roslyn left journals? Maybe I can find them! "That's part of why I stopped by. Some years are missing, and I wondered if any backups were here."

Nora's face fell. "I'm so sorry, dear. I loved your mother, but she could be so terribly old-fashioned. After she left me the shop, I redid the computer system. Her files were so well-protected, I just got rid of them."

Roslyn didn't have to feign disappointment. "It's all right. You had no way of knowing I would come back for them."

"Would you like to come in and have a cup of tea?" Nora gestured toward the other room. "I could tell you about your mother, and I would love to hear about your father. It's clear Roslyn didn't marry the man she was with when I knew her. I can't say I'm sorry for that. He was amazing and talented, and he adored her, but she never quite felt the same way about him."

Snookems barked then whined, and Roslyn was grateful for the excuse. "I don't know that Snookems is up for sitting that long. Rain check?"

Nora chuckled. "You are different from your mother. I can't imagine her ever naming her dog Snookems."

A pox upon you, Bliss. Roslyn gave Nora a polite smile and promised to return then rushed out the door.

Her thoughts spun as she hurried down the moving sidewalk toward the train station. For a few moments, she had almost convinced herself that Old Roslyn was her mother. That would be normal, and she could deal with it. But she had to face the fact that Old Roslyn was real, and somehow, Old Roslyn was *her.*

She didn't think she would fall asleep that night, but she did.

Twenty Years Ago

"When are you going to admit that you're packing for Arachne?" Gavin asked as Roslyn put a pair of pants into her second travel case.

He didn't sound angry. He sounded resigned and even a little amused. Still, Roslyn felt guilty for even going to Arachne. *With Jack.*

"I'm not packing for Arachne. I'm packing for Orpheus— where we're moving. Remember?" Roslyn pushed a button to rotate the clothes in her closet. *When did I get so many?* "We can't bring everything we have, so I'm being selective."

Gavin stared into her suitcase. "You're packing clothes. Only clothes. Specifically, your roughing-it pants and shirts, none of your professional attire or formal wear."

Roslyn glanced around their luxurious apartment filled with the genuine Old Earth antiques that felt like home to them. They had spent years acquiring the right accoutrements, and they had no way to move so many expensive items without drawing attention to themselves. Wherever she went, she would miss the place. *No, not "wherever." Orpheus. I'm going to Orpheus.*

"Well, we're hardly famous on Orpheus. We're not going to need all that formal wear." To prove him wrong, Roslyn grabbed the first suit she saw off the rack and shoved it into her travel case. "You should start packing too."

"I'm not going anywhere. You're going to Arachne, and I'm staying here."

"No, I'm not!"

"You just packed the lime-green suit Bliss got you for your last birthday. You hate that suit. If you had any intention of going somewhere you would wear a suit, you would have packed literally any other thing in your closet."

Roslyn looked Gavin in the eyes for what she realized was the first time since she had seen Jack. "I don't want—"

"You do." Gavin had a small smile on his face. "It's okay.

71

I always knew he would come back someday, and you would go with him. It's how it goes with us."

Somehow, his acceptance of her abandonment made red-hot anger rise inside her. "So that's it? I say I'm going to stay. I say I'm going to fight for us, and you're going to throw it all away? You say you love me. Why don't you fight for me?"

Gavin's smile grew wider, but his eyes were sad. "Because I won't win. And I have never learned to lose gracefully, so it's better if I step aside."

Roslyn felt something on her cheek. She reached up to touch it, and when she pulled her hand away, it was wet with tears. "I don't deserve you."

He shook his head. "We don't deserve things or people. That's not how the world works." He kissed her forehead. "Now finish packing and go to him before he changes his mind."

She hated that her primary thought as she finished packing was that Jack was going to see her with puffy eyes.

"Roslyn."

"Blueboy."

Roslyn was standing outside the ship that Jack had sworn he had not stolen. She had worried it would be difficult to find, but Jack was never one for secrecy, and no one else would dare name their ship the *Night Thief* after the unlucky zodiac sign. She had found the ship and only had to face one last gatekeeper.

"So you're coming after all," Cobalt said.

"Did Jack say I wasn't?"

"No, he said you would be by in the morning." Cobalt looked at his datapad. "Which I suppose fourteen thirty technically is."

Roslyn sighed. Of course Jack knew she was coming. She hated being that predictable to both Jack and Gavin. "Look,

I know you hate me, but can we do the usual get-along-for-Jack's-benefit thing?"

"I don't h—"

A figure ran down the gangway of the ship. "You came!"

Roslyn felt some comfort in the excitement in Jack's voice, as if he had not been one hundred percent sure she would come. He swooped her off her feet, and she let herself get caught up in the feeling of Jack's—*Jack's*—arms around her as her heart beat faster and a huge grin spread across her face.

When he finally put her down, she nodded to where Cobalt had been standing, though she was too focused on the heat of Jack's hands on her waist and the glint of excitement in his brown eyes to see if Cobalt was still standing there.

"Blueboy said you knew I was coming."

"We-ell, I might have exaggerated a bit for his benefit."

Roslyn arched an eyebrow. "You? Exaggerate? Perish the thought."

Jack's lip turned up in the half smile she was so fond of. "So you're in?"

"You knew I couldn't resist Arachne."

He leaned so close to her she could feel his warm breath on her lips. "And me?"

"And y—"

A *thud* filled the air as something landed at Roslyn's feet. She looked up, ready to glower at Cobalt for ruining the moment. Instead, she saw Gavin, still holding onto the straps of the travel case, standing only a few inches away. He was out of breath and sweaty, as if he had run all the way from their apartment.

"Got room for one more?" he asked.

Jack had stepped back from Roslyn. He laughed, a bitter sound that did more to shake Roslyn out of her romantic haze than Gavin's presence. "Always room for a fellow Transient." Jack turned and walked back up the gangplank. "We leave at dawn."

Roslyn stared at Gavin openmouthed for a good minute, and he gazed back at her, expression blank.

"What are you doing?" she finally asked.

He stepped close to her. "What do you think? I'm fighting for you." Then he picked up his travel case and walked onto the ship.

CHAPTER 12

Twenty Years Ago

COBALT KNEW HE WAS GOING to die. He was vaguely aware he was dreaming, but somehow, that knowledge didn't make him feel as secure as it usually did.

He wasn't certain of much else. He didn't recognize the strange green sigils on the cold stone ground, or the blond woman brandishing the knife. The air smelled damp, almost misty, and instinct—or maybe the blonde's gas mask—told him to keep his breaths shallow. He tried to sit up but found ropes cutting across his arms and gut.

Soft voices came from his right, and he didn't need to turn to know Jack was next to him. Cobalt turned his head but couldn't make out the two forms beyond his brother. The one talking to Jack had a woman's voice, and the other was either as unconscious as Cobalt had been or was keeping silent.

Cobalt's head pounded. Someone must have hit him. Maybe the blonde—she looked strong. He felt like he should recognize her. He muttered the word that came to mind when he looked at her. "Cuttlefish."

Her head whipped around, even though he hadn't thought he had spoken loud enough for her to hear. She strode over to where he lay and crouched next to him, pressing the knife against his face. "Don't call me Cuttlefish."

He inhaled, and the motion brought his cheek close enough to the blade to draw the tiniest sliver of blood. It felt hot on his face, contrasting with the cool air. "What does it matter what I call you? You're going to kill me anyway."

The woman smiled. "That's right. I'm not one of you anymore."

Cobalt suspected she was trying for a cold, cruel smile but couldn't quite pull it off. *She doesn't want to kill me.* "Cuttl—"

"*Don't* call me that." She stood up, pulling the knife away, pushed a button on her wristpad, and held it up to her mouth. "Can we end this now?"

He couldn't make out the words on the other end of the line, so he turned to Jack. If he had only a few minutes left to live, he wanted to spend them with his brother. Jack, though, was deep in conversation with the woman on his other side.

A burst of resentment flared in Cobalt's chest. *Who is this girl to steal my brother from me?*

Before he could make any further effort to identify her, the blonde who did not want to be called Cuttlefish stopped speaking to her wrist. "Okay, everybody. Time's up. Any last words?"

"You only need three of us, right, Tegan?" Jack asked. "So you could let one of us go?"

"Trying to save yourself, Jack? Why am I not surprised?" The blonde—whose name was apparently Tegan—stepped toward Jack. "Just for that, I'm happy to let you die first."

"I wasn't asking for me."

Her eyebrows rose. "You're willing to sacrifice yourself for your lady love? That's new."

Cobalt looked at Jack, expecting to see one of his crazy plans in the works, but the only expression on Jack's face was steadfast determination.

"Please," Jack said. "I'm begging you, Cuttlefish."

Tegan's face shut down, and Cobalt realized she had considered Jack's words until he pulled in the hated nickname. "Sorry, Night Thief. My orders are that she dies, even if the rest of you don't. But I'll tell you what... you can die first so you don't have to watch her die."

Jack closed his eyes, and Cobalt didn't think he'd ever seen his brother so defeated. But as Tegan approached, Jack looked up and laughed. "I love you. I'll find you," he said to the woman at his side. Then he turned and met Cobalt's gaze. "See you tomorrow, Blue."

Tegan grabbed Jack by the hair and pulled his head back, exposing his throat. As she brought the knife toward it, Cobalt squeezed his eyes shut and turned his head away. He prayed for death so he could forget the choking gurgle that was Jack's last breath and the scream of the woman who apparently had the courage to watch her lover die.

He kept his head scrunched against his chest through the abrupt end to the woman's cries, until he felt it being tugged upward. The woman was strong enough that he didn't think he could have fought the pull of her hand, even if he had wanted to. But where Jack went, he followed, even into death. He barely felt the pain when the sharp blade sliced into his jugular and an eruption of red flashed before his eyes.

Present Day

Cobalt woke up choking, and he could still taste his own blood flowing down his throat. He quickly checked to make sure he didn't have a giant gash in his neck, but the skin was perfectly clear. After he gasped a few times, the air came more smoothly.

"What is with you?" Jack asked. He was in the cot on

the other side of the cell, fiddling with a datapad he had convinced the guard to give him. Jack had pled boredom, but Cobalt suspected his brother had a plan. He wondered what kind of plan could involve a datapad that didn't connect to the datasphere, but he knew better than to ask his brother aloud.

"Bad dream," Cobalt said. He couldn't explain to Jack the visions that had started when he saw the woman on the detective's screen and had turned into full-fledged memories as he slept. "Memories" was the right word for what he had experienced. He had no doubt that woman, Tegan, had killed him once before and most likely wanted to do so again.

"Blue." Jack looked up from what he was doing and gave Cobalt a look almost as serious as the one he had given Tegan as he begged for his love's life. "You have been acting weird since we got arrested. You're making dire proclamations and having nightmares. It's not like you."

What would you say if I told you I believed you now? That there is some girl waiting for you out there? "Maybe I'm just pissed at you for getting us into this mess."

"Well, if that's all." Jack flashed a grin. "I think I've got a solution."

"Does this solution involve hiring a lawyer and getting us acquitted of all charges?"

"Don't be ridiculous. You know me better than that."

He did. In fact, he had known his brother for at least another lifetime, it seemed. Possibly many lifetimes.

This should all seem weirder to me than it does. He was a practical, scientific sort. He should know reincarnation was impossible. Yet he had one dream, and he was certain he had lived before. Maybe he was grateful to latch onto any explanation for why he acquiesced to Jack's plans so quickly. He had apparently been doing so for more than one lifetime.

"You ready?" Jack asked, the grin on his face growing wider.

"For what?"

"This." Jack pressed a button on the datapad, and sirens wailed outside the cell, accompanied by flashing red lights. *Wooo-eeeee-ooooo-eeeee.*

"Come on!" Jack jumped up and peeked around the edge of the cell.

I guess the force field's down. Trust Jack not to look for guards before *doing whatever he did.*

Footsteps sounded in the hall, not of guards but of all the other prisoners escaping their cells.

"Are you insane? You can't let everyone out! There could be dangerous criminals in those cells." Not willing to let his exasperation delay their escape, Cobalt rushed over to his brother and followed him into the quickly filling hall.

"That's what I'm counting on." Jack slipped between the criminals, and Cobalt had to push people aside to keep up. "Serious criminals will be a higher priority to recapture than we are."

"We stole diamonds from ZimmerCorp. I'm pretty sure we're near the top of the detective's list of people to track down."

"Shhh. I think I turned off the cameras, but they might have listening devices not on the datasphere." Jack ducked down and fiddled with a panel on the wall. "That's also why we're taking the heating ducts."

Cobalt closed his eyes. "Of course we are. Do you realize what the ambient temperature will be in there?"

Jack lifted the panel and set it aside. "About a million degrees? It'll get us out of here, and that's all that matters."

A tattooed arm pushed Jack out of the way of the opening. "Thanks for the escape for me and my buddies." The beefy man gestured behind him to four equally large men, none of whom would fit easily through the heating vents.

If we have to go behind them, we're sure to be caught.

A glint of metal flashed in one of the prisoners' hands, and Cobalt realized they didn't have a choice.

"Hey, I opened the vent. I'm going first." *Jack's going to argue with them. Of course.*

"What did you say to me?" The prisoner lurched forward, and Cobalt thought he would have to watch his brother die for the second time that day.

"I said I'm going first." Jack didn't seem the least bit scared, but then, he never did. "I'm the one that broke us out, which means I'm the ones with the building plans, which means I'm the one who knows the way out. You and your buddies can follow me." Jack offered a wink to the prisoner he had just stupefied with logic then ducked into the vent.

"I'm with him," Cobalt said, following his brother before the pack could recover enough to stop him. As the twins crawled through the vent, arguments over who got to go next echoed behind them.

"How did you break into security with a datapad that didn't connect to the datasphere?" Cobalt asked.

"Palmed the wireless transmitter from my handcuffs. They should really be more careful with those things."

"You do know where you're going, right?"

"Of course. I even scheduled a stop to pick up our stuff from evidence."

"Is that safe?"

"Blue, if life were safe, would it be any fun?"

Cobalt knew better than to argue with that.

CHAPTER 13

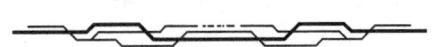

Present Day

GAVIN PULLED THE HOT DOG out of his MRE heating bag and stared at it. He wondered if he would be better off if he skipped to the survival portion of the adventure then decided against it. For one thing, the food was probably more nutritious than anything he would find in the forest, despite its odor and appearance, and for another, he knew the survival benefits to the constipation that resulted from MREs. Oh sure, he would hurt like hell in the buttocks for the next twenty-four hours, but he wouldn't leave behind biological remains.

Yeah, but they're not going to be chasing us for a week, and they're going to be following us on vid that whole time. There is literally no benefit to eating this slop.

Gavin forced his mouth open, his stomach threatening to upchuck his digestive juices if he had to smell that half-salty, half-plastic odor any longer. He took a bite of the hot dog, and the scent amplified a hundred times in his mouth. Bile rose in his throat as he chewed, and he needed every ounce of training in his life to swallow the hot dog. *One bite down, about seven more to go. Cronos, I wish I had some Tabasco sauce.*

He looked over at Archon, who was humming to himself

as he stirred jalapeño cheese paste into his piping-hot noodles. Gavin inhaled and marveled that the cheese, while still half-salty and half-plastic, was not nearly as stomach turning as the hot dog. He had lobbied hard for that cheese—well, actually, he had handed it over pretty quickly, but he had lobbied in his heart—but it comforted him to know it wouldn't taste much better than the hot dogs.

He stared down at the pseudo-meat in his hands. *That's a lie. The cheese wouldn't taste* good, *per se, but it would be a world of improvement over this monstrosity.*

Gavin took about three minutes of deep breaths between each bite, but he choked down the rest of the hot dog. The last few cold bites were even less palatable than the first few had been, but the important thing was that he ate it.

"Hey, man."

Gavin had been so engrossed in his eating that he had missed Archon coming over to him. That didn't bode well for his performance in the competition.

"I can't believe you ate that whole thing. You look positively green." Archon held out a package. "Here, eat the pudding to wash out the taste. You deserve it more than me. Let me have the granola I saw in your sack."

Gavin felt a smile light up his face, though he knew it wasn't as bright as usual, given his current state of nausea. "Thank you." He dug in his MRE box for the granola and traded it for Archon's dessert.

Pudding required some preparation but fortunately didn't need to be heated. Gavin poured the accompanying packets of water and coffee grounds into the chocolate mush and mixed them up with the provided pestle. The granules made a grinding noise as he mashed them, and he knew the substance would be gritty and not at all like the smooth pudding his mother made for him. It might remove the lingering taste of hot dog from his mouth, though, and that was all he cared about.

As he lifted his first spoonful of pudding to his mouth, a

large figure came rushing out of the forest toward him. He started and dropped his cup, grabbing the knife from his belt and aiming it at the newcomer, and could hear Archon mimicking his actions behind him.

The new arrival held up his hands in a gesture of surrender. "I'm not here to capture you. I need help."

Gavin thought he recognized the man as the champion from Terpsichore—Jesse something. Gavin held out a hand for Archon to stay back and gave Jesse a level stare. "What do you want? We're supposed to stay separated."

"I know, I know, but it's my partner! He got stung by one of those red wasps, and he's having trouble breathing. I think he's allergic."

Archon stepped forward next to Gavin. "I'm allergic too. I've got an allergen spray in my bag. Let me get it."

"No, man, you don't get it. I already tried that. It didn't work." Jesse's brown eyes were like saucers, and his hands were trembling.

Sometimes that happens, a calm voice at the back of Gavin's mind said. *At this juncture, you need to apply the spray directly to the windpipe.* Gavin didn't know how he knew, but he was certain he could apply an allergen spray at the last minute and still save someone's life.

Gavin reached out his hand to Archon. "Give it to me. I know what to do."

Archon handed over the spray, but Jesse knocked it out of Gavin's hand. "You can't possibly know what to do! You're not a medical professional. I came to find you to get the code phrase to get us out of here."

A prickle formed at the back of Gavin's neck. "What?" *Wait. Who was Jesse's partner again?*

"Look, I wasn't paying attention. I figured Abe was, so we'd have it if we needed it. But now Abe can barely breathe, and he can't tell me. He's going to die."

The world entered slow motion for Gavin, and he could see two parallel worlds opening in front of them. In one,

Abe really was dying, and his partner was desperate for assistance. In another, it was some trick to get Gavin to say the words that would remove him from the contest. In the first case, he would say those words or at least give a hint faster than his father would appreciate. In the second case, he had no intention of being played for a fool.

"Let me see Abe." Even Gavin's words seemed slow to him, though he spoke at a normal pace. "Let me see if I can help him. I don't know him that well, but he wouldn't want to leave the competition if he didn't have to."

Jesse reached out to shake him, and Gavin couldn't react quickly enough to stop him from grabbing hold, and his head shook back and forth. *Bop-ba-bop-ba-bop.*

"You don't get it," Jesse said. "I don't want to be here anymore. I thought it was all great, winning the competition for my region. But now we're going to die. We're for real going to die, and I just want it all to be over."

I could just tell him the words out of order or something. He could put it together fast enough to save Abe.

"Gavin, what's wrong with you?" Archon put a hand on Jesse's shaking arm. "We have to help him. The code phrase is—"

All at once, Gavin's full senses returned to him, and he reached out to clamp a hand over Archon's mouth. "Show me Abe." His voice brooked no opposition.

Jesse relaxed all at once. "Yeah, he didn't think you'd fall for it." He gave a rueful smile. "Though he'll be pleased to know that the weakest link nearly gave himself up."

Archon sputtered. "What did you call me?"

"Not now, little one," Jesse said. "Grown-ups are talking."

"Having the generosity to try to save a fellow soldier, especially one who has treated him with disrespect, is not a sign of weakness," Gavin said. "It shows a greater strength than someone who will cheat to win can ever understand."

Jesse shrugged. "It's hardly cheating. It's just a bit of

trickery. If it were cheating, they would disqualify us for it, but that other team got taken out, and we didn't."

"Other team?" Archon seemed dumbfounded.

"Oh, yes." Jesse's gleeful grin made Gavin want to vomit more than the hot dog had. "You won't be seeing Clio or Erato around anywhere. They were so eager to try to save Abe and so angry when they found out they'd been duped."

Gavin shook his head. "You're never going to win the competition this way. The judges rate you on your attitude and team-spiritedness as much as your cleverness and survival skills."

"All we have to do is make sure we're not captured," Jesse said. "If we stay free and the rest of you louts get nabbed, they'll have to give one of us the prize."

"That's a pretty big *if*," Archon said. "Especially coming from cheaters. What do you plan to do? Bribe the guards with your MREs?"

Jesse smiled. "We have our ways. But bribing the guards... hadn't thought of that. I bet we could think of something they want."

I'm sure Abe has thought of something. Gavin held out his hand. "Well, no hard feelings. You tried to trick us. You failed. Let's try to have a good and honest competition from here on out."

Jesse sneered at him and glanced down at the ground to where the pudding had fallen. Though the heavy dessert stuck to the sides of the carton, Gavin didn't want to eat what remained in the upside-down package. Jesse made sure of that as he stomped on the white container, grinding the brown paste into the dirt. "Enjoy that hot dog aftertaste. You're going to be experiencing it for a while."

CHAPTER 14

Present Day

WILL TURIN COLLAPSED ONTO HIS bed and wondered if he should bother to do his homework.

Homework. Cronos, I can't believe I went back to university. I'm... God, I don't even remember. Three hundred ninety-three years old? Three hundred ninety-four? And that's just in this lifetime. He didn't really regret it, though. After all, Lexi was at university, and it had been too long since he'd seen her.

Once upon a time, when the Turin siblings had been drinking and lamenting their terrible taste in significant others, Roslyn had asked him why he loved Lexi of all people. He would always remember what he had told her.

"Lexi is *happy.* You and I, we're angry. Cuttlefish is disgusted. Gavin and Bliss are always sad. Jack is most happy when he's surprised, and Cobalt's constantly afraid of what Jack's going to do next. I'm not sure Detrick has real emotions. But Lexi, in her natural state, is just happy."

"Yeah, until you tell her she can't be famous," Roslyn had said. "Then it's all me-me-me diva rant."

"She enjoys the diva rant," Will had said. "And there you go, being all angry again."

Will loved Lexi all the time, but he enjoyed her most at this point in a life cycle, when she still thought she had a chance at becoming famous. Soon enough, the memories would come rushing back, and along with them would be Demitrius's edicts against them drawing too much attention to themselves. Then would come Will's least favorite time of being with Lexi, the part when she went into denial. But she evened out eventually, and they would go on joyrides among the moons. Lexi would play at any little coffee shop that would have her, and he would be a freelance journalist for the fringe elements of the population, and for a little while, he would be happy too.

She used him. He knew it. He was her tagalong lackey, but he'd always hoped that someday, her carefree, narcissistic happiness would rub off on him. For over three hundred fifty years, they'd gone on that way until the last time, when someone had to go and fuck it all up.

Twenty Years Ago

"They're dead." Lexi reeled back from Will's office door and collapsed on the sofa. Her breathing was so shallow, he wanted to suggest she put her head between her knees. "All of them are dead."

Will hadn't meant for Lexi to overhear his vid call with his contact on Arachne, but he hadn't tried to hide it from her, either. He hadn't known he would receive word that one of his fellow Transients had killed four others, and Lexi's unfortunate penchant for eavesdropping had reared its ugly head at the worst time. He'd wanted to break it to her gently.

"They're not all dead." Will got down on his knees in front of her and used his most soothing tone. "*We're* not all dead. I'm still alive, and so are you. Detrick's fine. Cuttlefish is—"

"Cuttlefish is the one that killed them!" The pitch of Lexi's voice rose with every word. "And she's going to come after us next!"

"Relax. Deep breaths." Will reached out to lay a hand on her shoulder, but she slapped it away. "I have contacts. I can make us secret identities deeper than Tegan can find. We can slowly and secretly research what she's up to."

"I don't want to slowly and secretly research what she's up to!" Lexi screamed. "I want my life. My. Life. I want to be the famous singer I deserve to be, and if I can't have that, I want to at least be alive!"

Will took the deep breath he knew would better serve Lexi. "You're overreacting. They're going to be fine. They'll be reborn before you know it, and soon, you'll be telling me to stop talking to my sister via vid so I can come hear you sing."

"Are you listening to yourself? Your sister is dead, and you're like, 'Oh, it's fine. I'll talk to her in twenty years.'"

He closed his eyes and let himself feel the pain for a moment. He would miss Roslyn, but he needed to take care of himself and Lexi. But she was right about one thing... until they knew what Tegan was up to, they had to operate under the assumption that she would come for them next.

Will sat back, the tops of his feet sinking into the super-soft carpet. "We should call Bliss."

Lexi reached out and shoved him. "How can you think of *her* when I'm in distress?"

Ow. Will rubbed the spot on his chest Lexi had hit, probably harder than she had intended. "Someone should tell her what happened, Lex. She doesn't have all my resources to hear about these kinds of things."

Lexi stuck out her lower lip. "Oh, and I suppose you'll want her to go on the run with us too. I'll have to see her annoying face every day."

"Lexi." Will never knew what to do with her when she was like that—angry and scared and jealous all at the same time. Being anything but confident in all things was so un-Lexi. She was acting the worst he had ever seen her, though, and he suspected she was focusing on the familiar sensation of needless jealousy of Bliss because she couldn't face the fact that Tegan had killed Roslyn and the others.

"Fine, call Bliss," Lexi said. "Forget me. I'll be fine."

Will wanted to stay and reassure her, but he needed to call Bliss and get cover identities for all of them before Tegan found them. "You *will* be fine, Lexi. I'll take care of you."

After picking up his datapad, he carried it into the bedroom then sank down on the mattress, or tried to, anyway. He had sat on Lexi's side of the bed, which she liked to keep rock-hard.

Like her heart, Roslyn said in his mind.

"Call Bliss," Will instructed his datapad.

A few seconds later, Bliss's face appeared on the screen, her round eyes brimming with tears.

"You heard," he said.

"Tegan called me," Bliss said. "She wanted me to know she wasn't one of us anymore, and she had a bloody machete as proof."

"What? Did she say what her plans were?"

Bliss shook her head, and strands of her long black hair stuck to her wet cheeks. "She couldn't talk long. Something about Phedre overhearing."

"Dear, darling Mother. I might have known this was one of her plans." Will tapped his finger on the side of the datapad. "Roslyn told me some stuff about what they found there. I might have known Mother would get wind of it and involve herself. Didn't think she would kill anyone over it."

Sometimes Will liked talking to Bliss better than talking to Lexi. Bliss listened to things rather than ignoring them to maintain her blithe ignorance, or hysterical sadness, in this case.

"What are you going to do?" Bliss asked.

He summed up his plan for going into hiding. "You can come, too, if you like."

"Go into hiding. With you and Lexi." Her tone was very dry.

"She'll be a pain at first, but she'll get over it. I think it's safest for all of us."

"No, Will, you know what's safest for all of us?" A haggard voice Will barely recognized as Lexi's came from the doorway.

He looked up and could only see the shadowed outline of his girlfriend in the bright light pouring in behind her. But he recognized the red glow of his laser pistol in her hand.

Will dropped the datapad. "Lexi, what are you doing?"

Lexi waved the pistol around, aiming it at his midsection. "The only way we're safe is if we're dead. Rebirth is the deepest hiding we know."

"Okay, I know you're upset, but—"

"No buts! I'm done with this Transient thing. Being part of the group apparently gets you killed! I'm going to die, and when I come back, I'm not going to remember any of this, and I'm going to keep it that way. I'm going to be famous, and no one is going to stop me!"

"Lexi, don't—"

She moved the pistol toward her mouth. "Good-bye, Will. Don't try to find me." She put the gun between her lips and pulled the trigger.

Will dove across the room but not fast enough to stop her. The stench of burning flesh assaulted his nose as he watched a red laser beam emerge from the back of Lexi's neck, burning a hole in the ceiling as she fell.

As he clutched her body to his chest, the tears that hadn't come for Roslyn and the others streamed down his face. He didn't know how long he sat there—long enough for Lexi to go cold—but eventually, he realized someone was calling his name.

"Will! What's going on? Will!"

He stumbled to his feet and picked up his abandoned datapad. "Bliss."

"I thought I heard... Is Lexi okay?"

"No." He swallowed. "No, she's not okay. She decided she was safest if she was dead. Or I dunno, maybe not even safest, just something. I don't know. She's dead. She shot herself right in front of me."

Bliss stared at him for several moments then gave him a sad smile. "I'll go find her for you."

Will's eyebrows scrunched together, then he realized what she had said. "No. Absolutely not. You can't leave me too."

"You know I'm always drawn to the other Transients in new lives, even before we have memories. I'll be born near one of them. It might even be Lexi. I'll find her, and you can find us."

"If Tegan is after us, we are not safer reborn. We won't have our memories. We'll be vulnerable."

"I know." Bliss somehow didn't look sad anymore. She looked resolved. "But we remember things more quickly when we're with each other, and I can help with that."

"Bliss—"

"I've made up my mind. Good-bye, Will. Find me on the other side." She pressed a button on her datapad, and her image disappeared.

And just like that, he was alone.

Present Day

Lexi had said not to find her before she died, and he had ignored her. He told himself she wouldn't mind when she remembered, because she knew he would come after her no matter what. Sometimes, though, Lexi could be oblivious to other people's feelings and intentions, particularly when they contradicted hers. But he also knew from experience that someone was going to tell Lexi she couldn't be famous, and she took it a lot better from him than from Demitrius.

He knew he should look for his fellow Transients. They were old enough to regain their memories, which meant they would be easier to find, and Tegan and Phedre would be searching for them too. He wished he knew more about what they wanted on Arachne, but all he knew after twenty years of research was they hadn't found it the first time around, which meant his fellow Transients were still in danger.

Will hated to miss the time with innocent, carefree Lexi, though. He told himself he would start looking for the others soon, and he hoped they would forgive him if he was too late.

CHAPTER 15

Present Day

"You gave Jack Zhao a datapad while he was locked in your electronic cell?" Tegan didn't have much in the way of height, but Polanski's guards had shrunk in on themselves so much that she felt as though she were looming over them.

Their boss, though, stood straight and tall. "Agent O'Leary, the datapad was not connected to the datasphere. We had no reason to believe he could use it to escape."

Tegan wasn't surprised to get to Ariadne and discover Jack and Cobalt had escaped. She was angry about it, though, and she planned to take her anger out on anyone who crossed her path between now and the time she found them again. "So how did he escape, then?" She made her voice as sickly sweet as she could.

"Um." One of the guards swallowed. "It seems the prisoner took the network chip out of his handcuffs and connected it to the datapad. He then used it to hack into the prison's system."

"Idiots!" Tegan wanted to kick something, but everything in the room was cold steel, and she didn't want to damage her toes. *Or look unprofessional.* "Did it occur to you that these prisoners had committed a train heist that required technological genius to pull off without getting caught? Why would you give them anything?"

The guard stood up a little straighter. "Well, ma'am, he couldn't have been that much of a genius. He did get caught. Besides..." He coughed. "The prisoner kept saying he was bored. He was really annoying."

Tegan gritted her teeth. Jack could be very irritating when he put his mind to it. He was certainly irritating her at the moment. She knew she should have apprehended them herself instead of reporting them to the local authorities, but she couldn't have made it to Ariadne on time. They would have disappeared into the woodwork as quickly as they surely had now.

"It doesn't matter," Polanski said. "We'll have their picture plastered on every vid screen across the system. Someone will turn them in before you can blink."

"You will do no such thing." Tegan did not need Demitrius getting involved because Jack and Cobalt had become the most wanted criminals in the system. "*I* will make quiet inquiries, and *I* will handle this."

Polanski opened his mouth, but Tegan silenced him with a glare. "You've made it clear you have no idea how to handle these kinds of situations. We have no way to hack into their datapads to see where they were going, because we don't even have their datapads. They made it out with their gear. I don't know how you plan to explain your actions to ZimmerCorp, but I suspect they'll want your badges."

"We'll just refer them to you, I'm sure."

Tegan snorted. "Good luck with that." *They'll call OBI, and they'll have no record of a Tegan O'Leary.* She could appreciate the irony of her being forced into the role of a con artist to catch con artists, but she had a higher purpose, which Jack rarely did. And Cobalt went along for the ride, which made him guilty by association. She still hoped she wouldn't have to kill them again, though at least three

Transients needed to die, and Phedre would never be the one to get her hands dirty.

When she got back to the *Spirit*, she was about to call Detrick when she received an incoming call. A tremor passed through her when she saw the brown-haired woman on the screen. She was not looking forward to reporting her failure.

She pressed the button on her datapad and said, "Phedre."

The perfectly put-together woman who appeared on the screen looked enough like her daughter, Roslyn, that Tegan could see the family resemblance. "Tell me you have something," Phedre said.

"I had Jack and Cobalt in custody on Ariadne, but some idiotic detective let them escape before I could retrieve them." Tegan spoke through clenched teeth, and only someone who knew her well would notice the tremor in her hands that meant she was more frightened than annoyed.

"Really? That's disappointing. That's the only lead you have?" Phedre's voice was light, but it belied the aura of menace Tegan knew lay underneath.

"Gavin's on Bellerophon. You can see him yourself if you turn on your vidscreen. He's in the games."

"If he's in the games, you can bet Demitrius will get involved any moment now." Phedre's tone said it was somehow all Tegan's fault.

Tegan swallowed. "Yes, ma'am."

Phedre looked straight at Tegan, seeming to peer deep enough to see what was left of her soul. "You're working on a limited schedule. You need to capture the Zhaos and the Ibori boy before I get the information I need. If you don't, well, I only need blood from three Transients, and you and Detrick will work as well as anyone."

Tegan's fists clenched until her knuckles went white. "I've got Detrick researching Bliss and Lexi. Maybe—"

"I know exactly where Bliss Bhanushali is," Phedre said. "She's attending university at Chora, and I have reason to believe she is accompanied by the Ibori girl. You will leave them alone."

Tegan sighed. "Because if Lexi and Bliss are together, Will has undoubtedly found them."

Phedre nodded. "My son has never understood our purpose, and unlike the rest of them, he has memory enough to be wary."

"I'll get you Jack and Cobalt," Tegan said. "And I'll find a way to get Gavin off Bellerophon. You can count on me."

"Just remember... I need your obedience or your blood, and I'm not particular as to which. And don't try running to your fellows for help. They hate you more than they hate me."

She knew the others would never forgive her for what she had done, but the reminder still stung. But she wasn't the one who had made them enemies. They were the ones who had kept her heritage from her, not realizing she was willing to fight for it.

"I'll get them," she said again.

Phedre raised an eyebrow then hung up.

Tegan called Detrick. "I need you to keep a track on every train or spaceship that leaves Ariadne. I want to know if Jack and Cobalt leave the moon."

Detrick blinked at her several times. With anyone else, she would assume they were upset over her rudeness, but with Detrick, she knew he was processing what she was saying.

"You want me to track *every* ship?" he asked. "But some ships leave illegally and don't leave flight plans. And some private vessels move from one place to another on the planet. Do you want them? What about orbiting vessels? I don't think you've fully considered what you're asking me, Tegan."

Tegan took a deep breath. She could tell Detrick was on the verge of getting overexcited. It didn't happen often, but when it did, the fallout could be unfortunate. Last time, she hadn't been able to get in touch with him for four days, and when she finally did, he had tripled his gun order.

With this particular stimulus, he was more likely to refuse to find anything for her for several days, but she needed him on point.

She put on her most calming tone. "No, Detrick. You don't need to find all those ships. Just the major ones with passenger manifests. Though no one has skills like you do, so if you wanted to try to hack into any of those illegal vessels and get a passenger manifest, I'm sure it would be a great demonstration of your skills."

Tegan held her breath, waiting for Detrick to either agree or refuse. She hated that she used him that way. He was on the autism spectrum and couldn't function well in the world, and she wanted to protect him, which was why she needed him to work hard on finding Jack and Cobalt. Phedre would not hesitate to kill them both and make the rest of their incarnations miserable if they couldn't find her other Transients to sacrifice in their place.

"I could do that," Detrick said slowly. Slowly was good. Slowly was not overexcited.

"Thanks, Detrick." Tegan gave him a wide smile. "You're the best."

She hung up and rested her forehead against the cool steel of her ship. Things were not going according to plan, and part of her wondered if she didn't deserve exactly what she was getting.

PART II

CHAPTER 16

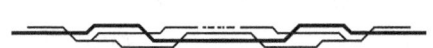

Present Day

ROSLYN HAD NOT HAD A dream in two weeks.
She didn't know what to make of that or how to handle it. She had thought that if she had a past life in which she was some amazing woman who went on interstellar adventures and had two attractive men competing for her attention, her current life would change. But it didn't. She was still a server who would spend the rest of her life walking her best friend's latest vanity mixed breed, and she would never go to Orpheus, much less the heavily guarded research station of Arachne. Roslyn had wanted to visit the black moon even before the dreams had started, and she wondered if Past Roslyn had made it there. Maybe the fool girl's ship had exploded before she made it. After all, she must have died somehow, or Server Roslyn would never have been born.

Though they couldn't change her life, she wanted the dreams back. They were an escape from her dreary existence, but she had no idea how to make them return. She pondered changing her diet to increase dreams as she walked Snookems home from the dog park. He'd had a doggie play date with a cockapoo that had consisted of the dogs ignoring each other in favor of barking at the passersby while Roslyn listened to the cockapoo's caregiver drone on about her relationship woes.

Roslyn almost wanted to get into a relationship of her own so she could return the favor. She had never been very interested in dating other boys of her station, and boys above her station were strictly off limits. Though she'd always assumed she didn't want to lock herself into her life as a server by marrying one, she realized she was in love with a boy from either her dreams or her past life. Either way, she was crazy, but she couldn't shake the feeling that she would never love anyone except Jack.

"Hey, dog-walking girl!" someone with a strangely familiar voice called from behind her.

When she spun around, she saw two identical men in blue jumpsuits jogging toward her. She didn't have to take in the shiny black hair, honey-colored skin, and almond-shaped brown eyes to recognize Jack and Cobalt Zhao when she saw them.

Roslyn opened and closed her mouth a few times. She had to be imagining them. Nora had known Old Roslyn, but those two had jumped out of her dream and into real life. She wondered if she were dreaming, but the dog leash Snookems was pulling on dug into her hand in that real-life way that meant she was really facing the boys she had only seen in her dreams.

They came to a stop when they reached her. "Jack," she said, grateful that the dreamy way she usually said the name in her head was replaced by a dumbfounded disbelief at the insanity of the situation. "Cobalt."

Cobalt—funny how she could tell them apart—raised his eyebrows at her. She glanced down at the name tags on their jumpsuits, which identified them as employees of a local personal cruiser repair shop. Jack's tag spelled out his name in bold, digital lettering, but Cobalt's read Blue.

Oops, Roslyn thought. *I need a distraction before he asks questions I can't answer.*

So she said the first thing that came into her mind. "My name is *not* 'dog-walking girl.'"

Cobalt's brow scrunched, and he looked about to say something—probably that *his* name wasn't Cobalt—when Jack spoke up instead.

"Well, I don't know your name. I only know that you're walking a dog. It seemed as good a way as any to get your attention." He gave her a wide grin.

Cobalt's face returned to even neutrality. Apparently, he was going to let Jack handle the interaction. *Yes,* Roslyn thought, *Blueboy always lets his brother do the talking.*

"You could have asked," Roslyn said. The indignation seemed to hide her astonishment well enough. *He should know my name,* a deep part of her thought. *We were lovers on and off for centuries.* Except she wasn't sure if that was true.

Jack let out an exasperated sigh. "But I couldn't get your attention that way. Look at all the people on this street."

Roslyn looked around at the road, empty except for the three of them, and raised an eyebrow.

"All right, so maybe just 'Hey, you there!' would have sufficed."

"Perhaps." Roslyn gritted her teeth. It wasn't his fault she resented her server role or that he had played a role in her nightly fantasies until two weeks previously. "Did you want something?"

Jack gave her his brightest smile, the one Old Roslyn had so often believed was reserved for her alone, only to find out it wasn't. "Blue and I were having a debate, and we wanted your opinion. We were split, you see, so we needed a third." He met her eyes, and for a moment, his smile fell, and a puzzled expression came over his face.

"Destiny," Cobalt said. "Jack's a firm believer that we make our own, but I'm starting to think maybe we don't have any choices about anything."

Jack snapped his fingers, and the grin returned. "That's

right. Blue's all convinced that we're going to die violently for our many crimes, and I say we can get away with anything if we're determined enough."

"Can you?" Roslyn was disappointed to find her voice a bit breathy. "How many crimes are we talking here?"

"More than you can imagine." Jack's eyes held a twinkle as they refused to meet hers.

"Well..." Roslyn considered the question. "I guess I believe that we make our own choices in life, but sometimes, being who we are, we can't help but go down certain paths. So while we may choose our own destinies, sometimes we don't have a lot of control over our choices."

Wow, Roslyn, that was surprisingly choice-centric of you, a girl who constantly insists she has no choices.

Jack stuck out his lower lip. "Well, that's not helpful at all. Total cop-out."

Roslyn shrugged. "It's what I've got." She waited to see if they wanted anything else, but neither twin met her gaze. Her desperation to continue the conversation turned into awkward silence. She turned to walk away. "Come on, Snookems."

Jack let her get almost a block up the road before he called after her. "Hey, dog-walking girl!"

Roslyn stopped.

"What is your name?"

Rosie, she wanted to say, because that was who she was, or who she should be, to Jack. But she wasn't. Not to that Jack. *Or am I?*

"I'm Roslyn," she said.

When he didn't say anything further, she continued up the street.

"It's all real!" Roslyn said to Dr. Tanner at her appointment later that afternoon. "I visited Nora, and she knew the old Roslyn—said I looked just like her! And I met Jack and

Cobalt, and something they said made me realize I've been feeling so grumpy and trapped, but I don't have to. I can fight! I passed that test fair and square. I should be at university, and I'm going to get there."

Dr. Tanner didn't look at Roslyn. She tapped her stylus on her pad several times before speaking. "Roslyn, I want you to tell me about these individuals you met, the ones you say were Jack and Cobalt."

"They *were* Jack and Cobalt. They even had name tags saying so. Well, Cobalt's said 'Blue,' but they're probably hiding out after some crazy scheme of Jack's—"

Dr. Tanner tsked. "I need to show you something." She turned her datapad around, and Roslyn saw the opening credits for a vid show appear on the screen.

"The Bellerophon Games? I don't watch them, but Mrs. Bhanushali does. I don't understand what they have to do with—" Roslyn cut herself off as Gavin appeared on the screen. "He's real too! This proves what I've been saying! I knew—"

"Roslyn, I'm afraid all it proves is that you may be more ill than I had realized," Dr. Tanner said.

Her arms and legs went cold. "What do you mean?"

"I think it's obvious what's been going on. You are unhappy with your life, so you have imagined a different one for yourself. You even went to the point of cheating on a test to try to make other people believe you."

"I didn't cheat! I—"

"You said yourself that you ran into these boys on a route that you take every day, and that they wear name tags."

Where is she going with this? But Roslyn knew where Dr. Tanner was going. She was trying to prove that Roslyn's memories were a lie. "Yes."

"And your mistress watches the Bellerophon games, which you must have seen her watching a number of times. You saw Gavin on the show and incorporated him into your fantasy."

"It's *not* a fantasy! I didn't make all of this up!"

"I don't think you did it intentionally." Dr. Tanner's voice took on a tranquil tone, but Roslyn didn't find it soothing. "I thought at first that you simply needed help admitting you cheated because you were unhappy. It's what your friend Bliss asked me to do for you."

"Bliss... thinks I cheated?"

"Of course she does. Everyone knows you cheated. There's no question of that. But I'm starting to think maybe you don't realize you cheated. Maybe these delusions go deeper, and you honestly believe them. That's very concerning."

Roslyn's breath came faster, and she grasped for anything to hold onto. "What about Nora? She knew me from before, from my past life. I *recognized* her."

"Oh, Roslyn, surely by now you've realized you can't trust your own mind. But I did do a little research into your mother. She wasn't always a server. She used to own a small antiques store, but she gave that up when she fell in love with your father."

Roslyn gripped the armrests of her chair and shook her head over and over. "No, Nora said she went to Arachne, like she did in my dreams. And it wasn't my mother. It was *me*."

Dr. Tanner's brow furrowed, and the corners of her mouth turned down. "Roslyn, I need you to listen to me. None of what you're imagining is real. It's all a delusion. A fantasy. I can help you, but you need to let me."

Roslyn rocked in her chair as tears stung the corners of her eyes. *I can't be crazy. Can I?* She knew Dr. Tanner had to be right. Reincarnation wasn't real, and she could easily have seen those boys and pulled them into her fantasy. With the revelation about her mother, and not even Bliss believing her, she had to acknowledge Dr. Tanner's version of events made a lot more sense than hers.

"What do I need to do?" Roslyn's voice was small and unsteady.

"I'm going to give you a prescription. I want you to have

it filled right away. Tomorrow morning, I would like to have you check into the hospital so we can get these delusions under control."

"All right." Roslyn felt defeated, and just half an hour earlier, she had felt on top of the world.

That night, Roslyn dreamed again.

Twenty Years Ago

Roslyn looked out over the rocky black surface of Arachne and wondered if she had made a mistake coming there. She wasn't concerned about the forbidding landscape and makeshift tents that would be her home for the duration of the exploration. The two men standing to either side of her were what concerned her.

Traveling with both Gavin and Jack in the Zhaos' small ship had been intense. She had tried to keep her distance from both of them, which was completely impossible, so she had spent most of the trip in silence. The pair were civil to each other, of course. Though they were rivals for her affection and complete opposites in temperament, they were both Transients and, as such, understood each other better than either would ever understand a human. For his part, Cobalt had spent the entire trip glaring at Roslyn, probably because he blamed her for having to give up his bunk to Gavin and share with his brother.

"You must be the new recruits!" A beautiful woman with a blond ponytail came over to greet them.

Funny how I'm always more likely to notice a woman's attractiveness when Jack is around, Roslyn thought. She didn't want to be a jealous shrew, but history had taught her that sometimes beautiful women really were out to get her, paranoia or no. *Why am I putting myself through this again? Oh, right, the adventure. And because apparently I'm*

107

a glutton for punishment. And because she loved Jack, even when she hated herself for it.

The woman's blue eyes sparkled as she eyed each of them. She paused for a moment before choosing Roslyn to hold her hand out to. "I'm Dr. Hannah Carriger, the leader of the expedition."

Roslyn returned the woman's handshake, trying to keep a frown off her face. "I'm—"

"You look awfully young to be the leader of the expedition." Jack inserted himself between Roslyn and Dr. Carriger.

Right. He likes to do the talking, and Blueboy always lets him, Roslyn thought. *Gotta remind him that's not how it works around me.*

"Hannah, was it?" Jack's smile was all charm, and Roslyn felt whatever hope she had that things would be different that time die in her chest.

Dr. Carriger did not look impressed. "*Doctor* Hannah Carriger, yes."

"Forgive my associate here. He thinks he's charming." Roslyn's sickly-sweet tone reminded her of Tegan, and she wasn't sure that was a good thing. "I'm Dr. Roslyn Turin, archaeologist. This is Dr. Gavin Ibori. Medical doctor, that is. We heard you needed help in the clinic."

"We do." Dr. Carriger pursed her lips and considered Gavin for a moment before adding, "Any expedition always has the danger of new maladies, and a doozy of a bug has hit a few of our members."

Roslyn nodded. She wasn't really worried about illness. The other Transients sometimes caught human diseases, but they were half human while she was a full-blooded... whatever they were. "Cobalt Zhao answers to the title of 'mechanical genius,' so if you've got any machinery on the fritz, just let him know. And Jack..." She sighed, hating to describe his skill set when she was annoyed with him. "Jack can do anything."

"Except talk to educated women, apparently," Dr. Carriger said.

Jack yelped, but Roslyn smiled. She was going to like Dr. Carriger. "We all have our strengths and weaknesses."

Dr. Carriger held out an arm toward the camp and headed in that direction. "I'll give you the tour." She tossed a grin back at Roslyn. "But first I'd like to show you something. I'm an archaeologist, too, so I know how excited you are we finally get to uncover something completely unique. Something I might even call *alien*."

Cobalt coughed behind Roslyn, and she caught Gavin giving him a dirty look.

"Alien?" Roslyn asked. "Do you mean that literally? Do you think we've found our first evidence of alien life?"

"Well, I don't want to jump to any conclusions. A lot of work still needs to be done. I haven't ruled out the possibility that a group of humans landed here in the early days of our arrival and died out. After all, I don't know every Old Earth language. That would be impossible."

Not so impossible, Roslyn thought. Her jealousy lessened a bit at having an advantage over the other archaeologist. *Though I suppose she didn't have the fortune of living on Old Earth for centuries.*

"But the artifacts we're finding don't look like any technology from the days of the migration." Dr. Carriger lifted the flap of a tent and gestured for them to enter. "And our preliminary chronology estimates indicate they predate any human settlement on Orpheus."

Roslyn stepped inside the dark tent, and at first, all she could see were a few glowing green spots hovering over what appeared to be the outline of a table.

Dr. Carriger said, "Lights," and as the voice sensor responded to her command, Roslyn could see the glowing green spots were sigils carved into stone.

"See?" Dr. Carriger's eyes were wide, her face flushed. "These stones appear to be some kind of technology. We're not sure what each of them does yet, but human devices are made out of metal or plastic, not solid stone!"

"May I hold one?" Roslyn asked.

Dr. Carriger seemed to have anticipated Roslyn's question, because she was already handing her a pair of gloves. "I know I don't have to tell you to be careful."

Roslyn reached out and picked up an egg-shaped rock she could hardly believe was a device of some kind. She eyed the symbols and begged them to become familiar to her. Demitrius had taught her all of the language once then had taken it away until such time as he deemed her worthy of it.

A tear formed in her eye. The egg, whatever it was, was her heritage, and being so close to it made her want to know where she came from more than she ever had before.

"It's remarkable, isn't it?" Dr. Carriger said, but her voice was distant as a stronger voice rose in Roslyn's mind.

"*Elleks. Tsufo. Kel.* Repeat." It was Demitrius's voice, and he was identifying the symbols.

"*Elleks,*" she whispered. "*Tsufo. Kel.*" The symbols flashed in her mind, and she recognized them among the symbols in front of her. *The language is coming back to me!*

Before she could appreciate it, pain erupted in her skull. She barely had the sense to place the precious artifact back on the table before she clutched her head and screamed.

"Roslyn!" Gavin's arm caught her as she fell. She would know Gavin's arm anywhere.

"Rosie!" And Jack. "Rosie!"

She held onto his voice, the panic in his tone her only solace, until she passed out.

Present Day

Shut up, Snookems, Roslyn thought as she woke up. She could hear the dog before she even opened her eyes.

Really, though, she was grateful to the dog for rousing her. Her splitting headache was only a fraction of the one she'd had in the dream. She wondered if Old Roslyn had died of it. The pain had certainly felt the way she imagined an aneurysm might feel.

Except Old Roslyn didn't die. There is no Old Roslyn. It's all some delusion I made up. But the words didn't ring true. The dreams felt so real.

Snookems was still barking, and Roslyn's head needed a moment to clear before she realized someone was knocking on her third-story window.

Had she been more awake and in less pain, she might have been frightened, but in her muddled state, the logical thing was to pull back the curtain and see who was on the other side.

The light was dim, but Roslyn would recognize the thin frame and devil-may-care smile anywhere. *Jack.*

CHAPTER 17

Present Day

"**S**HE KNEW MY NAME, JACK. My real name."

Jack didn't understand why Cobalt kept repeating that. *I mean, sure, rando dog-walker-girl Roslyn called him Cobalt when his tag clearly read Blue, but Cobalt and Blue are synonyms. Cronos knows I use them interchangeably.*

"I seriously doubt the dog walker is a secret corporation spy," Jack said.

He didn't know what had made him call to the girl on the street. Usually, he and his brother were content to manage their arguments themselves, especially when they were on the run from the OBI and ZimmerCorp. Jack didn't know why his and Cobalt's faces weren't broadcast all over the moon, but he decided to be grateful that Cobalt's plan to hide out as cruiser repairmen was working.

"Or maybe you don't want to believe it," Cobalt said, the accusation clear in his tone.

"Why wouldn't I want to believe it?" Jack asked, though he knew Cobalt was right.

Something about the girl had called to him. It wasn't her straight brown hair or her I-don't-give-a-crap-about-my-clothes-because-I'm-a-server attire. He had met hundreds of prettier girls who put effort into their appearance. Maybe he was fascinated by the way she talked back to him or the way she put serious thought into a question posed to her by some guy on the street.

"I don't know." Cobalt ran his hands through his hair. "All I know is you've spent every minute since we got back using your not-inconsiderable hacking skills to research this girl. That's not like you."

No, it's not like me, Jack thought. *I'm waiting for my girl to come along, and it can't be this Roslyn. I'm interested in her, sure, but if she were my girl, I would recognize her. Wouldn't I?*

"I'm researching her because she knew your name, remember?" He pointed at the screen, which had several bullet points of notes, a few pictures, and a dossier of school records. "I'm trying to figure out if she has corporate ties. Which she doesn't."

The more he looked into Roslyn, though, the more he knew his words to Cobalt were a lie. He wanted to know more about her because she reminded him of himself in some ways. She had a life a lot of people on Daedalus would give their right arms for. She was a server, but she was well kept with all those legally mandated benefits. All she had to do for the cushy life was walk a dog, but she wasn't happy. He wondered if she would go along with a plan to rob a train just because she could.

Cobalt pointed at the screen. "Would you look at what you're reading? The girl is by all accounts a genius. Maybe not on your level, but she can speak at least five languages and apparently knows more about dead painters and computer engineers than I can imagine anyone wanting to. Yet she was denied admission to university. You think if a megacorp offered her the opportunity to get off this polished rock in exchange for spying on some criminals, she wouldn't jump at the chance?"

Jack sighed. Cobalt had a point. "Then why would she call you by your real name and give herself away?"

"Because she's an amateur, obviously. She didn't expect to have to interact with us."

Tapping his finger against the side of his datapad, Jack considered that, but something didn't feel right about Cobalt's response. He looked at his usually calm and sedate brother and wondered at his rigidity. "There's something you're not telling me."

"On any given day, there are a million things I don't tell you, but that doesn't mean I'm wrong about this girl being trouble."

Jack twisted back and forth on his swivel chair. "Okay, you may have a point. I've got an idea. I'll go talk to her and see if I can get a better insight into her motivation." *And I'll get to talk to her again.*

"That is a terrible idea," Cobalt said. "If she is a corporate spy, you'll be playing right into her hands."

"Please. It's the middle of the night. Who's she going to call now?"

"You want to go visit her now?" Cobalt rolled his eyes. "Of course you do. Like the creepy stalker you've already made yourself out to be today."

Jack grinned. "Her bedroom's on the third floor. Any chance you know where I can get a set of lift-off boots this time of night?"

"Jack!"

Though he thought it might be his imagination, she sounded happy to see him. He hoped Cobalt wasn't right about her having some nefarious corporation-driven plot to have him arrested.

"Can I come in?" he asked. "These boots are kind of hard to balance in."

She looked surprised for a moment then looked out the window at his power boots. "Oh, sure. Hopefully, it'll make

Snookems stop barking." She backed up, giving him room to get inside.

He looked around the surprisingly pink and frilly bedroom. He would have expected something more utilitarian, maybe in red, for her, but maybe the décor was as much her choice as the dog—who had stopped barking—had been.

"How did you know it was me and not C—Blue?" Jack asked.

Roslyn studied him for a moment, and he could tell a million thoughts were going through her head. He found that he wanted to know every one of them.

"You're not all that similar looking" was all she said.

He laughed. "We're identical twins."

Giving him a small smile, she said, "Only on the outside."

She cringed and put her hand to her head, but he didn't think the reaction had anything to do with him. Her eye twitched, as though the muscle was spasming, and he realized she was in pain. He wanted to reach out to her, but somehow he suspected that might put him over the top on the creeper scale, if showing up at her bedroom window hadn't done that already.

"Why are you here, anyway?" She sounded tense and guarded.

Not surprising since she's in pain and I showed up in her bedroom in the middle of the night. But it feels like more than that. Like she knows better than to rely on me. But that's impossible. She couldn't know he lost interest in things as easily as he breathed.

"Blue's worried you're some kind of corporate spy sent to destroy us so you can get into college and escape your meager existence."

Roslyn let out a bark of laughter. "Someone's been doing their research." She pulled back and scrunched her eyes shut with a sharp hiss of breath. "Look, do you mind if I sit down? My head is killing me."

Jack nodded as she sank onto the mess of frilly lace comforter and pink sheets. "You're not angry."

She shook her head. "No. Just surprised there was that much to find on someone who's going to be a dog walker for the rest of her days." Her breath hitched, as if she wanted to say something else but thought better of it.

"Yes, well." Jack didn't want to tell her the lengths to which he had gone to find out about her, and not just because he didn't want to creep her out. He didn't want to tell her about his nefarious talents, yet at the same time, he wanted her to know everything about him. He felt, on some level, she would understand. "Maybe life will surprise you."

She gazed up at him, and for a moment, he felt like she already knew all his deepest secrets and didn't care. His throat went dry, and his hands trembled. He looked down at his palms and saw they were sweating, and his mind dredged up the word for the feeling that had washed over him: *fear*. He was terrified of the slight girl in front of him. Somehow, he knew she didn't care about his past, but he wasn't sure what that meant. *Does it mean she would like me anyway, despite my chaos and indiscretions? Or does it mean she doesn't care about me?*

"Surprises aren't always good," she whispered, and her thoughts were a million miles away.

Jack swallowed and decided to focus on the reason he'd come. "So when you said I did my research, did that mean you *are* a corporate spy?"

Roslyn snickered, and it turned into a whimper as she slid down and rested her head on what looked like a very soft pillow. "I don't know why you would think that." She closed her eyes, and for a moment, he thought she wasn't going to open them again. "I mean, I guess I do. But I'm not a corporate spy. I just wondered how you knew I wanted to go to university and put an end to the *meagerness* of my existence. Why would a corporate spy be looking for you, anyway?"

"You don't want to know."

"Perhaps not." A small smile graced her lips.

"How did you know Blue's real name if you're not a corporate spy?"

The smile fell. "*You* don't want to know."

"Fair enough."

She lay with her eyes closed for long enough that he thought maybe she had gone to sleep, but somehow he could not make himself leave. He listened to her steady breathing, how it intermixed with his short, stuttered breaths in a crazy kind of perfect rhythm, and he didn't want to ever walk away.

"You never answered my question," she said after a while.

Her voice should have surprised him, but instead, its cadence drifted perfectly into the silent music he had created in his head. "What question was that?"

She opened her hazel eyes, and they held a challenge in them. "Why are you here, Jack? You said Cobalt suspected me of something, but that doesn't explain why you're here instead of him."

His entire mouth dried out that time, and the trembling in his fingers intensified. He couldn't face the question standing, so he sank onto the frilly comforter next to her feet, all the while waiting for a protest from her that never came.

"I don't know," Jack said, surprising himself with his honesty. "I don't know why I'm here. Pulling crazy stunts, that's totally me. Showing up in strange girls' bedrooms in the middle of the night, wearing rocket boots, is a new one."

"Is it?" She sounded dubious and suddenly closed off.

"*Yes.*" He felt like he needed to justify himself to her, to bring her back to him, but he couldn't explain about his girl, the one who was waiting for him, the one who couldn't possibly be Roslyn, because if he had met *her,* he would *know. But Cronos, right now, right at this moment, I want it to be Roslyn so badly.*

117

He felt a hand on his arm, and he realized he had buried his face in his hands. She had sat up next to him, her hazel eyes positively glowing with sympathy and something else he couldn't quite name or didn't want to name.

Her breathing was as unsteady as his. He withdrew his arm from Roslyn's warm touch, hoping putting some distance between them would help, but it only made him feel fainter. He brushed a strand of hair out of her face, letting his hand linger on the silkiness, and suddenly, the world came into focus. Or at least *she* did. The rest of the world didn't matter. She leaned just the slightest bit closer to him, and he felt himself falling toward her.

A hail of what sounded like scattershot against the windows pulled Jack out of his haze. He pulled back from her and shook his head.

Roslyn's eyes were round and terrified. "What *was* that?"

Jack groaned. "Blue. He's probably spent the last half hour calculating the exact trajectory of throwing a handful of pebbles against a window three stories up to sound like the most terrifying thing he could think of. I should go see what he wants."

It was a stupid thing to say. Cobalt wanted them to get out of there before Roslyn's alleged spy plan came to fruition. Jack was going to accede to his brother's wishes, because he knew if he stayed there any longer, he was going to betray the love of his life.

Cobalt stared up at the apple tree outside of Roslyn's window and resented it. It was *spring*, for Cronos's sake. During spring, apple trees were supposed to have blossoms, not apples. But the crazy-rich people on Ariadne wanted to have fresh apples in the spring, so they genetically engineered their trees to cycle off-season. It was unnatural.

He wasn't really angry about the trees, he told himself. He was angry with Jack for dragging him there in the middle of the night to chase after some girl who probably wanted to see them jailed or worse. But then, he wasn't really angry with Jack, either. He was angry with himself for being pulled along on another wild goose chase for the sake of that girl. *Roslyn. Her name is Roslyn.* Somehow, the dog-walker server girl roused a series of feelings in him—anger, resentment, frustration—he didn't understand.

That was a lie. They reminded him of how he'd felt when he saw the blond woman on the screen in the detective's office. He saw her, and thoughts that felt like memories pounded through him. He saw Roslyn laughing, crying, and screaming. He saw her hanging out on some derelict spaceship with him and Jack like she was as much one of them as they were to each other, and he loved her. He saw her railing at his brother, and he pitied her. He saw her kissing Jack, and he resented her.

Cobalt did not, as a general rule, like his emotions. He had been through the requisite emotional skills training in school and knew that emotions were not technically good or bad, but they still felt irrational to him. He needed to stay calm, to think with his head. If he didn't, Jack's emotions would rule their lives.

But lately, he felt like he was all emotion, and irrational emotion at that. He was imagining whole lives with people he had never met. He feared that when he went to sleep that night, he would dream some vivid memory about Roslyn. In short, Cobalt hated the apple tree because Roslyn made him afraid to sleep. Though that made a lot more sense before he put it into words. He kicked the tree stump. *Stupid tree.*

He wondered how long Jack would be up there *and* what he was *doing* up there. He'd said he was going to interrogate Roslyn for possible corporate or OBI ties, but Cobalt knew better. He had never seen Jack like this about a girl, and he wasn't sure hacker-stalker was a good look on his brother. Judging by the visions Cobalt hated to call memories, he knew the odds were good that Roslyn was *the* girl, the one Jack was so obsessed with saving himself for.

But Jack didn't seem to remember her. At least, not the way Cobalt did. Jack clearly felt some kind of connection to her, but when Cobalt had suggested they had met before, he had dismissed it, citing their lifetime residence on different moons. Cobalt didn't understand why he had the new memories and Jack didn't, when Jack figured so prominently in all of them.

Cobalt kicked the tree again. He hated feeling out of sorts. Jack was supposed to be the crazy, emotional one, yet Cobalt was the one having the nervous breakdown. *Roslyn has to be a corporate spy. That's what makes the most sense. These "memories" are crazy fantasies that my too-idle brain has created. That's the logical answer, and it's what I'm going to focus on. And that means Jack has spent way too long up there, if she hasn't had him arrested already.*

Cobalt looked for his brother's shadow in the window and didn't see it. He didn't see anything moving up there at all, except for some flickering light. *Crap.* He looked around for some small stones. *If I throw these at the right angle, I should be able to make an adequate noise.*

Pop-pop-pop-pop-pop. The rocks hit the window, and Cobalt cursed under his breath. The entire world would be aware of their presence, but at least the sound had the desired effect.

Jack stuck his head out the window a moment later. "Cronos, Blue! You trying to wake the whole house?"

"No, just trying to get you out of there before you get arrested."

Jack was already climbing out the window and activating the boots to float back down. "Relax. Servers are allowed to have visitors, you know."

"Yes, great. I'm sure the authorities will see us as run-of-the-mill visitors, climbing in the third-story window in the middle of the night."

"Well, we were until you decided to see if you could mimic projectile weapon fire," Jack muttered. "Though I suppose it's just as well I wasn't caught. No doubt the Bhanushalis would love to get Roslyn married off to some normal fellow. It would be another server for their paddock."

Cobalt felt his eyebrows drift up to somewhere around the stratosphere. "You're getting married now?"

"Blue! Don't be ridiculous. I just met the girl." Jack got quiet for a moment then said, "I like her. But I don't think she's the one, you know? I would know if she were the one, wouldn't I?"

"You're asking the wrong person." Cobalt was aware even as he said it the words were at least half a lie.

Jack nodded. He was silent the rest of the way home.

CHAPTER 18

Present Day

After two weeks in the forest, Gavin was the worse for wear. He had tried using his utility blade to shave off his growth of beard a week ago, but a slice or two in his chin had convinced him to embrace the scruff. The stink was harder to deal with, but it had been days since he had seen the one river that meandered through the forest. Hanging around the river was a surefire way to get caught.

If Archon's appearance indicated anything, the viewers of the games were not getting a treat, looking at them. Gavin's friend had always been the perfect clean-cut soldier before, with a smoothly shaven chin and a crew cut refreshed every week or two. After a day or two of survival training, he might have appealed to women—or men—who liked the rugged look, but after two weeks, Gavin wondered if his friend shaved all the time because he couldn't grow a decent beard. Wisps of uneven hair floated from his chin, and his hair grew unevenly.

He also didn't smell any better than Gavin did, but the stink didn't make it through the cameras. Some tech experts had experimented with sending scent information through vid screens along with sight and sound a few years back, but complaints about headaches had squashed that beta test.

Actually, now that he thought about it, that experiment had been over forty years ago. He wasn't sure why he remembered the story so vividly, almost as if he had been there. Regardless, people watching the games should be grateful they weren't smelling what he was.

Beards aside, they were traveling around in full forest camouflage, with leaves covering their hats and clothing, almost making it difficult to see past the falls of green hanging off them. They had adopted the natural garments over the first week, making themselves look shoddy over the vid screens. Then, as soon as they knew the trackers were no longer watching, they redid their "costumes," making sure to take foliage from a variety of different places.

A rustle sounded in the trees.

"Hey," Archon whispered. "Did you hear that?"

Gavin motioned for silence, trying not to feel exasperated with Archon. He saw no point in having a battle buddy he'd known for his entire life if they couldn't take advantage of predetermined nonverbal communication. But he understood too. He hadn't used his voice in a week, and sometimes at night, he feared it would go rusty.

Archon scrunched up his nose at Gavin then pointed in the direction of the noise. Gavin tried to identify what had made the sound. It didn't seem large enough to be fellow competitors or the team chasing after them, but he couldn't be certain someone wasn't making a noise to lure him in. The rustling also seemed larger than a rabbit or a squirrel, something that could make a decent single meal. It could be a deer, which would be a mixed blessing. On one hand, it had been a long time since the summer blackberries they had found that morning, and they'd had to make sure to eat only a few of those to leave their tracks clear. On the other hand, a deer was large, and they didn't want to cut out what they needed and leave behind a body. Nor did they want to carry around a moldering deer carcass.

He nodded that they should investigate. Archon moved slowly forward and pushed aside the foliage.

Shit, Gavin thought.

A larger form than he anticipated was in the clearing on the other side of the branches. It had four legs, though it was standing up on its rear two, using its massive claws to dig into the bark of a tree. Its black fur coat glistened in the sun, and its massive horns rose a good five feet above its head. Gavin thought it looked beautiful, but at the same time, he knew he was in very grave danger. It was a trimper, a deadly predator that could see them as well as they could see it.

Gavin took a deep breath. *We can handle this.* They'd had ample training in wilderness activities. *Stay calm. Back away.* Maybe the horned bear would not see them as a threat or as food.

He felt a rustle to his left, and he moved only his eyes to see Archon. His battle buddy's blue eyes were wider than Gavin had ever seen them, and he realized his friend was losing his cool.

Don't sweat. Don't move, Gavin thought. *It can smell your fear.*

But Archon couldn't read Gavin's mind, and beads of sweat formed on his brow. "We've got to get out of here," he said under his breath.

Gavin gripped his friend's arm tighter, so tight his knuckles lightened. He knew that the tension would draw the trimper's attention, but he was more concerned about what would happen if Archer ran.

The trimper came down from the tree to stand on all four feet. Gavin's best guess put it at six and a half feet tall without the horns, making it taller than Gavin and giving it over half a foot on Archon.

Gavin ran his finger up and down his friend's arm in as

soothing a motion as he could. *I'm not afraid, and you're not afraid, and it's not afraid. No one is afraid, and soon it will go away and leave us alone.*

The motion that he'd intended to calm Archon had the opposite effect. He supposed men didn't generally stroke each other's arms, but he didn't have another calm way to communicate stillness. His wrist wrenched as Archon broke free and tore across the forest.

The trimper snorted, and Gavin imagined a mythical fire bull with smoke coming out of its nose. It brushed one front paw along the ground, then with a pounce almost like a cat, it sprinted toward them. Gavin braced himself for impact, knowing he was about to die, but either his attempts to remain still had worked better than he could have imagined, or the trimper wanted a bit of a challenge. It tore off into the woods after Archon.

For what must have been only five or ten seconds but what felt like an eternity, Gavin watched the trimper close in on his friend. As the right horn pierced his friend's side, Gavin had a feeling of déjà vu and the strangest thought. *Fucking Jack. I can't let him die.*

He didn't know where the thought had come from or what it meant, but the exact anatomy of the trimper flowed through his mind. He knew where the muscles were and what each one did. He knew the exact location of every bone in its body and, more importantly, where it did not have bones covering major arteries. And with expertise that his father had always desired of him, he grabbed his survival knife and flung it toward the trimper with unexpected accuracy.

Blood spurted from the trimper in every direction, and it reared on its hind legs as it squealed an unearthly noise. Gavin half expected Archon to be pierced upon the beast's horn, but apparently, the impalement hadn't been complete. *Good,* he thought as the trimper collapsed to the ground in a pool of its copper-scented blood. *Maybe there's still hope.*

But he didn't see how there could possibly still be hope.

He had seen the trimper's sharp ivory horn stab his friend in the gut, and he knew that some of the blood on the ground over there did not belong to the trimper.

He darted over to his friend, relived to see Archon's chest still heaving, albeit with substantial effort. His blue eyes were glassy, and his skin was tinged green.

"I'm calling for extraction," Gavin said, though he had no expectation that his friend would hear him.

Archon made a weak noise.

"What?" Gavin dropped to the ground next to his friend.

"Don't," Archon said breathily. "You could still win. You... you killed a trimper. That's got to be, like, a million points."

"I don't care if I win if you die, you moron," Gavin said. But on some level, he must have still wanted to win, because he wasn't saying the words that would get them out. Or maybe he was in as much shock as Archon, because his brain was not feeling at all like his brain. Instead of trying to figure out how to get a doctor for Archon, it was trying to *be* a doctor and analyze what needed to be done to save his friend's life.

But I don't know what to do! the panicky part of his brain said. *I don't know how to cauterize a wound or staunch bleeding or stitch up internal organs.*

But even his thoughts deconstructed themselves. As he stared at his friend's wound, he realized he didn't have to quit the game or watch his friend die. He knew what to do.

CHAPTER 19

Present Day

WILL BOUNDED UP THE STAIRS to the third floor of Lexi's dorm, whistling as he did so. The last two weeks had been the best he could remember in a long time. He and Lexi were together. He seemed to be having an easier time convincing her to go out with him than he had in some previous lives, and already they were practically inseparable. And Bliss was around, which was always nice. She had always been Roslyn's best friend, but in some ways, she was his too.

He reached Lexi and Bliss's room and took a moment to observe the digital board hanging on the metal door. "Lexi, meet me at 3. We're going shopping, bitch," the one closest to the top read. He glanced at the time on his datapad: 3:05. So much for surprising her. He supposed he should have called first, anyway. Lexi didn't really like surprises. He was about to walk away when he heard a familiar voice on the other side of the door.

"Stop calling me. I'm not talking to you."

Only one person had that sarcastic tone, and he hadn't heard her voice in over twenty years.

"I know you're not talking to me!" Bliss's voice came

through the door. "What I don't know is why! Don't you owe me an explanation?"

"I don't know," Roslyn said. "I think you're the one who owes me an explanation. Why did you tell the professors I cheated? Why did you get me referred into therapy instead of university? They think I'm crazy, by the way. I'm waiting for someone to pick me up to take me to the loony bin."

"I was trying to help you!" Her voice sounded as if she was crying. "You'd been saying crazy things, and you cheated on that test!"

Will placed his hand on the door. He wasn't sure exactly what Bliss and Roslyn were arguing about, but he could guess. Roslyn always got her memories back first and most clearly. It was part of being a full-blooded Transient. And when they first came back, they could look like insanity to an outsider.

"I did *not* cheat on that test!" Roslyn's roar created static over the interplanetary line. "And how is keeping me a server for the rest of my life helping me? Do you want to keep me as much your pet as Snookems is?"

Will closed his eyes and leaned his forehead against the door. He wanted to reach out to his sister to comfort her. *A server. I can't believe she was born a server.* More than anything in the universe, she would hate that. She, who only ever wanted to go somewhere she had never been before, was stuck in a cage.

He wanted to tell her it would get better. The system couldn't hold a Transient as a server forever. They had been born into servitude before and always found ways to break free. He wanted to reassure her he knew she hadn't cheated on the university entrance exam and that the unnatural knowledge that had come to her was perfectly natural, for them, at least. But mostly, he wanted to see her face.

He knew he shouldn't and most likely wouldn't be able to. Lexi and Bliss had probably locked the door, so if he pressed the sensor, it would alert Bliss to his presence instead of opening. Bliss would hang up her call to see who was at the door, or she wouldn't hang up and would ignore Will. Either way, he wouldn't get to see Roslyn.

But he had to try. He pressed his hand to the door, and it swung open. Bliss was lying on her bed. She turned to see who had opened the door, and he barely registered the puzzled look she gave him. His gaze followed the angle of her neck to a datapad tilted slightly away from him, but he still recognized the girl on the viewscreen.

His throat felt tight, and a tear formed in his eye. Maybe he should have looked for Roslyn instead of Lexi. He had trusted that Roslyn would find her own way, as she always did, but his sister looked so lost and helpless. Her cheeks were red and tearstained, and he doubted it was because she was so happy to see him. Roslyn only cried when she was angry.

"Will?" Bliss said. "Do you need something? I can get off this call."

He shook his head, as much to stop staring at Roslyn as to indicate a negative. "No, no. Of course not. Stay on your call. I was looking for Lexi. I'll just leave her a note."

His eyes found Roslyn's once more, and before he could back out of the room with as much grace as was left to him, she said, "Will? Your name is Will?"

"Oh, yes, I'm sorry, Roslyn. How rude of me!" Bliss held up her datapad so Will could see it straight on. "Will, Roslyn. She's my best friend from home. Roslyn, Will. He's dating Lexi."

Roslyn reached out to touch the screen, as if she could somehow reach Will's face through it. "Do I... Do I know you?"

Bliss brought the datapad back to face her. "I told you about him, I'm sure. He's been hanging around with us a lot."

"And he's dating Lexi? Is he psychotic?" Roslyn's words didn't hold quite their usual sarcastic bite, but they sounded enough like his sister that he was content she was feeling better.

"No, of course he's not psychotic! He's very nice. He just—"

"Has terrible taste in women," Roslyn said. "I get it. I apparently have terrible taste in men."

Will snorted. *She does indeed.*

Bliss glanced back and forth between Roslyn and Will. She apparently didn't know whether to focus on Roslyn's words or Will's reaction to them.

"I would tell you all about it," Roslyn continued. "But I'm mad at you. And you'd probably say I was crazy."

Bliss focused on Roslyn. "If you have a boyfriend you're not telling me about, I will personally come home to Ariadne and feed Snookems a diet of beans."

"I don't have a boyfriend," Roslyn said, but even Will could tell she wasn't telling the whole truth.

Bliss squealed, and Will wanted to stay and hear the whole story. *Is it Jack? Gavin? Some entirely different human boy whose heart she's destined to break?* He wanted to hear everything.

Wait, no, scratch that. He didn't want to hear about his sister's love life. He just wanted to hear about *her*. But he had already given too much away, and he needed to get out of there. To the tune of Bliss's high-pitched entreaties to know more about the man in Roslyn's life, Will crept out of the room.

Lexi studied the digital representation of the dress on a figure designed to mimic hers exactly. "I'm just not sure." It was a nice-enough dress. The red would complement her skin tone nicely and maybe even bring out the mahogany flecks in her eyes, but the sweetheart neckline was so last year.

Her friend Steff groaned. "Come on, Lexi. That's like the

fiftieth dress you've tried on, and you don't like any of them. You do realize the winter formal is months away."

"Just because everything looks perfect on you, Miss Blond-Haired-Blue-Eyed-Hourglass, does not mean the rest of us are so fortunate." Lexi shifted through the touch screen to another dress. *Have I looked at this blue number already? I wonder if it comes in green.*

"Yes, because you're such a hag." The petite Steff rolled her eyes. "I would absolutely die if I were five-foot-nine and had legs almost as long. Will will love you no matter what you wear."

Lexi flipped past a few more dresses. "Who says I'm taking Will to the winter formal?"

"Um, duh. You guys are perfect for each other."

How can I explain to Steff the strange way Will makes me feel? The boy seemed to adore her, and that was great. She loved it when a guy would do anything for her. But at the same time, he anticipated her wants almost too well, to the point that she wondered whether he was stalking her to learn her preferences.

Not that that would be such a huge deal. She was worthy of a stalker and was perfectly capable of stringing him along while keeping him at arm's length in case he became violent or something. What mattered was that when she was around Will, the strange voice of her doubts became louder. It kept telling her she couldn't be famous, and she couldn't knock it down, not when Will was around.

She hated the look he got every time she mentioned her inevitable fame. His smile would dim, and he would refuse to meet her eyes for a few seconds. Then he would look back and agree with her. He didn't believe in her, not really, and it drove her mad. He probably pretended to agree with her to get into her pants, which would be fine if her self-doubts didn't get louder. She hated that Will had so much power over her, which meant that sooner or later, she was going to have to call it quits. *Probably before winter formal, since*

Steff's right. It's months away, hardly a blip on anyone's radar. But if I want a one-of-a-kind dress, I need to get my order in soon.

"Maybe something short." She reselected her filters and ran dresses over the fake Lexi figure almost faster than the eye could see.

Steff sighed.

Whatever, Lexi thought. *She can wait if it means I look perfect.*

"I picked out my dress," Lexi announced as she paraded into the dorm room. "No doubt you've been here studying like a little ferret the whole time."

Bliss looked up from her datapad. She wished she could say she had been studying, but she had been searching for information on Will, though she'd reached a major stumbling block. "What's Will's last name?"

Lexi mumbled something from inside her closet then stuck her head out. "Why?"

"Did... did you just say 'Turin'?" Bliss asked.

"Yes, then I said, 'Why?' but I notice you're ignoring that part."

"Turin is my friend Roslyn's last name." Bliss pulled up a picture of Will then one of Roslyn and arranged them next to each other. She gasped. They didn't look identical, but the family resemblance was hard to deny.

"So? Who cares?" Lexi said. "I've got the same last name as one of those chumps in the Bellerophon Games, and you don't see me making a big deal out of it."

"Look at this." Bliss held up her datapad for Lexi to see.

Lexi pursed her lips. "That's Will and... his sister? Why am I interested in this?"

"'That's not Will's sister," Bliss said. "That's my friend Roslyn. She was born a server on Ariadne. I've known her my entire life. She doesn't have any siblings."

"O-kay," Lexi said. "So two people you know happen to look similar. Big whoop."

"They have the same last name."

Lexi put her hands on her hips. "So, what? You think it's some kind of galactic conspiracy?"

"All right, I know it sounds crazy, but what if Will was never looking for you or me? What if he approached us—"

"Me. He approached me. You butted in."

"Right, he approached *you*, but what if he was looking for his sister the whole time? What if he was born on Ariadne, and his parents smuggled him off so he could have a chance at a better life? And now he's looking for the sister he left behind?"

Lexi flopped down on her bed. "Cronos, Bliss, can you be any more self-centered? You're saying Will is interested in me because he wants to get to *you*?"

Bliss felt heat rise to her face. "No! I mean, I'm sure he really likes you. I just—"

"Besides, if he were looking for his sister, he would be on Ariadne, not here."

Rolling onto her back, Bliss said, "You're right. I know you're right. It's an insane theory."

Lexi made an offended noise in her throat. "I did not say it was insane. You're right. Something is off about Will, and you and I are going to find out what it is."

"What do you mean?"

"I mean dust off that extremely unfashionable trench coat I've seen lurking in the back of your closet, because you and I are about to become detectives."

CHAPTER 20

Present Day

TEGAN WISHED SHE HAD FRIENDS.

Scratch that. She'd had friends once. They'd betrayed her, and she'd betrayed them, and it sucked. She had Detrick and Phedre. She didn't need anyone else, though they weren't really satisfying company. One had all the social skills of bread mold, and the other threatened to kill her on a regular basis.

Maybe I can get Detrick to build me a robot friend. He'd done some experimenting with AIs in the past, and while he couldn't get along with the things to save his life, maybe she could. It would give her someone to talk to, anyway. *Someone who would never, ever call me Cuttlefish.*

Twenty Years Ago

Tegan's datapad bleeped, and she let out a heavy sigh when she saw the scowling brunette come up on the screen. Her finger hovered over the face for a few seconds before she pushed the button to respond. "Go away, Phedre. I'm not interested in any of your plots."

"Oh, but I think you are this time" came the silky voice over the line. "You see, your fellow Transients have betrayed you."

"You always say that, and it's never true." Tegan pressed a few buttons on the *Spirit*'s cockpit, trying to get the cabin to air out. She'd let Detrick come aboard last week, and the place still smelled of disinfectant.

"Have you heard of Arachne?" Phedre asked.

"Sure. The tabloids are full of it. Mysterious moon discovered by joyriders, cloaked by ancient alien technology."

"Exactly." Tegan wasn't looking at her screen, but she could hear the smug smile in Phedre's voice. "Ancient *alien* technology. Sound like something you would want to know about?"

"Yes. In the event ancient alien technology actually existed, I would absolutely want to know more about it."

"You mean you haven't heard?" Phedre could try to make her sultry voice sound innocent, but she never quite succeeded. Years of duplicity had settled on her vocal chords, and Tegan suspected even the hungriest child would balk before accepting candy from Phedre. "I mean, I would have thought with you being so close to your fellow Transients and all, you would have at least *heard*—"

"Spit it out, Phedre."

"Well, your dear friends who would never betray you are already there, studying whatever Demitrius left for us to find."

Tegan barked out a laugh. "You'll never make me believe Lexi is on an archaeological expedition to a secret moon." As soon as the words were out of her mouth, she realized what Phedre would say next.

"And can you really imagine Roslyn and Jack wouldn't be on such a mission?"

She couldn't, and she knew that if Roslyn and Jack were there, Cobalt was too. Which meant a third of the Transient population was researching their heritage while the rest of them were left in the dust.

"They'll tell us about it when they find something." *I hope. Cronos, I hope.*

"And who is this 'us' you're referring to?" Phedre asked. "Gavin's on the trip, and you know Roslyn tells Bliss and Will everything."

"And what Will knows, Lexi knows." Tegan heard something snap, and it wasn't until she felt the burst of pain and the blood dripping down her finger that she realized it was the stylus in her hand.

She shouldn't really be so angry. She was used to being on the outside. The rest of them had their interconnections and their little love triangles, and she was the one they forgot. They gave her cute nicknames like "Cuttlefish," but they didn't think of her if she wasn't immediately in their presence.

"So I guess the only ones who don't know about the plan are you and Detrick," Phedre said. "Gee, do you think they put you in the same category as Detrick?"

Tegan nearly ended the conversation right there. She knew Phedre was trying to get to her. Of course the others didn't think of her the same way they thought of Detrick. She was capable of basic social interaction. Besides, Phedre shouldn't use Detrick that way. His autism wasn't his fault, and to treat him like less of a person because of it was cruel.

Underneath Phedre's misdirects and manipulations, though, was a layer of truth. Her fellow Transients didn't think of her or respect her. They knew she was as desperate as any of them to learn about their heritage, perhaps even more so, yet they didn't think to tell her about the discovery. They didn't want her help, but Phedre did. On some level, all Tegan wanted was to be wanted.

"Okay," Tegan said. "I'm listening."

Present Day

Tegan didn't know if she regretted listening to Phedre that day or going along with all her nefarious schemes since. Certainly, Tegan's actions had driven a wedge between her and her fellow Transients. *But wasn't that wedge there all along?* The fact that she wasn't sure should have said everything, but it didn't.

She adjusted her vidscreen to show the Bellerophon Games. She couldn't get to Gavin, so she figured she could check up on him that way. Though she'd expected to have to rewind to the last footage featuring him, he was right there in all his glory.

As he moved through the trees, she admitted to herself that she liked him best in soldier mode. Based on the pre-contest interviews, he liked being a soldier about as much as he always did, but that had never stopped him from signing up for what he deemed necessary wars. *And when he's cleaned up, he looks damn good in uniform.*

He wasn't cleaned up in the scene Tegan was watching, but he pulled off the scruffy, uneven beard and sweaty, war-torn greens better than that friend of his. Looking closer at the smear of red on the screen, Tegan decided just about anyone would be doing better than the friend, who had blood gushing from his side.

Gavin rushed over to his friend's side and rummaged around in his pack until he pulled out what looked like a lighter, a canteen, and a sewing kit, and Tegan smiled. If Gavin was performing emergency field surgery, he had to remember who he was, at least a little. Phedre was convinced she needed activated Transient blood for the ritual, and Gavin looked like a perfect candidate.

Gavin had explained it to Tegan once. The Transients always began life looking, even on a molecular level, just like humans. In their late teens, around the time they got their memories back, they developed other markers of the alien species they belonged to.

"Does that mean if we died before the markers showed up, we wouldn't reincarnate?" Tegan had asked.

Gavin hadn't been sure, but he suspected they wouldn't. Yet another reason not to die, as far as Tegan was concerned. But she was glad Gavin was getting his memories back. When she killed him again, he wouldn't die permanently.

CHAPTER 21

Present Day

"ROSLYN, WOULD YOU LIKE TO tell the group why you've joined us?" the therapist asked.

I'm here because my psychologist is a traitor who doesn't believe me about anything, Roslyn thought, but she didn't say it. The nice, amber-skinned woman with her big, soulful brown eyes seemed sincere. She didn't deserve Roslyn's bitterness. "Not really," she said.

"Now, Roslyn, we're all friends here."

The woman's black hair gleamed like Bliss's did. Bliss might have been a traitor who'd landed Roslyn in the hospital, but she was her friend. These other patients, sitting in a circle, wearing the requisite white uniforms of drawstring pants and shirts that tied in the front, were probably nice enough, but Roslyn didn't want to be their friend.

Roslyn sighed, knowing she had to say something. She summed up her basic experience with the university test, leaving out the craziness with the dreams and the past lives. She finished with "Honestly, I think they're just calling me crazy because they don't want to send a server to university."

The therapist gave Roslyn a level gaze then made a note in her chart. No doubt it said something like "Patient is intransigent. Will not admit to delusions in front of random people she doesn't know."

Maybe that was the problem. She had trusted Dr. Tanner, and the woman had sent her off to a place full of strangers where everyone was on suicide watch. Each patient had a hover-droid following them everywhere they went, transmitting images to some voyeur. Roslyn couldn't eat, sleep, or even shower without a gleaming silver bot with a red laser eye staring her down.

She didn't get to do any of those things very often, though. During her intake, the administrator had handed her a schedule indicating her days would be regimented until her therapists deemed her sane enough to go home. She had hoped she could spend more time sleeping, because that meant dreaming, which meant spending more time with Old Roslyn. *And Jack.*

Roslyn had almost believed Dr. Tanner was right about her delusions until Jack had shown up in her bedroom. They must have a real connection, not one she had fabricated. She wondered if he would come back and find her gone, and what he would think if he knew where she was.

On top of all that, she was worried about Snookems. She couldn't quite believe it, but she missed that damn dog.

Some of the patients nodded and smiled at her words, but they moved on to other topics. She suspected most psychiatric patients, her included, were primarily preoccupied with their own problems.

Finally, after a long day of group therapy, art therapy, individual therapy, and a boatload of pills shoved down her throat, Roslyn retired to her single room. She wondered how she had swung that, considering most people had to share. The Bhanushalis must have been feeling generous toward their dog walker, or else Dr. Tanner had told everyone she was too dangerous for a roommate. Either way, she was grateful for the privacy. She stared at the blank white walls and willed herself to fall asleep.

Twenty Years Ago

"Rosie! She's waking up! Rosie, say something!"

"Wh-What happened?" The world—or rather, Jack's face—spun into focus as Roslyn awoke inside a strange room. *Wait, not a room. A tent.* She was in a large beige tent with several metal poles holding it up along the edges.

"It was very strange."

Roslyn turned her head to see the blond woman who had spoken. *Dr. Hannah Carriger. Leader of the expedition.*

"One minute, you were looking at an artifact, and the next, you were on the ground, bleeding out of your nose."

"May I have a word with the patient alone?" someone with a deep voice asked. *Gavin.* No doubt he had already asserted himself as chief medical staff person in the short time he'd been there. *At least, I hope he has.* She didn't want to explain to anyone else what had happened.

"I'm staying," Jack said as Dr. Carriger obligingly headed toward the tent flap.

"You're not." Gavin pointed after the archaeologist. "Go find your brother and make sure he hasn't gotten into any trouble."

Jack grumbled and left.

Roslyn watched him go. "You realize he's more likely to get Cobalt into trouble than out of it, right? Cobalt's probably just gawking at the machinery."

"I know." Gavin sat down on the edge of Roslyn's cot. "I wanted to talk to you alone."

"I shouldn't have made you come." The words rushed out of Roslyn's mouth. "I shouldn't have said you should fight for me. That was stupid and thoughtless of me. You—"

"You didn't make me come. I chose to come. I knew Jack was here, and I knew what that meant," Gavin said. "Besides, that's not what I want to talk about."

"Oh." Heat rose to Roslyn's face.

"I don't think it's safe for you to be here, investigating these artifacts. Demitrius taught you about our heritage, language, and technology, then he blocked your memories of the lessons using some highly advanced brain surgery techniques that, quite frankly, I don't understand."

"Not surprising since you were never a brain surgeon." Roslyn gave her words as understanding a tone as she could.

"I've done enough research on brains to know that whatever he did was beyond human technology. I imagine Caramrilla was involved. Just looking at these artifacts, not even researching them, is making you remember some of what Demitrius taught you. It's trying to break whatever block he put in, and I'm afraid of what the consequences will be."

"I'm not leaving! I want to know where we come from as much as the rest of you, and I'm not going to just take off and leave you here." *And leave Jack here.*

"No, I'm not saying you should." Gavin ran his hands over his shaven head. "I would never ask that of you. I know this kind of archaeology dig is what you live for. I just don't want this one to kill you."

Roslyn placed a hand on Gavin's. "It won't. I'll be careful. I'll just dig and clean, and I won't look closely at any of the symbols."

Gavin turned his hand over and held hers. "Why don't I believe you?"

"I have no idea, because I don't want to die here any more than you want me to. Probably less. This is the first adventure I've gotten to go on in forever, and I don't want to spoil it by dying."

"I know." He gave her a small, sad smile. "I love you."

She gave him half a smile in return. "I know." She cleared her throat. "Now, am I cleared to leave this tent in pursuit of safe adventure that will not cause my head to explode?"

Gavin gestured toward the tent flap. "Go find him."

"I wasn't... I mean, I don't..."

"Just go, Roslyn."

She tried to ignore the sting of tears as she ducked under the tent flap. She had made a mess of everything. *Why couldn't I love Gavin? That would have made everything easier.*

Emerging, she saw what must have been the center of the camp. It was a more bustling place than it had been when she had passed out, with at least a dozen people ducking in and out of tents or standing around the central fire, drinking something out of travel mugs.

She didn't have too much time to analyze the scene before Dr. Carriger pounced on her. "You look like you could use a drink."

"Somehow, I don't think Dr. Ibori would approve of my consuming alcohol so soon after a head injury," Roslyn said.

Dr. Carriger linked her arm with Roslyn's and led her toward the fire. "Well, fortunately for Dr. Ibori, alcohol is in short supply here. The good news is we have something that tastes just as bad without the lovely buzz."

Roslyn laughed. "Oh, well, then, order me up some of that."

Dr. Carriger stopped outside one of the tents. "Mess hall." She ducked inside, and Roslyn followed.

The mess hall was surprisingly small and empty, considering the bustle outside. "Where's the food?" Roslyn asked.

"The government's trying out some new liquid rations on this expedition." Dr. Carriger led her to what looked like a keg on a metal stand. She grabbed one of the travel mugs next to it and held it up to the tap, and a thick brown liquid glopped into the cup. When it was full to the brim, she handed it to Roslyn. "Three times a day, we get that, and it's supposed to have all the nutrients we need to survive. Sure isn't as satisfying as a warm bowl of oatmeal, though."

Roslyn made a disgusted face for Dr. Carriger's benefit.

She had been on any number of expeditions to various frontiers, and an all-liquid diet sounded preferable to some of the things she'd had to eat—or the times she hadn't had *anything* to eat.

She took a sip of the concoction and didn't have to fake the wrinkled nose. The drink tasted like a bran muffin without the sugar mixed with pure rubbing alcohol and mashed into a soggy paste.

"See? Told you," Dr. Carriger said as she got a mug for herself. "So tell me about your team."

"Well, Gavin Ibori was a celebrated surgeon on Ariadne before he came here, and Cobalt's been fixing machines since before he could walk. Jack lives up to his name—a real jack-of-all-trades, but you'll see he's absolutely brilliant at whatever he applies himself to."

"So you and Jack are—?"

"Together? I suppose, yes." Roslyn wondered at the reluctance in her voice. "But trust me, Dr. Carriger—"

"Hannah, please. We're all archaeologists here."

"Okay, Hannah." Roslyn took a deep breath. "Trust me when I say that Jack's and my relationship has no bearing on our work. When I say he's brilliant, it's not because I love him. It's because I've never met anyone with a sharper mind. I am aware of his faults, namely that he doesn't keep focused on any one thing for very long. I recommend keeping his days varied."

"And what about you? What's your expertise?"

"Largely Old Earth artifacts. Most recently, I ran an antiquities shop, where I acquired and appraised artifacts for select, wealthy clientele. It paid the bills, but it wasn't my passion. When I heard rumors of a potential Old Earth fringe colony out here on Arachne, I couldn't pass up the chance to see for myself."

"Yes, I saw your resume," Hannah said. "I was a bit concerned that an antiquities dealer might not have much to add to a live dig, but then I saw your reaction to those artifacts. You've seen that language before."

Roslyn took a long swallow of her rubbing-alcohol-slash-bran mix. She should have known Hannah would have questions about her reaction to the stones. "I've seen writing similar to that on the artifacts. Many of the Western languages from Earth contained similar rounded pictographs. I was simply trying to see similarities in the scripts."

Hannah nodded, but the corners of her mouth had turned downward. Whether she was disappointed in Roslyn's response or she suspected prevarication, Roslyn couldn't tell. After another few sips of "breakfast," Hannah perked back up. "Well, if you think it's like something you've seen before, that's closer than the rest of us have gotten. We'll have to schedule you for some time with the artifacts. That is, if you think you can look at them without passing out."

Is it me, or was her tone a bit snide? Roslyn scanned Hannah's face but couldn't see anything but sincerity in the crystal-blue eyes. *I must be getting paranoid in my old age.*

Roslyn excused herself and went to find Jack. She thought about bringing him a mug of glop, but if she knew him, he was already weaseling his way into the moon's black market to get himself some real food. She circled around the outside of the tents, searching for the best place for a back-alley deal.

She had the briefest warning of someone coming up behind her before hands covered her eyes and someone whispered, "Guess who?" in her ear.

"We-ell," she said, not giving her assailant the satisfaction of pretending to be scared. "I only know two people with hands that size and a voice like that, so I figure I've got a fifty-fifty shot of guessing correctly."

Jack spun her around to face him, and she floated toward him like they were in a ballroom instead of sneaking around behind tents in a ramshackle exploration site. "You wound me. Blue's not creative enough to come up with a gag that clever."

Roslyn laughed. "Ah, yes, exactly the cleverness I have come to expect from you. What are you doing hanging out back here?"

"Why, waiting for you, of course. I wanted some alone time."

Roslyn pulled back a bit, the smile not fading from her face. "And you're not trying to figure out who can get us real food on this rock?"

Jack grinned. "Well, maybe that too."

"I'll forgive you for lying if you get me some chocolate."

"Will you forgive me for lying if I..." He leaned forward and whispered delicious suggestions in her ear, the kind that were no doubt meant to set her body afire but filled her with solid contentment.

We're together. He cares about me. And maybe this time it will last.

CHAPTER 22

Twenty Years Ago

COBALT GLANCED AROUND THE UTILITARIAN tent he was apparently sharing with Jack and Roslyn on the desolate moon. *Great. I always love sharing quarters with them when there are no doors to put socks on. At least there are machines.* The dig site had dozens of machines that needed to be fixed or maintained or tweaked to perform at maximum efficiency. He almost forgave Jack for dragging him to the misbegotten rock.

"Okay, I talked to Hannah, and she has some assignments for us," Roslyn said to him and Jack.

Jack stretched in his chair, appearing to barely pay attention. Cobalt wasn't sure who the show was for. Both he and Roslyn knew that Jack paid attention to details, no matter his outward appearance.

"Remind me why you're in charge again?" Jack asked.

Roslyn made a noise of frustration in the back of her throat. "Because Hannah decided I was, and I didn't want to argue with her. Neither did you, as I recall."

"Because she didn't like him," Cobalt said.

Jack flashed him a grin. "I like a challenge."

Cobalt didn't need to look at Roslyn to know she was cringing. He wanted to make a face as well. It was early in the

Jack-Roslyn relationship cycle for him to be mouthing off to her and throwing other women in her face. Cobalt suspected his brother was acting out because Gavin's presence made him insecure, but Jack was a little over four hundred years old in their current lives and should have been too old for that kind of crap.

"Good, because Hannah needs help translating the runes," Roslyn said. "I would do it, but Gavin's afraid my head will explode, and I'm rather fond of my head. So, Jack, you're on translation duty. Help Hannah with whatever she needs. As for us..." Roslyn gestured to herself and Cobalt. "The explorers have found only this one site of artifacts, and they suspect more may be on the moon. What they've found here isn't enough for a proper settlement. So we're on scouting duty."

Cobalt raised an eyebrow.

"I think what my brother is trying to say is that he is a mechanical genius but not so much into the geographical speculation," Jack said. "Why is he going out with you?"

"Hannah said the terrain is rough out there," Roslyn said. "She thinks we might run into trouble, and she wants someone with me who can repair the rover."

Cobalt nodded. That made sense.

Jack leaned forward in his chair. "All right, fine. Leave me alone. I won't get lonely or anything." His tone was light, but he often whined about being abandoned whenever he and Cobalt separated. Cobalt suspected he had a deep fear of abandonment, though Cobalt had never left him for long, not in the thousands of years they'd been brothers.

"Relax. It's only two weeks," Roslyn said. "Gavin's here, and you're sure to make friends with some of the other explorers. They're all genius adventurers too." *Just stay away from the women,* Cobalt suspected she wanted to add. "That's all, really. Cobalt and I leave in the morning. Jack, you can report to Hannah whenever you feel like it. Just please feel like it sometime in the next couple of days, okay?"

Cobalt got up to walk out of the tent. If he was going to spend two weeks alone with the rover, he wanted to check it out before he left. Out of the corner of his eye, he saw Jack approach Roslyn and wrap his arms around her. "If you're going to be gone for two weeks, we need to make the most of our last night together."

"Really, Jack?" Roslyn managed to make her voice sound breathy with anticipation and sardonic at the same time.

Cobalt sped away from the tent as fast as he could. He didn't want to listen to what came next, be it an argument or something they enjoyed more.

I'm going to be alone with Roslyn for two weeks. That should be interesting. Roslyn thought he hated her. He didn't. In many ways, he loved her like the sister he didn't have, but he didn't understand why she let Jack treat her the way he did.

Don't I? After all, Jack treated Cobalt the same way, and part of his disagreements with Roslyn were that she made him look too closely at his relationship with his brother. Jack was more loyal to Cobalt, certainly, but Jack made all the decisions, no matter what Cobalt wanted to do.

Cobalt walked a bit faster. He could spend two weeks in silence. It wouldn't be the first time.

Present Day

Cobalt woke to find his brother sitting at a desk, staring at his datapad, and checked the clock to make sure he had the time right then looked out the window to make sure he was still on Ariadne and hadn't somehow ended up in Bizarro World. As he approached, he realized Jack had dark circles under his eyes. Either he had been up for hours, or he hadn't slept at all.

"What's wrong?" Cobalt yawned.

Jack didn't look up from his datapad. "I've been doing some research."

"Roslyn again?" Cobalt moved to the coffee maker and turned it on. Within seconds, it was dripping a delicious steaming beverage into a cup.

"Nah, I'm done with her. How much information can there possibly be about a slave who walks a dog, anyway?"

After waiting until the coffee machine had filled two mugs, Cobalt handed one to his brother. "You seemed very interested in her yesterday."

"Eh. That was yesterday." Jack flipped his datapad so Cobalt could see it. "Take a look at this."

Cobalt squinted, trying to make out whatever Jack was trying to show him. It looked like some kind of oddly put together spaceship. Then he figured out the problem. "It's upside down."

"Oh. Here." Jack handed over the datapad.

The ship looked to be of an old design, and the words "Transcendent Spirit" arched across the hull. As soon as Cobalt read the words, a spark lit in his mind, and he could see the interior of the ship in its full glory.

Glory? he thought. *That's a piece of space junk. Should have been replaced by a newer model years ago.* Somehow, he could picture himself walking its corridors, upgrading its engine, and hanging out in its mess hall. But he wasn't pulling up memories from a blueprint. He had the same feeling about the ship as he did about Roslyn and the blond woman hunting them, as if they were memories of a life he'd never had. "I wouldn't buy it" was all he said as he handed the datapad back to Jack.

"Well, of course you wouldn't, but I think you'll be very interested in who did." Jack swiped on his pad a few times then flipped it back around. That time, it was right side up, and the image of the blond woman made Cobalt flinch.

The grin fell from Jack's face. "One of these days, you're

going to have to tell me why you're convinced this woman wants to kill us. Anyway, her name is—"

"Tegan O'Leary." The name sprang into Cobalt's mind as he stared at the brown liquid in his mug. *Known to her friends as Cuttlefish.*

"You've been doing your research," Jack said. "You want to tell me what you've found?"

Cobalt didn't say anything.

"Okay, fine, be unhelpful." Jack flipped past a few more pages on his datapad. "I've got a bunch of pictures of her. The weird thing is when they were taken."

"Let me guess. Twenty years ago, and she looked exactly the same then as she does today."

"Well, yes and no," Jack said. "I've found the registry for the *Transcendent Spirit* over the past *one hundred years*, and in every single registry, the license picture of one Tegan O'Leary looks exactly the same. She's registered in a bunch of different places over the years, which is why it's taken me all night to piece all this together."

"What do you plan to do with this information now that you have it?"

Jack gave him a strange look, as if surprised he was so calm about everything. Cobalt didn't know how to tell his brother he was starting to suspect that all of them—him, Jack, Roslyn, Tegan, and possibly others—were immortal beings who reincarnated. He wasn't even sure he believed it himself, especially since Jack didn't seem to remember any of it. If his memories were anything to go on—and he wasn't sure they were—he and Jack had been as inseparable in their previous lives as they were in their current one.

Eventually, Jack shook his head. "I'm going to go find her, of course."

Cobalt blanched. "You want to find the woman who wants to kill us?"

"Blue, think about it. The woman has found the secret to

immortal life. We could get it from her and either sell it for millions or use it ourselves."

Booming words rose in Cobalt's mind, loud enough to make him flinch. "Above all rules, remember this: Let *no one* know we exist."

"What is with you?" Jack asked. "You've been jumpy all morning. No, since before that. Since we got arrested. It's not like you."

"Getting arrested? No, it's not." Cobalt sighed. Being deliberately obtuse wasn't going to solve the problem, but if Jack didn't have the same memory flashbacks as he did, he wouldn't believe them. Cobalt's best plan was to behave as normally as possible. "Jack, we've got a good thing going here. A good job. A stable job. We don't need to go mucking that up."

"What we need is a spaceship." Apparently, if Cobalt behaved normally, Jack would go back to ignoring him.

"I am *not* stealing a spaceship."

"Relax. We don't need to steal one." He gave Cobalt a beautiful, brilliant, terrifying grin. "We've got enough diamonds to buy one."

"This is not going to work," Cobalt muttered.

Jack sighed. Sometimes—almost all the time—his brother was so negative. "That's a bad idea, Jack" or "That's crazy, Jack" or "That will get us arrested or killed, Jack." *Doesn't he trust that I would find a way out of any trouble we got into?*

He didn't know why Cobalt was being so negative about the plan. It was simple—they would walk in, buy a spaceship, and fly out. From there, they could leave Ariadne and gather the information they needed about Tegan and the *Transcendent Spirit.* Cobalt shouldn't be down on the idea, especially since he couldn't suspect Jack's reasons for wanting to get off Ariadne so fast.

That Roslyn girl. She attracted him in ways no other woman ever had, and he couldn't have that. He wanted to... No, he *needed* to remain loyal to his girl, and he knew if he stayed on Ariadne, he would keep seeking out Roslyn, and there was no way he would stay true. Going after a crazy woman Cobalt was convinced wanted to kill them seemed as good an excuse for leaving as any.

The diamonds made a deep clanking sound as they knocked against each other in the backpack he carried them in. He had considered getting a case to protect them, but he concluded diamonds were unlikely to damage each other. Besides, he liked the idea of carrying a spaceship's worth of diamonds in a simple rucksack.

Jack let Cobalt look at the ships while he studied the people. He wanted the salesperson most desperate to make a sale and least likely to question two nineteen-year-olds walking in with a bag full of diamonds, so not the manager or the uptight brownnoser who was featured as salesman of the month. *No, how about that guy in the corner? He looks a bit shy, but he's definitely glaring at the employee of the month.*

Jack meandered over to the man. "Hey. My brother and I are looking to buy a ship. Can you help us?"

The man looked around as if expecting to find another object of Jack's address but, finding no one, shrugged. "Sure, I can help you."

"Awesome." Jack gave his best grin. "Don't worry. We don't need too much in the way of information." He jerked his thumb back toward Cobalt. "My brother knows everything there is to know about spaceships."

"I hope he's not looking for a job," the salesman muttered. He held out his hand. "I'm Dennis Weyover."

With a name like "way over" and an attitude like that, it's no wonder you don't make many sales, Jack thought, but he kept his smile up and shook the man's hand. "I'm just waiting for my brother to pick the one he likes."

153

Weyover raised his eyebrows. "You don't care?"

"Oh, I have veto power." *Come on, Blue. Get back here. I don't want to have to make small talk with this putz all day.*

As if he could hear Jack's thought, Cobalt meandered in Jack's direction.

"Well?"

Cobalt put his hands in his pockets. "I looked over the two-man vehicles. I think that one is our best bet."

Jack wasn't surprised to see his brother had passed over the stodgy, cheap Aeon and the sleek speeder Elitu in favor of the practical, mid-priced Argon. "You sure? Not the Elitu? You know I like to go fast." *Translation: We might have to run away from the spaceship with the psycho that wants to kill us.*

"The engine on the Argon is more reliable. You can't go fast if you can't go anywhere. At least you'll be happy to know that the only Argon they currently have with the specs I want is red."

Jack grinned, and Cobalt rolled his eyes.

"We're naming it *The Rose*." Jack didn't know where those words came from. He had envisioned a red speeder but hadn't realized he'd had a name picked out for it. As soon as he said it, though, he knew it was the right choice.

Cobalt blinked at him a few times then nodded, as if the name choice made sense to him. Maybe it did. Either way, a few signed papers and lost diamonds later, they had a ship, and they were off on the next adventure.

CHAPTER 23

Present Day

GAVIN WAITED WHILE ARCHON SLEPT, certain the guards would appear any moment. *Nothing to be done about that, though.* He skinned the trimper and cooked some of its meat over the fire he'd set up to sterilize his knife—no sense in wasting the meat or the fire.

Maybe it's better if we do get caught. Then Archon can get some real medical attention. Gavin had managed to staunch the bleeding and stitch up the wound pretty well, but the risk of infection was real. If he'd counted the days right, the contest was almost over. If Archon could make it to the end, he would probably be all right, but Gavin would rather not risk it.

Archon stirred and groaned. "Something smells good, which I guess means I'm not dead. Also, I hurt too much to be dead."

"You're not dead." *Thank God.*

Where did that come from? God is an Old Earth superstition.

Archon tried to sit up, grunted, and lay back down. "The last thing I remember, the trimper was coming right for me. How am I not dead?"

Gavin hated to lie with a passion he could never quite explain to himself, but he couldn't explain the rush of memories that had flooded him when his friend nearly died. "The attack wasn't that bad. Trimper only got you in the side. Field medicine training kicked in, and I was able to stop the bleeding."

"How did you get rid of the beast?" Archon managed to prop himself up on his elbows. "We don't have the kind of equipment we would need to go big-game hunting. Cronos, I can't believe they sent us on a survival mission somewhere with trimpers!"

"They probably didn't know it was here. It must have gotten into the area when they weren't paying attention. Trimpers can be surprisingly stealthy for such large animals." Despite his words, Gavin agreed with his friend. He would've thought the people running the games would be more careful. He hoped they hadn't let the trimper in intentionally in hopes of raising the vid ratings and, consequently, the money made. *Don't be cynical, Gavin.* "As for killing it, that was a lucky shot with a knife. I figured it had a big fleshy part with an artery in its neck like most mammals do." He shrugged, trying to appear more casual than he felt.

"You threw a knife at a trimper and killed it?" Archon leaned his head back, awestruck by the act. "You are totally going to win this contest."

Gavin snorted. "Only if we don't get caught, which I'm thinking we should. Field medicine can only do so much for your wound."

"No way, man. You are going to win this thing, and I am not going to stop you." Archon cringed. "Don't get me wrong. If I could get caught and still have you win this thing, I would be all about it. But I can't, and I'm not blowing your chance. Help me up."

"It's just a game. It says so in the title. And as I told you when you were spewing blood everywhere, I would rather lose and have you live."

Archon made a weak dismissive gesture with his hand. "I

can survive for a few more days." He deflated. "But maybe I should sleep some more now."

Gavin nodded. "I'll keep watch."

The fire flickered as Archon slept, and Gavin realized he had been conscious for almost a whole day, and a stressful day at that. Even though he knew it was a bad idea, he lay down on the cold ground.

I'll just close my eyes for a minute.

Twenty Years Ago

"So tell me about this disease." Gavin had learned his way around the small medical tent on Ariadne about as quickly as one would expect, given the size. *Though I've worked in smaller buildings on Daedalus. And less well-stocked ones.*

"What disease?" Emerson Raring, the medic in charge, asked. He had introduced himself as "only" a nurse practitioner, though Gavin had thought that an unfair assessment. He had met many NPs who knew more than most doctors. *Yet it took me longer to tour the tent than to realize that Raring is not among them.*

"Dr. Carriger said a strange disease is working its way through the scientists here." Gavin looked at the empty cots in the tent and thought perhaps Dr. Carriger had exaggerated the situation.

"Oh, yeah, it's weird," Raring said. "Happens to most people a couple weeks after they get here. They get this purple rash and flu symptoms for a few days, then they're fine. We've isolated some of the bacteria that are causing it but haven't had time to do much more than that."

Gavin looked once more at the empty beds and raised his eyebrows. He wasn't sure what Raring and his team could be doing that was more interesting than a brand-new infection.

Raring must have caught Gavin's look, because he

raised his hands defensively. "Hey, the archaeologists are short-staffed. They've been pulling anyone with a science background in to try to make sense of those weird glowing rocks, not that I have much to say about them. Hannah had high hopes for the new archaeologist on the team, but you've forbidden her from going near the things."

"Because she took one look at them and started bleeding out of her nose!" The heat in Gavin's tone surprised him, but he supposed it shouldn't have. He'd known he would catch flak for keeping Roslyn away from the artifacts, as she was the most qualified to analyze them. Gavin took a deep breath. "I can promise you I'm not going to be any help with the artifacts, either, but from my perspective, a new disease is as important a discovery. Let's take a look at it."

Gavin spent the next several hours looking through the rudimentary notes the field medics had put together on the bacteria. It seemed to have survived on the rocky wasteland for thousands of years with nothing to feed on, making Gavin question whether it should be called bacteria at all. The few studies the medics had done on the disease in the human body indicated that it didn't seem to attack any particular kind of cell, almost as if it were looking for something the human body didn't have.

After several hours of reading through notes, Gavin gave a grim nod. He needed more evidence to be sure, but he suspected it was a Transient disease, one designed—and he did suspect some kind of biowarfare—to attack his people. Humans might not be in any danger from the disease, but the Transients almost certainly were.

Present Day

Gavin felt something like the butt of a gun bump against his shoulder. He opened his eyes to discover that it was, in fact, the butt of a gun held by a soldier in camouflage.

"Gavin Ibori. Archon Derring. You have failed this survival expedition. Do you surrender?"

Gavin sat up slowly, holding his hands up so the soldiers could see he wasn't carrying any weapons. He wasn't going to attack or kill his captors for doing their job. His knife was on the other side of camp, anyway, buried deep in trimper meat.

Archon similarly had his hands raised, though he didn't sit up. "I know you guys haven't been watching the feeds, but I'm in a little bit of pain right now. You'll have to forgive me if I don't get up to greet you."

The soldier next to Archon looked down at the gash in his side. "I wondered how we managed to find you two. We watched the feeds for the first two weeks. You two knew what you were doing."

The one next to Gavin looked at the large lump of dead animal next to the fire. "Is that a trimper?"

"We'll go with you." Gavin rose to his feet, still keeping his hands where his captors could see them. "Just, please, get Archon medical attention."

The soldier next to Gavin motioned to his fellow, who holstered his gun and picked up Archon. "We'll take him to the holding station and call in a copter from there."

Though the march to the holding station took over an hour, the soldier carrying Archon didn't even break a sweat. Gavin felt a new appreciation for people in the military, but he still didn't want to join. If the last twenty-four hours had taught him anything, it was that he was meant to be a doctor. He didn't know where the memories came from, but they made him feel more like himself than he ever had during his childhood on Bellerophon.

The holding station was a small brick building on the edge of the survival zone. A barbed-wire fence stretched out in both directions from the back of the building, and

Gavin knew the implant that let the cameras track him also contained an electrified chip to go with the fence. Last year's victor had figured out a way to climb out of the sanctioned area and had survived in the adjacent wood. The games committee had updated the chips after that so the same trick wouldn't work again.

The inside of the station was one grimy room with a few cells with force fields to keep the prisoners in place until the end of the games. The white cells actually looked nice, with curtained showers and cots that looked far more comfortable than the ground Gavin had slept on for the last few weeks. Prisoners occupied two of the cells, and they were eating warm meals of meat, vegetables, and buttered rolls.

Two sets of prisoners plus the team Abe managed to get disqualified. That meant one team was still out in the wild, and the winner would be chosen from them. But at least it wasn't Abe. Gavin recognized him and his Terpischore partner in one of the cells.

"Well, hello," Gavin said with a smile. "Who's the weakest link now?"

CHAPTER 24

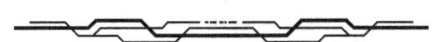

Present Day

L EXI INSISTED ON THIS STAKEOUT, *yet somehow, I'm the one doing all the staking out.* Bliss shifted in the passenger-side seat of her car, careful not to move her gaze from the window. *I'm also not sure how Lexi convinced me to let her drive.*

They'd been following Will for two days straight—two days of nothing but following the boy from class to dorm room to dining hall to class. He hadn't done anything outside the norm for a university student, and in the meantime, Bliss was neglecting her classes.

She had tried pointing that out to Lexi. "He's going to keep going to classes during the week. Why don't we wait and see if he does anything interesting on the weekend?"

"Because we need to see if he sticks to the schedule he claims he has." Lexi didn't need to add the "duh."

Bliss had sunk farther down in her bucket seat. "You just want an excuse to skip."

Lexi had grinned. "What do I need with music classes? I'm a genius without them."

Bliss sighed. *She* needed her classes, because she wasn't a genius without them. Her parents had told her corporations served an important role in society as job providers, but one of the first things she'd learned in her management class was corporations should employ as few people as possible to maximize their profits. All the other students had nodded, so Bliss raised her hand to point out the contradiction. The class had laughed at her, and the professor had suggested that if she wanted to be a philosophy major, she was in the wrong classroom. She had needed all her energy not to cry in front of the class.

I don't even have someone to discuss this with. She'd mentioned something to Lexi, and Lexi had laughed harder than the students had. Then she'd tried calling Roslyn, but Roslyn didn't even answer the call. She thought of her first conversation with Will and thought that he might understand her dilemma, but she didn't trust Will anymore. Bliss had never felt so alone in her life.

Lexi laughed at something on her datapad. "Look at the kittens!" She held out the image for Bliss to see, but she pulled it away too quickly for her to catch the caption. Bliss didn't understand the datasphere's obsession with cats. She had always been a dog person. Snookems loved her no matter what.

Bliss gazed out the window. She hadn't had a decent night's sleep in two days. Lexi insisted they stake out Will's dorm room at night, but though they were supposed to split watches, Lexi never managed to wake up for hers. *Just as well. I can't sleep in this car.*

She leaned her head against the window. Will's class was supposed to run another two hours. Maybe she could get a few restless winks in before he got out.

Twenty Years Ago

"This has been the worst week of my life!" Roslyn didn't bother with a hello when Bliss picked up the call. "Using the emergency connection to call you probably breaks interstellar law, but I can't take the silence anymore."

Unkind thoughts flitted through Bliss's head. *Really? Worst week ever? Worse than the first time Jack left you? Worse than every time Will has died?* And *Weren't you breaking interstellar law by hacking your way onto Arachne in the first place?* She didn't say any of them, though. Roslyn was prone to exaggeration and hopelessly in love with a criminal, and finding fault with either led to arguments. Bliss didn't want to fight with her best friend when she might not be able to talk to her again for months.

"What's wrong?" she asked instead. "Last time I checked, you were on your way to Ariadne with Jack and Gavin. I know Gavin can be the strong, silent type, but Jack definitely isn't."

"Oh, I'm here, but I'm stuck on a two-person mission with Blueboy, and he won't talk to me."

Maybe if you called him by his real name, he would be nicer to you. Bliss half listened as Roslyn continued to explain her assignment. She didn't understand the technical details, but Roslyn seemed more concerned about leaving Jack alone with some beautiful woman named Hannah, anyway.

"But enough about me," Roslyn said. "Tell me about you. Are you still on Daedalus?"

I talked to you two weeks ago. Where would I have gone in the meantime? Not all of us live at the beck and call of a cute boy who treats us like crap. "Yup, still on Daedalus, running the homeless shelter. We could always use some extra funds if you're getting hazard pay on your Arachne trip. With all the wealth we acquire, it's not like you need it."

"I'll bear that in mind."

Bliss's datapad beeped, and Will's face appeared in the corner of her screen. "Hey, Roslyn. Will is calling."

"Well, I know I can't keep you from my brother," Roslyn said. "I should get off, anyway. Tell him I said hi."

Roslyn's face blinked away, and Will's took up the entire

screen. Bliss's finger hovered over the datapad for a full five seconds before she pressed Respond.

"Hi, Will," she said, trying to keep her voice as steady as possible, though she could hear a touch of a squeak in her timbre. "What brings your face to my datapad?"

Will flashed her a grin. "Not much. Just wanted to say hi. How are things in your neck of the woods?"

"Oh, the usual. Running the shelter. Trying to give job advice to people and hoping the economy picks up so there will actually be jobs for all of them."

"Tell me about it," Will said. "I've been reaching ZimmerCorp and EndCorp. Looks like they may be paying liberal members of Congress to vote against workers' rights. I thought it was crazy—two megacorps working together on something?—but the more I dig, the more I find."

Mm-hm. Will always seemed convinced of the legitimacy of his findings, but despite his alleged detailed research, no respectable media outlet ever took his work. He meant well, though, and maybe the corporations did control the newspubs like he thought.

"Well, I hope you find somewhere to publish your research this time," Bliss said. "You're a brilliant writer, and you deserve to be heard."

Will flashed her a smile. "I miss you. You've got to come visit us on Orpheus soon. I love Lexi, but she can be pretty me-me-me. Sometimes I feel like you're the only one who understands me."

If I'm the one who understands you, why are you with Lexi and not me? "I talked to Roslyn today. She says hi."

He brightened. "How's Arachne treating her? She and Jack still the perfect couple?" He rolled his eyes.

"They're on the rocks already, from what I understand."

"I don't know why she puts up with it."

I do. It's the same reason you put up with Lexi and I put up with you. Love makes you stupid. Sometimes she even rooted for Jack and Roslyn. If they could finally make it work, anything was possible.

Present Day

Will's datapad beeped in the middle of class. The students in his periphery gave him sideways looks, but fortunately, he was sitting far enough back that the professor didn't notice. He glanced at the face in the top corner of his screen. *George. Crap. I need to take this.*

Before Will returned to university, he'd had a decently paying job with a tabloid called the *Orphean Inquirer*. He hated having his name associated with a publication known for stories about aliens and kittens laughing at their owners' jokes, but they were the only ones who would take his solidly researched pieces the rest of the world dismissed as conspiracy theories, and he needed to eat.

He had given his boss, George, some cock-and-bull story about how he thought the biology department had evidence of alien life. He planned to attend university on the company's dime and meet Lexi. That he had met Bliss as well was happy coincidence. *It's not like I'm not researching aliens. I'm just not telling George I am one.*

After two weeks of research, George wanted Will back in the office. His message from the previous day indicated that Will had one day to get back if he wanted to keep his job. Will was surprised George cared enough to call one last time, but he slipped out of class and pressed Respond as soon as he got in the hallway.

George's red-cheeked, gray-bearded face appeared on Will's screen. He did not look pleased. "Turin, I am not saying this again. Get your ass into the office in the next fifteen minutes, or you're fired." Then he hung up.

Will groaned and asked his datapad's AI how far the

Inquirer's office was from his current location. A slow, cheerful voice told him it would take him eighteen minutes to walk there.

Crap, guess that means I'm running. Will took off at a trot down the hallway, hoping beyond hope that Lexi and Bliss had gotten bored with their stakeout. He hadn't checked into the office the day before because he had seen Bliss's little blue speeder—with Lexi behind the wheel, of course—following him around. He'd been a model student, hoping that would keep them off his tail until they got their memories back, but he doubted it.

He picked up his pace when he got outside and glanced at where the vehicle had been illegally parked when he went into class. It was still there with two girls inside, though Bliss appeared to be sleeping, and Lexi was absorbed in her datapad. With any luck, he could sneak past them. *At a dead run? I don't think so. Even Lexi's not that unobservant.* He didn't have much of a choice, though, and could only hope their memories had returned enough that they wouldn't hate him when he told them the truth.

He ran down the streets of Chora, past glowing signs advertising bright fashions and hot nightspots, then darted across the street at the last moment, nearly getting himself run over by a red lifter in the process. He didn't look behind him to see whether Lexi was following. He had no doubt she was, and he could only hope that, since he was outpacing traffic, he would lose her.

Fourteen minutes after George hung up on him, Will exited the staircase and made his way into the *Inquirer's* office.

"Okay." He gasped for breath. "I'm here. What was so urgent?"

Will's boss was standing in the office alongside his secretary, Carolina, and a bevy of reporters, most of whom were wise enough to make themselves look busy. George clapped him on the back. "Just wanted to see where your priorities were, young man. Do you have a story for me or not?"

Young man? I'm, like, seven times your age! "We-ell..." The truth was he didn't have a story. He really should have come up with one, but he had been so distracted with Lexi and Bliss that he hadn't bothered. He had thought he would have more time. "I'm pretty sure the university's funding is coming from—"

George slammed his fist on Carolina's desk hard enough to make the datapad lying on it jump. "Cronos take you, man! I don't want any more of your political-conspiracy crap! You promised me aliens, and I want aliens!"

"My political-conspiracy 'crap' has a large following!" Will said. "I'm trying to get some dirt on aliens, too, but I haven't found anything yet."

"Just make something up," one of Will's fellow reporters said under his breath. "It's what we all do."

"I don't make up my stories!" Will clenched his fists, and his face became hot. "I do thorough research on them!"

"Yeah, I know, I know." George put an arm around Will's shoulder. "You're a true believer, and that's what makes you great. But aliens on college campuses? That's not your kind of thing. I should have known better than to assign you there."

"Sir, I promise you, I have looked into—"

George guffawed. "You've spent all your time hanging out with a couple of university women. I can't blame you for that, of course, but I can't let you do it on the company's dime. I'm going to have to—"

"They're the aliens!" Will regretted the words as soon as they were out of his mouth. *What am I doing? I can't publish that. Demitrius would kill me! Like, permadeath kill!* Unfortunately, the words were already out there, so he figured he might as well save his job before he got erased from existence. "Bliss and Lexi are part of a group of rare reincarnating aliens who have infiltrated humanity. I'm

167

waiting for them to recover the memories of their past lives so they can give us firsthand experience of human history."

"What the actual fuck!" The automatic glass doors slid open with barely a *swish*, but the woman storming in through the gap was as loud as a thunderclap.

"Lexi." Will closed his eyes. He should have known if anyone could catch up to him in that traffic, it would be Lexi. No doubt she'd left the car double-parked and running so she could race up the stairs after him. She wouldn't care if Bliss's car was stolen.

No, she took the elevator, a calm part of his mind thought. *I didn't hear anyone on the stairs behind me, and Lexi never takes stairs if she can help it.*

"An alien? You think I'm an *alien*?" She had moved in front of him and was shoving him repeatedly in the chest.

Will felt his mouth fall open as he struggled to think of something to say. George grinned at the unfolding drama, and Will's fellow reporters gathered around. He thought he even caught the blinking red light of a camera in one of their hands.

"Of course I don't think you're an alien," Will said in as soothing a voice as he could. "I just—"

"What you just did was tell *that man*"—she pointed at George—"that I am an alien. Cronos, I knew you were some kind of conspiracy nut, but I didn't know you were absolutely insane!"

George reached out to put his arm around Lexi. "Now, young lady—"

But Lexi would have none of that. She twisted her arm up to block George's. "Don't you 'young lady' me! You're some pathetic tabloid journalist. When my father hears about this, he'll put you all out of business so fast you won't even feel it come out from under you. And as for *you*..." She pointed a finger at Will. "If you ever come near me again, I will make your life so miserable you will regret ever knowing me." She spun on her stiletto-heeled boot and stalked out of the office, her exit only slightly marred by her having to wait for the door to open.

"Alien, huh?" George said. "Seems more like a she-cat to me."

It'll be fine, Will thought as he buried his head in his hands. *She'll get her memories back, and she'll come back to me. I hope.*

CHAPTER 25

Present Day

DETRICK STARED AT THE SCREEN, waiting for it to beep. He did his best to keep his thoughts blank.

Phedre told him he had no life of the mind. He didn't know what that meant. Tegan always responded that his mind was such a fraught place that deadening it made his life easier. He wasn't sure what that meant, either. He just knew that Tegan was nicer to him when Phedre was around. Or maybe she only seemed nicer by comparison.

He sometimes wished he had people other than Tegan and Phedre in his life—nicer people, like Bliss. She used to call him sometimes and ask about his life. She was always interested in hearing about his research, though she was less interested in the guns.

Will used to call, too, usually with research puzzles. "Find the connection," Will would say. "I know it's there." Detrick once tried to explain to Will that coincidence was a statistical fact. Will didn't believe him, but he also found some lovely coincidences, so Detrick forgave him.

The others mocked him or didn't care. *Poor Detrick, all alone in his apartment. Too scared to leave,* Lexi or Jack would say. That should offend him. Tegan always raised her voice when he repeated it to her. To Detrick, it was simply an acknowledgement of fact. He was too scared to leave his apartment.

They were once his friends, or at least his fellow Transients. Detrick wondered if he should regret it, but he didn't. He still had Tegan and his apartment and his screens and his guns. He didn't need more than that.

Twenty Years Ago

The datapad played a little song.

Detrick cringed. He hated music. Music took mathematical perfection and tried to add emotion to it. Mathematics, he understood. Emotion, he did not. Music, he could put in neither category, so it bothered him.

Bliss must have set it up when she was here twenty-three days ago. He took a deep breath. Twenty-three beautiful days of no human interaction were about to come to an end.

He looked at the datapad. Tegan's face appeared with a blinking light around it, and he pushed the respond button.

"We're working for Phedre now," she said without preamble. She had a lock of hair in front of her face, which annoyed him as much as her words.

Detrick blinked. "You don't like Phedre. You said she was the worst person you had ever met, Transient or otherwise."

"Yeah, I did." Tegan tried to blow the lock of hair out of her face, but the strands only shifted slightly to the right. *Or left. My left, her right.* "But she's also the only one telling us the truth right now. Did you know Roslyn and her coterie were on Arachne?"

"Yes."

"See, no one tells us—" Tegan stopped as she processed what Detrick had said. "Wait, what? Why didn't you tell me?"

Detrick had a hard time with emotion, but he had learned that inflection as a form of self-defense. He had made her angry, but he didn't know how. "You told me not to tell you about Will's research anymore. You said Will was a crazy conspiracy hound, and you didn't need to hear his insanity spouted from two sources."

"And you heard about Arachne from Will?"

He nodded.

"Are you nodding? I can't see you nod when you insist on keeping the datapad flat on the table."

Detrick held the datapad up to his face and nodded again. "Will asked me to do some research on the place Roslyn was going."

"Well, you have to stop doing research for Will," Tegan said.

Detrick shrugged. "Okay. I'll call him and tell him."

"No, don't do that! He'll know we're working for Phedre!"

He put the datapad back down. "You said we are working for Phedre."

"We are, but we don't want Will to know."

Detrick felt a headache forming at the base of his neck. *This is getting people-y. I hate people-y things. They make me think words like people-y, and people-y isn't a word.* "Okay, I won't tell Will. And I won't give Will information. What should I say when he calls?"

"You know what would be really helpful?" Tegan asked. "If you could give him false information."

His breathing seemed to echo through the apartment, though he knew it was a sonic impossibility. "I don't understand."

"I know you don't." Tegan sighed. "Just don't answer when Will calls. Can you do that?"

He nodded again.

"Detrick..."

He picked up the datapad. "Yes, I can do that. Do you need anything else?"

"Yes." Tegan grinned, and Detrick felt a spark of warmth inside. "Send me everything you have on Arachne and keep researching. Classified and unclassified datasphere. I want to know everything there is to know about that place before I get there."

Present Day

Beep.

Detrick jumped.

His eyes snapped to the screen that had made the noise. *Aha.* Someone—almost certainly Jack and Cobalt—had used the diamonds from the robbery to buy a spaceship.

"Call Tegan."

CHAPTER 26

Twenty Years Ago

ROSLYN'S HEAD ACHED WORSE THAN she could ever remember it hurting, though she had to admit that the pain impeded her memory some. As an alien being, she was less susceptible to human diseases than the people around her. She'd had a cold or two in her time, but all the really serious conditions bypassed her. She rarely even felt symptoms like headaches or nausea, but she was beginning to understand what people who got migraines complained about.

The pain was centered behind her left eye, and with every beat of her heart, it radiated along her blood vessels into every corner of her skull. Meanwhile, the liquid lunch she'd consumed threatened to eject itself from her body with every breath. She wondered if those maladies were related to the purple rash she'd noticed on her stomach a few days ago and had spread to her arms and legs in the intervening time. Hannah had said a strange disease was affecting members of the colony, but she'd assumed she would be immune.

"Roslyn? Are you listening to me? Roslyn?" Cobalt waved a hand in front of her face. His eyebrows furrowed with concern.

I must look bad if Blueboy is worried about me. She had let him drive that day and had slumped over in her seat, not capable of much more action than that for the last several hours. She straightened up in her chair, each motion sending violent spasms through her abdomen.

"Sorry." Her voice came out as a croak. *When did my throat get so dry?* "What do you need?"

"We're back." He frowned at her for a moment. "I let you sleep because I thought you were tired, but you're sick, aren't you?"

"Don't be ridiculous. I don't get sick." Everything—the timbre of her voice, the pounding in her skull, the roiling in her stomach—belied her words, and Cobalt wasn't an idiot.

"I think we should get you to Gavin," he said.

She cringed, and a tear fell down her cheek. *Gavin. I treated him so terribly. He shouldn't be here.* She couldn't bear to see Gavin right now. "I want to see Jack."

"I'll go get him," Cobalt said. "But you should go see Gavin straight away."

The thoughts *Blueboy's being nice to me?* and *Blueboy can't tell me what to do!* clashed in her head. She pushed against her seat, forcing herself to her feet, though she wobbled a bit. "I want to see Jack," she repeated. "It's on the way. Then we can see Gavin." She had no idea if Jack was on the way to Gavin. She didn't know where Jack was.

"Do you..." Cobalt let out a polite cough. "Do you need help walking?"

"No!" *Maybe.* "I'm fine." *I'm not fine.* She took a deep breath and instantly regretted it. The rush of air down her throat reminded her how dry it was, and the effort made her head ache.

The light in camp was dim, for which she was grateful. If someone shined a bright light in her face, she was pretty sure her eyeballs would explode. *That doesn't sound so bad. At least then it would be dark.*

Cobalt followed along behind her, and she was grateful for it, though she would never tell him that. She wasn't one hundred percent sure she wouldn't pass out as she walked between the tents. *I'll just go see Jack, then I can sleep.* She stopped and closed her eyes, swaying on her feet. A few more tears fell down her cheeks. *It must be the pain.*

Roslyn headed for the main research tent, the one Hannah had shown them when they first arrived, and pulled back the flap. For a second, she was blinded by the brightness of the lamps. She blinked a few times, and flashes of color splashed in her sight as her vision adjusted, but they didn't stop her from seeing what she needed to see: Jack and Hannah locked in what could only be described as a passionate embrace.

She stood there staring at them, dumbfounded, but they were so engrossed in each other that they didn't notice her. *Of course not. The light's all in here, so I'm not letting any in.* For some reason, that thought struck her as funny, and she laughed.

That got Jack and Hannah's attention, but Roslyn didn't have the energy to process their responses. She dropped the tent flap before they could be anything more than startled.

She felt a hand on her shoulder. *Blueboy.* She reached up and clutched his hand. "I have to... Gavin?"

"I thought you wanted to see Jack."

She laughed, a crazed sound even to her ears, and pushed his hand off her shoulder then continued along the row of tents. Out of the corner of her eye, she saw Cobalt flip up the tent flap. He cursed under his breath as a figure burst out past him.

"Rosie!"

Roslyn didn't turn around. "Forget it, Jack. I'm done. We're done. I'm going to see Gavin now."

"Rosie, let me explain! It's not what you think!"

"That would be a lot more convincing if you had a shirt on right now," someone said with a sarcastic voice.

Is Blueboy taking my side? It was too much—the headache, the stomachache, the rash. Jack, Cobalt, Hannah. The tears, the pain, the dizziness. She had to stop.

I can't stop. Jack will think I'm listening to him. Then, more distantly, she thought, *I'm sick. I need to get to Gavin.* She took another step forward, but the world was spinning too fast.

"Rosie!"

"Roslyn!"

As her head hit the ground, she was surprised to find it could hurt more than it previously had. Then the world went dark.

"What do you mean, 'she's dying'?" were the first words Roslyn heard when she awoke.

Jack. She felt as if her heart had spoken the word as she recognized the voice.

No, she told her heart. *We are done with him. He's betrayed us again and again. We're done.*

Roslyn tried to open her eyes, but even that slight motion hurt more than she would have thought possible. She whimpered and settled back against the bed. The hard pillow wasn't doing anything to ease her headache, and the bars under the thin mattress dug into her back.

"I mean the bacteria seems specifically designed to target Transients, to attack the parts of us that are different from humans." She knew that voice too. Gavin.

"*We* didn't get sick," Jack said, the accusation clear in his tone. "And the humans did. How could that be, if it wasn't supposed to attack them?"

"Our anatomies are very similar to humans', as you are well aware." Gavin kept his voice calm and rational, but Roslyn knew him. He only got that calm when a patient was about to die, as a way of distancing himself from the situation. "And not everyone who catches the disease becomes symptomatic. As far as I can tell, our hybrid DNA helped us fight off the disease more easily. As a full-blooded Transient, Roslyn was more susceptible."

"Okay. It's okay." Jack sounded as though he was trying to reassure himself. "She may die, but she'll come back. We always come back."

"No," Gavin whispered.

In the moment of silence that followed, Roslyn felt as though she should care about what Gavin had said, as if it somehow affected her, but her head ached too much for her to put together how.

"What do you mean, 'No'?" Jack spoke almost as softly as Gavin had, but his tone held a world of menace.

"I mean the disease attacks the cells that make her different from humans, the ones that let her reincarnate," Gavin said. "If she dies of this disease, I don't think she's coming back."

A clang of metal rang through the tent, then Jack yelled far too loudly, "Take it back!"

"Jack, put the scalpel down," Gavin said, still infinitely calm. "We both know I can take you in a fight. Besides, stabbing me won't change anything. She'll still be dying."

Something made a *clack-clack* noise against the rock floor. "You say that so calmly. I thought you loved her."

"I do love her," Gavin said. "Don't you, of all people, tell me what I feel. But making a scene won't save her. The only thing we can do is wait and hope. She might pull through this."

Jack let out a defeated harrumph.

"Go home, Jack. Get something to eat. There's still time."

"I'm not leaving her." Roslyn could picture Jack setting his jaw. He appeared devil-may-care on the outside, but when he decided to be stubborn, nothing could move him.

"Jack—"

"I'm not. Leaving. Her." Footsteps moved toward Roslyn, a chair thunked by her bedside.

Go away, Roslyn wanted to say. *I'm done with you.* But her head was too heavy, and her mouth was too dry. She drifted back into the black.

Present Day

The sound of the morning wake-up call rang through the psychiatric hospital. Roslyn opened her eyes and lay in bed, unwilling to get up and face her day.

Maybe there really is something wrong with me. Maybe I'm depressed. Isn't unwillingness to get up a sign of depression?

The edge of her sheets was wet. *Great. I'm even drooling in my sleep now.* When she reached up to clear her face, she realized the wetness had come from both sides. *No, I'm crying in my sleep.*

The dream about Old Roslyn had hit her quite hard. She had wondered how Old Roslyn died, and now she knew. She'd caught some weird alien disease that had killed her and her ability to reincarnate. *If that were true, though, how am I here?* The story had begun to unravel, as Dr. Tanner had said it would, once Roslyn had the tools and medication to look through the fog.

Roslyn showered and dressed, moving so slowly she expected an orderly to come in and yell at her. All the while, tears streamed down her cheeks, tears for the old Roslyn dying on an alien moon, and tears for Current Roslyn, giving up on any belief she'd once had she could be anything other than a server.

She sat through her morning art therapy and group skills training with a sense of determined anticipation until it was finally time for her one-on-one session with the brown-eyed therapist.

"I didn't want to talk about this in front of everybody," Roslyn said. "They'll think I'm crazy, and I've had enough of that. But I want to get better. I'm going to tell you everything that's been going on with me."

CHAPTER 27

Present Day

J ACK SAT IN THE PILOT'S seat of his new spaceship and
stroked the dashboard. His *Rose* was even red on the
inside, or at least had sufficient red accents to be tasteful.
"Next stop, Bellerophon."

"Bellerophon?" Cobalt climbed out of the engine pit and
sat down in the copilot's seat. "Why are we going there?"

As he flipped the toggles above his head to release the
landing brakes, Jack said, "Well, the way I figure it, we're
looking for a woman who has a spaceship and wants to kill
us, right?"

Cobalt strapped himself in. "Right."

"Well, the *Transcendental Spirit* or whatever—"

"*Transcendent Spirit.*"

"Or whatever... has got to have some decent weapons."
Jack pushed the button to initiate automatic takeoff. "So I
was thinking Eurydice."

"No."

Jack frowned as the ship taxied itself out of the hangar
on Ariadne Station. "This whole automatic-spaceship thing
is kind of a drag. Tell me this thing has a manual mode."

Cobalt grabbed Jack's hand before it could search for the
appropriate switch. "Did you hear me, Jack? I said, 'No.'"

Jack leaned back in his chair. *Might as well let the ship get itself into orbit while I have this argument.* "I heard you. I was ignoring you. Look, Eurydice is the only place we're going to get military-quality guns for the *Rose* from people who won't ask too many questions."

Cobalt ran his fingers through his hair. "Remind me why we're going after this woman—"

"Tegan O'Leary."

Cobalt's look said, "Of course I know that, you moron," which was weird. Jack was the one who'd found the woman, and Cobalt was terrible with names. "Remind me why we're going after *Tegan* again."

"She wants to kill us," Jack said. "Or at least, you're convinced she does. Do you want to spend the rest of your life hiding out from her?"

"Yes! Yes, I do! We had a good thing going on Ariadne— decent jobs on a moon a hell of a lot better than Daedalus. And you liked that Roslyn girl, right? We could have been happy there." Cobalt's face was flushed, his breathing rapid.

I can be self-centered, but I know my brother. He's been acting weird since the police station, and this is not just about the train job. "Blue, I am going to ask you again, and I want an honest answer this time. What is *wrong* with you?"

Cobalt dropped his head and hands between his knees and muttered something.

Jack leaned closer to him. "Did you just say, 'I think we're immortal beings who reincarnate'? Because that doesn't make any—"

The wail of a siren interrupted Jack, and a voice sounded over the ship's speakers. "Jack and Cobalt Zhao, you are under arrest for the theft of one million credits of diamonds from ZimmerCorp and for escape from a legitimate Ariadne holding facility. Please exit the spacecraft with your hands up."

"Shit," Jack and Cobalt said in unison, and both sat up and manned their stations.

"Stupid police with the access codes to every publicly sold ship," Jack muttered.

"You disabled their access to everything except the speakers, right?" For someone who had wanted to stay on Ariadne a few minutes ago, Cobalt sure seemed in a rush to get off.

"Of course. What do you take me for? I left them access to the intercom so we would know they were coming. Aha!" Jack pushed the button labeled MANUAL at the bottom of his array of controls. His dashboard opened, and a steering mechanism slid out. "Brace for takeoff!"

Jack knew he only had a few seconds before the police figured out they couldn't hold his ship in place, so he throttled forward at full thrust, clearing the last bit of the hangar and flinging himself into the emptiness of space.

Except space wasn't so empty around Ariadne Station. The three sets of train tracks that led to Daedalus, Bellerophon, and Orpheus spiraled around the ship, making flight that much more complicated.

"Woooo!" Jack looped around the tracks faster than the bulky police ships could.

"Incoming!" Cobalt yelled.

Jack glanced at the viewscreen and realized he was on a collision course with a train coming into the station. He pushed the controls down, and the *Rose* shot straight up. The sudden movement rocked him and Cobalt. "That's why I wanted the Elitu," he said. "Smoother turns."

"I stand by my choice." Cobalt flipped a few toggles, which Jack assumed rerouted power to engines or navigation. "I presume you have a plan?"

"Working on it." The downside of evading the train was it put the *Rose* in open space, which made it easier for the police vessel to catch up to them.

"Jack and Cobalt Zhao," the voice over the speakers said. "This is your last chance to surrender."

Before Jack even had a chance to surrender—not that

he was going to—something rocked the *Rose*, and the ship slowed.

Cobalt hissed. "They hit our port thruster with a sonic pulse. I can fix it, but it'll take a bit. Dodge them as best you can." He darted out of his seat and headed down to the engine pit.

Jack tried to head back toward the train tracks, but the difficulty turning right created problems. The massive police ship bore down on them. *Wait, that's it. It's massive and doesn't have sensors everywhere.*

He slowed the *Rose*, making it appear as if the shot had hindered him more than it had. As the police ship approached, Jack pulled a similar maneuver to the one he'd used to avoid the train, except that time, he went down.

A thud came up from the engine pit. "Hey!" Cobalt called.

"You said to dodge them!" Jack pulled up underneath the police vessel, keeping pace with the larger ship. No way could the police spot them. Unfortunately, the police ship wasn't that much larger and less maneuverable than the *Rose*, and Jack had a hard time predicting its movements as it tried to get into a position where it could fire on him.

"How's that thruster coming?" Jack yelled.

"I just got down here! These things take time!"

The police ship got into a position where it could fire its rear laser at Jack. With the port thruster as sluggish as it was, he was barely able to dodge. "We don't *have* time!" he said.

"You're the genius! Figure something out!"

Jack silently cursed. *If I were a genius, I wouldn't have bought the ship with stolen diamonds.* But he would never say that for Cobalt to hear. "Our problems would be a lot fewer now if we had some guns on this ship."

"Because we need to up our number of crimes to include firing on a police vessel."

When Jack wrenched his ship to starboard to avoid another laser beam, the lack of balance sent the *Rose* into a tailspin. The smaller ship's back faced the front of the police cruiser, where the missiles—and more importantly, the tractor beam—were located. He switched his viewscreen to observe the rear of his ship, and sure enough, telltale purple beams emerged from the police ship's docking bay. "Shit, shit, shit, shit, shit!"

"Do I want to know what's going on up there?"

"Almost certainly not." Jack closed his eyes and braced for the impact of tractor beams, but to his surprise, nothing happened. He opened one eye and looked at the viewscreen. The police ship had turned away from them.

Never one to look a gift horse in the mouth, Jack moved full speed ahead, trying to put as much distance between him and the cruiser as he could. He looked at the viewscreen again as he limped away and saw the police cruiser had engaged with another ship. Taking in the old style, the bronze color, and the sleek lines, he didn't need to see the name to identify the *Transcendent Spirit.* He didn't know if he was more surprised that Tegan O'Leary had appeared or that she had saved them.

Before a minute had passed, the police cruiser had a laser hole in it, and the *Spirit* headed for Jack's ship. When the communications array beeped, he decided to answer the call. The pale-skinned blond woman he had briefly seen in the detective's office appeared on the screen. "Hello, Jack," she said. "Remember me?"

"Can't say that I've had the pleasure." As he spoke, he tried to keep the ship moving away from her, but the *Spirit* gained on him.

Tegan's brow furrowed in annoyance. "Are you really going to play that game?"

"Lady, I'm not playing any games. I know you're Tegan O'Leary because I did my research, but I have no idea who you are or why you're after me."

Cobalt clambered up the ladder to the cockpit. "Okay, I've got the thruster—" He stared at Tegan. "Hello, Cuttlefish."

Tegan gave him a not-altogether-pleasant smile. "Cobalt. It's nice to know someone remembers me."

Cobalt's face was deader than Jack had ever seen it. "It's hard to forget the person who killed you."

She nodded toward Jack. "Your twin seems to have."

"Yes, well." Cobalt shrugged. "Jack."

Jack didn't know what *that* was supposed to mean, but he decided to use Cobalt and Tegan's staring contest to escape. Cobalt had said he fixed the thruster, but Jack continued to move as if disabled, knowing Tegan would follow. He glanced at the clock. If he remembered the timetable right—and he did—a train should be leaving for Bellerophon any moment.

The train exited the station. *I need to time this just right.* He moved slowly toward the tracks, then just before the train crossed his path, he cut the comm line and darted across the tracks in front of it. As he went, he expelled the ship's garbage to hit the front of the train. Then he adjusted course and speed to move parallel with it. With any luck, Tegan would assume the explosion of garbage was their ship getting torn apart. If not, she wouldn't be able to distinguish his signal from the train's for as long as he kept pace with it, which he planned to do all the way to Bellerophon.

Cobalt dropped into the copilot's seat. "Are you insane? You nearly got us run over by a train!"

"Am *I* insane? You're the one who seems to know the woman who wants to kill us!" Jack put the ship back into autopilot. "I asked you before what was going on with you, and I think it's time for you to start talking."

CHAPTER 28

Twenty Years Ago

G AVIN LAY ON HIS COT in the tent he shared with the other medics on Arachne and stared up at the white canvas. He needed to get up soon, judging by the way the sun angled through the tent flap. When the alarm went off, he would get up, shower and shave, and go through as normal a day as he could, considering it might be his last day with Roslyn in it.

Raring's soft snores rose from the adjacent cot, and Gavin envied him his ability to sleep. Gavin hadn't slept so much as dozed in the past two weeks since Cobalt had rushed into the infirmary, carrying an unconscious Roslyn, with a hysterical, shirtless Jack on his tail. The purple rash on Roslyn's arms had clued Gavin in to the danger. Jack hadn't left Roslyn's side, and despite Gavin's assertions that the best thing any of them could do was take care of themselves, Gavin had abandoned sleep.

After the morning alarm finally went off and he performed his ablutions, he headed toward the mess tent. He wasn't in a hurry. Roslyn's case was the only one that required his skills, and he couldn't do anything to help her. Besides, watching Jack spend days at Roslyn's side like the dedicated lover he never was raised Gavin's hackles.

Someone approached Gavin as he siphoned the gloop they called food there into a travel mug. He glanced up to see Hannah Carriger standing by his side. He didn't know how to feel about her. She seemed like a competent-enough archaeologist, but Roslyn hadn't been gone for more than a few days before rumors of Dr. Carriger and Jack carrying on an illicit romance circulated through the camp. Gavin had thought Dr. Carriger and Roslyn had been striking up a friendship, and it surprised him that the doctor would betray her fellow archaeologist in that manner.

"Can I help you, Doctor?" Gavin asked. "Perhaps get you a mug of this refreshing breakfast?"

Dr. Carriger scowled. As Gavin studied her, he realized she looked worse than she had when they'd landed about a month ago. Her eyes were as puffy as he knew his to be, and something in their depths spoke of desperation. "I need you to make Jack come back to work."

Gavin laughed, and the bitterness in the sound surprised him. "I can't make Jack do anything. Nobody can, except maybe Cobalt. Try him."

She bit her lip and looked away. "Cobalt won't talk to me. He'll do what I tell him to—exactly what I say and no more—but he won't answer any questions or say anything."

"Can you really blame him?" Gavin took a sip of his grainy drink. It really was one of the most disgusting things he had ever tasted, and he had eaten military ready-to-eat meals in dozens of armies.

"You're all blaming me because your precious Roslyn is ill," Dr. Carriger said. "But it's not my fault. She was sick before she even found out about Jack and me."

"Roslyn's not just ill. She's most likely dying."

"Oh, don't exaggerate. Lots of people have gotten this disease, and no one's come even close to dying."

Gavin slammed his travel mug onto the table next to him. "Are you calling me a liar, Dr. Carriger? You know as well as I do that no one was laid up for two weeks with this disease."

Dr. Carriger held up her hands and took a step back. "No, I'm not calling you a liar. I just don't understand what the big deal is. It's a weird disease, but to everyone else, it's been no worse than a bad cold. Which means this has to do with the big secret you all are keeping."

"Secret." Gavin's voice was flat.

"Yes, secret. You all show up here in your fancy ship, a new freelance team to help with the research. Roslyn immediately recognized the symbols on those alien devices. I know she did. She passes out, and when she wakes up, not only will she tell me nothing, but she refuses to even look at the artifacts again.

"So she gives me Jack, who as far as I could tell was the cabin boy of the party, except he's not. He starts detecting patterns in the rocks I never would have noticed in a million years. We were so close to knowing what the symbols are, what these devices do. And now he won't help me!"

"That's all this is to you, isn't it?" Gavin asked. "An archaeological find. Some discovery to get your name in the journals and maybe the history books."

Dr. Carriger threw her hands in the air. "Of course that's what it is! What is it to you? Life or death?"

Gavin couldn't explain to her what Arachne was to them—their history, their future, and maybe Roslyn's forever grave. "And what about Jack?"

"What *about* Jack?"

Gavin felt his lip curl. "Is he just another tool to you? You seduce him in hopes he reveals all these secrets you're so convinced we're keeping?"

"It's not like it was hard," Dr. Carriger said.

Gavin turned his back on her. "Good luck with your research, Dr. Carriger. It sounds like you're going to need it."

He closed his eyes as he walked away. Roslyn needed hope and love to sustain her through the illness, and thanks to that woman's selfish ambitions, all she had was a broken heart. Once upon a time, Gavin would have prayed, but he had fallen out of the habit along with humanity, so instead he sent out a thought to Roslyn's spirit. *Please, Roslyn. Please pull through this. You're so strong. You're the strongest person I know. Jack's stupidity has never broken you before. Make it through just one last time.*

As Gavin approached the infirmary tent, a black-clad figure rushed out at him. Jack neither looked nor smelled well after two weeks of flat-out refusing to leave Roslyn's side for any reason. His emergence could only mean one of two things, and he was smiling. *Smiling.*

Jack reached out to clasp Gavin's hand. "Her fever broke. Raring says she's going to make it."

Present Day

Gavin opened his eyes with a strange sense of invigoration. He didn't know what to make of the dreams he'd been having, where he was a doctor exploring Arachne, of all places. All he knew was if he stayed in his cage, he would spend all his time mulling over dreams and abilities that made no sense. He needed to focus on things that mattered, like Windla. The best way he could think to do that was to fulfill his father's wishes and win the games.

He studied his first obstacle: the force field. Though he'd trained in survival techniques, no one had ever taught him how to escape from a cell. The assumption was if he ever ended up in one, he deserved to be there. Maybe in this case he did as well, but he would still try to get out.

Gavin, Gavin, Gavin, came a voice from the back of his mind, a voice he recognized as belonging to Jack from his dream. *Nobody, not even a constant do-gooder like you, should be without the basic knowledge of how to short-circuit a force field. You never know when you might be caught behind one.*

189

Now, this won't help you with a really good barrier, but for a low-grade one, here's what you need to do.

And suddenly Gavin knew. He made sure the guard was still glued to his datapad and reached into the grate around the force field. His fingers were thick, so it was difficult to get to the wires, but eventually, he felt them—the thick one, the thin one, and the braided one, just like Jack had said. His fingernails weren't long, but they were enough to snap the braided wire. The force field fizzled out with a crackle of lightning and a boom of thunder.

Thanks for the warning about the noise, Jack, Gavin thought as the guard stood up.

"Hey, what's going on over there?" The guard picked up his Taser and made his way over to Gavin's cell.

Gavin was prepared for a physical fight. He dodged the Taser and used his newfound medical knowledge to hit the guard on the back of the neck at just the right angle to knock him out. Unfortunately, the poor man was going to have a very bad headache when he woke up in a few hours, but by then, Gavin planned to be long gone.

"Hey!" Abe yelled. "Let us out too!"

Gavin looked Abe and Jesse up and down. "Why should I?"

Jesse grinned. "Because the other guards are about to come rushing in here any minute, and I have something in my gear that will take care of them."

Though Gavin knew he shouldn't trust them, some inner nobility argued that letting them out was the right thing to do. He snapped the braided wire on Jesse and Abe's cell then turned to the other trapped pair. "You guys want out too?"

"Naw, man," one said. "We've got showers and real food in here. We're going to accept our loss."

Gavin shrugged and joined Abe and Jesse as they went through their equipment. He didn't bother grabbing anything except his knife because he only needed to survive a few more hours out there, and he thought he could handle anything once he escaped. *A trimper kill and a few dreams of competence, and we're overconfident, aren't we?*

As soon as he got his hand around the hilt of the knife, the door to the holding facility flew open, and three armed guards rushed in. With a grin larger than Gavin had seen on him yet, Jesse rolled what looked like a grenade at the oncoming guards.

"Hold your breath!" Abe called as a gas emerged from the canister. "It's neutralizer!"

Are you insane? Gavin wanted to shout, but he had to hold his breath. *Neutralizer causes a violent reaction in ten to twenty percent of cases!*

He was thus not surprised when one of the guards got a crazed look in his eye and ran toward Jesse. Still not breathing, Gavin moved in behind the guard and knocked him out in the same way he had taken out the guard by the force field. He glowered at Abe and Jesse, but they ignored him and ran out into the clear, fresh air.

"I hope you're pleased with yourselves," Gavin said after a deep inhalation once he had joined them outside.

Abe and Jesse laughed and gasped simultaneously.

"That was awesome!" Abe said. "Where'd you learn to do that?"

Gavin wished he could explain, but he wasn't sure. He took the strange new memories as they came, but once the contest was over, he suspected he would have some deep thinking to do. Windla would help him sort it out.

Except... When he thought of Windla, his feelings for her paled in comparison to his memories of the Roslyn girl. Though Old Gavin had known he could never keep her, his attachment to her made every relationship Gavin thought he'd had in this life feel weak.

Of course, I also feel strongly about Jack, though those feelings aren't nearly so positive. He couldn't continue down that line of thought at the moment, though. He needed to focus on getting away from the guardhouse before reinforcements arrived. He could worry about Jack and Roslyn another time.

"Hey, Gavin, wait." Abe jogged over to him. "Why'd you let us out? Jesse told you all you needed was in his bag. You could have left us to rot."

Gavin looked Abe straight in the eye. "Because you deserve a shot at winning as much as I do." He moved a few steps away then turned back. "And when I win this thing, you'll know it's not because I cheated or had an advantage in knowing how to disable a force field. You'll know it's because I deserved to win." And with that, he disappeared into the forest.

CHAPTER 29

Present Day

BLISS BHANUSHALI DIDN'T UNDERSTAND ANYTHING anymore. She had come to Chora as the celebrated daughter of a megacorp CFO, destined to take his place in the business world. Only a few weeks later, she had all but flunked out of her business classes, felt something akin to love for her roommate's boyfriend, had lost her best friend, and might be an alien who reincarnated.

When Lexi had run back down the stairs from the tabloid office—just as Bliss had found a parking spot, of course—she had told Bliss what Will had said about them. Bliss wanted to chalk it up to Will being some stupid tabloid journalist, but she couldn't.

Once, a long time ago, she had done a genealogy project for school and learned that her family used to be Buddhist. They believed in reincarnation and that the soul was ever on a quest for Nirvana. No one believed anything like that anymore, but Bliss had always thought the idea sounded rather nice. She wondered sometimes if maybe it was true. It would explain why she felt so close to Roslyn, Will, and Lexi before she even knew them.

As she had slept in the car, she had dreamt of something more real than a spiritual closeness. She had witnessed a different time, one in which she knew Roslyn, Will, and Lexi for real. They were still the same people, with the same names and faces, which wasn't how reincarnation was supposed to work. She tried to dismiss the vision as just a dream, but she felt in her bones that they were real.

Bliss had skipped her management class to sit in her car outside a dilapidated apartment building in a run-down-but-not-too-bad part of town. She had done research on Will Turin, investigative reporter for the most disreputable tabloid in the system, and found his address, and she had been outside his building for an hour, trying to gather the courage to get out and knock on his door. Contacting him on the datasphere would have been safer and easier, but she needed to talk to him in person.

She stepped outside of her car and made her way to the building. Though she was a little surprised that she was able to get past the building's nonexistent security, she supposed that she shouldn't be, given the neighborhood. She was less amused by the lack of an elevator since Will lived on the fifth floor, but she made her way up the stairs.

When she reached his floor, she took a moment to catch her breath. The hallway hosted only four doors, so apartment 5B was easy to find. She raised her hand to knock on the door then pulled her fist back against her mouth. *Do I really want to do this? Whatever I find out, it's going to change everything.* She took what felt like the hundredth deep breath of the day. *I have to. Whoever I really am is on the other side of that door.*

She knocked. The person who opened the door did not look like the Will who had visited Bliss and Lexi at the university, but the Bliss growing in her head every moment, the one who was somehow more than a megacorp CFO's daughter, recognized the disheveled hair and offbeat attire of the real Will Turin.

"I didn't expect to see you here," he said.

She looked past him into the apartment and could make

out a sofa and a coffee table and behind them, a small kitchen. They were, if not clean, at least tidy. "Yes, you did," she said.

Will ran his fingers through his hair, mussing it even further. "Maybe I did. Or at least, I hoped. But I figured it would be a couple of weeks until enough of the memories came back. I just—"

"Look, can I come in?" Bliss had the distinct impression Will would be happy to ramble in the hallway forever, and she wanted to have the conversation in private.

Will stepped back and held out his hand, indicating that she could walk past. "I'm going to need some coffee for this," he muttered, making his way to the kitchen.

Bliss started when she saw the wall of his living room. A giant screen covered the surface, and it could have come out of any conspiracy theorist's wall in a vid, except usually, fictional conspiracy nuts hid their walls in secret rooms. News articles had red circles with lines pointing to photographs, which pointed back to other stories. "ZimmerCorp to Purchase Land on Bellerophon" one headline read, and it had a line connecting it to a story about ImriCorp sponsoring a dance school on Ariadne.

If anyone else had such a wall, she would make excuses to leave right then and there, but it was Will. She didn't know him or understand him, not really—or at least, not yet—but something inside her knew she could trust him.

"You aren't going to offer me any?" she asked as he poured himself a mug of steaming brown sludge. *He makes it strong,* she thought, or maybe remembered.

"You don't like coffee," he said. "And I don't have any tea. I can get you some water."

"No, thanks." Bliss took deep breath number one hundred one.

Will looked at her expectantly. Apparently, she had to start the conversation.

"So here's the thing. You told some guy that Lexi and I were aliens who reincarnate—"

"Which Demitrius is going to kill me for," Will muttered.

"Pardon?"

"Nothing." Will took a sip of his coffee then cringed as if it was too hot, though Bliss realized it was probably cold since he had brewed it before she arrived. "George latched onto the idea is all. Actually wants to see the story. I tried backpedaling, reminding him I didn't write alien kind of stuff, but he paid for two weeks of university to finance an alien story, so he wants to see it. Fortunately, no one will believe it."

"It's true, though," Bliss said in a very small voice. "Isn't it?"

Will looked her straight in the eye. "Yes, it is."

Unsure where to look, she felt something heavy rise in her chest and try to burst out of her, except it had nowhere to go. "Oh Cronos. Oh ancestors. How can that be true? How can I be one person now, have been another person before, and—?"

Will came over and put a hand on her arm. "Let's sit down, and we'll talk about this. I'll tell you from the beginning."

Somehow, Bliss let Will lead her to the couch, because before she realized she had moved, she was running her fingers along the red corduroy of the sofa. The grooves in the material felt rough under her fingers, and for some reason, that calmed her.

"Humans have yet to find life on other planets, but it exists, somewhere out there. A few thousand years ago, by human reckoning, an alien ship went on a mission near Earth, and something went horribly wrong. The engines of the ship failed, and the one person on the ship who knew how to fix them died in the accident. The aliens decided to kill themselves in order to return to their planet."

"Because they reincarnate," Bliss said. "*We* reincarnate."

"Exactly." Will gave her a bright smile. "What they didn't realize was that they were only a few systems away from a species they had a lot in common with."

"Humans."

"Right. Instead of being reborn light years away on their planet, they were reborn on Earth to human parents."

"It's not just regular reincarnation, though, right?" Bliss asked. "I mean, I've started having memories of my past lives, and we look exactly the same and have the same names. That's not how reincarnation is supposed to work."

"Not as humans understand it, no. But we're not human. Or at least, only half. Our bodies re-form in the same appearance as our old bodies, and our names project themselves onto our parents. We're even born into families with the same last names. There's some mystical explanation for it, but Demitrius won't tell us what it is."

"I have so many questions," Bliss said. "Like who is this Demitrius you keep mentioning?"

"He was the captain of the vessel the aliens came on, and now he's our leader. He likes to make rules, and ordinarily, I'm not one for rules, but Demitrius is kind of scary."

"So that's who we are. The people from that ship."

"Not exactly," Will said. "You see, Demitrius has rules, and one of them is that Transients—that's what we call ourselves—aren't allowed to have children. But he broke that rule himself once, and consequently, he relaxed the rule for the others for a while. But after nine children were born to the original Transients, he reinstated the rule. You're the daughter of the science officer, Astrid."

"And who are you?"

Will laughed. "My story's a little more complicated. One of the women on the ship, Domina, was pregnant when they set off on the voyage, and she gave birth right around the time they realized the ship was stuck. She killed her baby along with the rest of them, and her baby ended up reborn on Earth too. Unlike we half bloods, she remembers her time on that alien planet, but unlike the rest of the crew, she has no idea what kind of mission they were on. Another of Demitrius's rules, you see, is silence on that topic. The baby's name was Phedre, and she's been obsessed with finding out what separated her from her people for longer than I've known her, longer than I've been alive, since she's my mother."

"And the other children?"

"Well, I told you Demitrius had one child. In her obsession, Phedre seduced Demitrius, hoping he would tell his lover everything. She really should have known better. Demitrius told exactly one person any of our secrets—his and Phedre's daughter, Roslyn."

"My Roslyn?"

Will nodded. "You're always born near one of us, and you tend to gravitate toward the rest. It's why you elected to die twenty years ago."

"I—I chose to die?" *What in the worlds happened twenty years ago?*

Will gave her a sad smile. "I'll get to that part later. For now, you wanted to know who all of us were. And when I say 'us,' I mean the nine of us who were born on Earth and don't remember the alien world at all, because we were never there. We don't even know its name. There are Phedre's children, Roslyn and me, though my father was human. Roslyn's the only full-blooded Transient among us. First Officer Obseverus had twins, Jack and Cobalt, and they've been a profound disappointment to him for hundreds of years. Dr. Camarilla had two children: Lexi, whom you know, and Gavin, whom you may have seen starring in the Bellerophon Games."

"Wow, my mother loves those. She keeps calling me and telling me that someone named Gavin is going to win. He's one of us?"

"Yes. Then there's you, of course, and finally, pilot Inktari's children, Detrick and Tegan."

Bliss concentrated for a moment, trying to bring up memories of those people. "Jack is... in love with Roslyn? And Gavin is too? I don't remember the others."

"The others will come back to you. Roslyn tends to get her memories back the fastest because she's full-blooded. The rest of us usually require cues. Now that I've told you all of this, the rest should come back pretty quickly."

"Oh Cronos!" Bliss put her hands over her face. "No wonder Roslyn hates me right now. I told the school administrators that she must have cheated on the university entrance exams. There was no way she could have known all that stuff about art history and archaeology. But she remembered from past lives, didn't she?"

"Yeah, art and archaeology have always been Roslyn's fields of expertise." Will twisted his lips. "I don't suppose you could tell me about her. I haven't talked to her in twenty years, except that moment in your room."

"She's a server." Bliss cringed even saying those words. "She was born into my family and assigned to serve me personally. I always saw her more as my sister, but I guess that doesn't make it any better for her."

"Cronos, she must hate being a servant." Will smiled. "But it won't last forever. We're going to have to figure out a way to get her out of there before everyone realizes she's not aging."

"Are we immortal, then?"

"Yep." Will's smile broadened. "I've been alive for three hundred ninety-three years this time around. I think that's the longest of any of us at the moment."

Bliss wanted to return his smile but found she couldn't. "Will, you said you would explain later, but I think I need to know now. Why did we all die twenty years ago?"

Will's smile faded as well. "I don't know all the details. I've been trying to find out more for twenty years, but Phedre and Tegan have kept a close wrap on everything."

"Didn't you say Tegan was one of us?"

"Yeah, she is. Or at least, she was. I'm not entirely sure what happened. What I do know is that Roslyn, Gavin, Jack, and Cobalt went on an archaeological mission to Arachne. They found something there related to us, to why we're all here and not on our home planet. Phedre found out about it and somehow recruited Tegan to her side, and where Tegan goes, Detrick follows. Tegan killed the four of them that were there, all in service to some discovery Phedre was trying to make. Since Phedre's still on Arachne, I suspect she hasn't found it and may well want to kill us again."

"Wait, if she didn't kill me or Lexi, why are we here? You said I killed myself?"

"Lexi flipped out and said she didn't want to wait around for Tegan to kill her. You hoped that your special power to find the rest of us might help us avoid Tegan this time around."

Bliss leaned back against the sofa, taking everything in. Will had given her a million things to worry about—Demitrius's rules, her betrayal of Roslyn, Tegan and Phedre's desire to kill them—but all she could think about was the man beside her. He had told her the most amazing, mind-blowing things about who she was and how she knew people. She wondered why he wasn't rushing to save the world or all of them from Phedre and Tegan. As their memories came back, they must be more at risk.

It's Lexi, came a certain voice from the back of her mind. *He wants to save us but not as much as he wants to save Lexi.*

She stared at Will, with his mussed dark hair and shining hazel eyes, and understood why she had felt drawn to him since she had met him. She'd been in love with him for thousands of years, and always, in all that time, he'd been in love with Lexi. She couldn't begrudge him choosing Lexi over his fellow Transients when she wanted to choose him over them.

He's not with Lexi right now. Lexi made that very clear.

And I don't have years of rejection weighing down my soul yet. This may be my only chance.

"Thank you," Bliss said. She leaned over and kissed Will.

CHAPTER 30

Present Day

TEGAN SWORE. SHE COULDN'T BELIEVE she'd lost Jack and Cobalt again.

Yes, you can. They had always been smarter than she was. What she couldn't believe was that she had blown a hole in a police cruiser to get to them. When Detrick had told her the police had found the Zhaos and were closing in on them, she had lost it. No way was she letting the Ariadne police capture them again. Those barely-better-than-rent-a-cops had proven how incapable they were of holding onto the twins.

Turns out I'm not any better. Tegan banged her hand against the dashboard of the *Spirit*. She needed to get out of Ariadne space. No doubt more police cruisers would come looking for her. Jack and Cobalt were almost certainly following the train to Bellerophon, so she wouldn't be able to pick up their signal until they arrived. She considered heading in that direction anyway but decided to head back to Orpheus instead so she could bring Detrick his accursed gun and regroup.

Once she had set her autopilot, she called up the most recent highlights of the Bellerophon Games. The first image that popped up was one of Gavin in a holding cell.

She inhaled through her teeth. *Not good.* If Gavin won the competition, he would get shipped out to Orpheus, where she might stand a chance of capturing him, but from the looks of things, he had lost his chance.

Tegan buried her head in her hands. Even if she caught Jack and Cobalt, she was dead, or Detrick was. *Which means I'm dead, because no way am I letting Phedre's greasy fingers anywhere near my brother. I should never have let her get them anywhere near me.*

Twenty Years Ago

"This is an interesting little ship you have here," Phedre said as Tegan welcomed her aboard the *Spirit*. "And such a cute name. Is that how you and your fellows think of yourselves? As Transcendent Spirits?"

Tegan gritted her teeth. She'd put up with a lot of guff from Phedre, but she would be damned before she let someone insult her ship. "It's what we aspire to be. And if you don't like the ship, you're welcome to seek transportation elsewhere."

"Of course I like the ship! It's going to help me fulfill my dreams." Phedre's voice was as smooth as butter. "You know that's what Arachne is, right? The answer to every question we've ever had."

She's trying to distract me. "Look, Phedre. Maybe this wasn't such a good idea. Us working together, I mean."

"I'm happy to walk away, if that's what you really want." Phedre ran her hand along the *Spirit*'s bronze hull. "But I don't think it is. After all, I have the government connections to get you passage to Arachne. You do want to go, don't you?"

More than anything, but Phedre's not the answer. Roslyn or Jack or Gavin would help if you just called and asked.

Tegan swallowed. *But then they would think you need them, but you* don't.

She grunted in acknowledgement. "Come on. I'll give you a tour."

Showing Phedre around didn't take very long. The ship had a few bunks, a privy, a small armory in back, and a cockpit in front. The *Spirit* didn't look like much, as Phedre's wrinkled nose made apparent, but it had been Tegan's home for over a hundred years. She'd shared it with all of her fellow generation of Transients at one point or another. The ship had so many memories that Tegan couldn't give it up if she tried.

When they got to the cockpit, she gave Phedre voice authorization access. With her first smile since her arrival, Phedre sank into the pilot's seat.

"That's my chair," Tegan said.

"Not anymore, it's not." Phedre's singsong tone belied the menace Tegan suspected lay beneath her benign expression. "Oh, come now, Tegan. You know I'm a better pilot than you are. I've been flying ships for far longer."

Tegan wanted to take back Phedre's voice authorization. She wanted to take back the entire arrangement, but she couldn't because she needed to prove to her fellow Transients that she could do things on her own, and she wasn't just some ferry they could visit when they needed a ride. She sat down in the copilot's seat and vowed to do whatever Phedre wanted.

Present Day

When Tegan had the courage to look at her datapad again, she almost laughed. Gavin was going head-to-head with some security guards, which meant he had escaped his cell. She breathed a sigh of relief.

He might win this thing after all. She did laugh that time. *Of course he will. He's got lifetimes of experience to draw on.*

As she chuckled, another thought struck her. Jack and Cobalt couldn't be headed to Bellerophon proper. They would never be allowed on the planet. *They must be going somewhere less legit. Somewhere like Eurydice.*

"Call Ant," Tegan said to her datapad. As the device made the connection across the datasphere, she whistled. Things were looking up.

CHAPTER 31

Twenty Years Ago

Roslyn lay in the same cot in the medical lab where she had spent the past four weeks. *Or so they tell me. I can only remember two of them. I spent the first two having delusions. If that is how being sick feels, I never want to contract another disease.*

"Can I please get up?" she asked Gavin for what seemed like the millionth time. "I'm better. I swear it. I can sit up. I can eat. I can count to ten in about four hundred different languages. I'm pretty sure I can handle walking across camp."

Gavin sat on the edge of her bed and ran a thermometer over her forehead. "Your fever's stayed down."

"It's been down for a week. The rash has faded. I'm *better*. You can't keep me prisoner here forever."

He tapped his finger on the thermometer, not looking at her. "You *are* better, but you still have that cough, and I'm worried about re-exposure."

"Gavin—"

"I don't think you realize how much you worried us." He met her gaze, his brown eyes still full of fear. "You almost died. For a couple of days there, I thought every breath you took was going to be your last. And if you'd died, you wouldn't have come back."

Tears welled in her eyes. She understood. Gavin had been terrified for her. Knowing how close she had come to dying forever, she was terrified for herself.

But she still couldn't take another day in that bed. Exasperated, she let out a breath and ran her hands through her hair. "You can't keep me locked up here forever because you're worried for me. You have to let me take risks again."

Gavin avoided her eyes again. "I know."

"Good, then I can go." Roslyn pushed away the sheets covering her.

He grabbed her hand. "I'll let you go on one condition."

Roslyn smiled. She had won. "Anything for you."

"Talk to Jack."

Her grin fell. "Anything but that."

"Roslyn..."

She lay back on the cot and turned her back on Gavin. "Can I at least get some better lighting in here? Because if that's the condition of my leaving, I'm going to be here for the rest of my natural life."

Gavin sighed. "He's been driving me—and everyone— insane. He literally would not leave your side the entire time you were sick."

"I know. I remember the smell." The first thing Roslyn had done when she was conscious enough to realize a very scruffy Jack was holding her hand was to tell him to get lost. She had heard him outside the medical tent more than a few times, but she refused to see him.

"He cares about you," Gavin said.

She turned over and glared at him. "Don't give me that! Jack and I were back together for like two minutes before he cheated on me this time. I'm done with him. I should have been done with him before, but he held Arachne in front of me like a carrot. And like a stupid horse, I fell for it."

"If it makes you feel any better, I think he and Dr. Carriger were just using each other."

"It doesn't." Roslyn lay flat on her back and stared up at the tent's off-white ceiling. "If he had to cheat on me, I would like it to have been for something real, you know?"

"I do know." Gavin's voice was barely above a whisper.

Roslyn felt heat fill her cheeks. She had never cheated on Gavin, but she had left him high and dry more times than she could count. "Since when are you all Team Jack, anyway?"

"I'm not. But he's been pestering me for days to let him talk to you. He's also not doing his job, so Dr. Carriger keeps asking me to ask him to do it. I figure I can get at least one of them off my back if you go talk to him."

"All right, fine. I'll talk to Jack. But I'm doing this for you."

Gavin stood up. "Thank you kindly."

Roslyn had never considered Arachne a bright place, but when she stepped out of the medical tent for the first time in a month, the light nearly blinded her. As her eyes adjusted, someone called, "Rosie!" and footsteps headed toward her.

She didn't look at him. There was no point. "Hello, Jack."

"Rosie! Cronos, you look—"

"Emaciated? Pale? Just generally terrible?" Roslyn had meant to save the bitter sarcasm for later in the conversation. *Or maybe I hadn't.* Either way, she realized how she must look to him. Her illness had taken a lot out of her, and she didn't want to think about what her hair must look like. *I should have asked Gavin for a brush.*

"I was going to say amazing. A million times better than the last time I saw you." Jack came into focus, and he looked much better than the last time she had seen him too. He had shaved, for one thing, and showered. "How shallow do you think I am?"

Roslyn raised her eyebrows. "Do you really want me to answer that?"

Jack sucked in a breath through his teeth. "Probably not. Look, can we go somewhere and talk?"

The petty part of her wanted to say no. They'd already had enough of a conversation to fulfill her promise to Gavin. She knew, though, that she would have to talk to Jack sooner or later. *Which is weird because I don't think Jack has ever wanted to have a serious conversation about our relationship in all the time I've known him.*

She followed him back to the tent they had shared with Cobalt before she left for the exploration mission and tried not to wonder if Hannah and Jack had shared it in her absence.

Jack turned to her as soon as the tent flap fell. In the dim light, she could barely make out the contours of his face, but she would still know that outline anywhere. "Rosie, I'm an idiot."

Roslyn crossed her arms. "You dragged me all the way back here to tell me that? It's not exactly news."

"I'm serious. I've treated you like shit our entire lives, and I don't know why you take it. You deserve a million times better than me." Jack ran his hands over his face and through his hair, leaving it mussed and surprising Roslyn. Though he pretended he didn't, he cared a great deal about his appearance. Looking closer, she realized he hadn't shaved in at least a day, and his shirt had some kind of grease stain on it.

Maybe my illness did affect him. Or he's upset about something else. He's never let me in before, not really. Why would he change now? "Again, not telling me anything I don't already know."

"I wish I could explain. I wish I could say I was afraid of commitment or something, not that that would be an excuse, but it might be a reason. But the truth is, I had forever. We had forever, and I didn't see the point of settling down when I could have everything." Her eyes had adjusted to the light, and the look he gave her was the saddest thing she'd ever seen. "But I can't have everything, can I?"

I will not cry. I will not. "No, you can't."

He started tugging at something inside his shirt. "I've realized it doesn't matter, though, because all I want is you."

The tears she had begged not to come welled in her eyes anyway. "You realize that's hard for me to believe, right?"

"Right. Right. I know. And that's why..." He dropped onto one knee and held something out to her. "I'm asking you to marry me, Rosie."

Tears stopped forming in Roslyn's eyes as her jaw dropped open. *I... What?* A million questions popped into her head. *Ha. Popping questions. But seriously, where did he get a ring on this deserted rock? Does Cobalt know anything about this? Does* Gavin? *And most importantly...* "Are you insane?"

Jack gave her a half grin, and for the first time that day, he looked like himself. "Maybe. But you knew that."

Roslyn shook her head, unable to cope with all the thoughts and feelings flooding through it. "Transients don't get married. Demitrius made that very clear. For us, it's not 'till death do us part.' It's till *permadeath* do us part. And you don't want that."

"I do. I'm done with all the other girls. I only want you. In this lifetime and in every other one." He looked up at her, and that time it was his eyes that had tears in the corners. "Don't you want that too?"

Yes. Oh Cronos, yes. But she couldn't say it, because she didn't believe he could change. He was upset about almost losing her, but that feeling would fade, and he would go back to the way he was. *Right?*

"I don't know, Jack," she said. "I—I need to think about it. Can I have a little time?"

Jack stood up and took her hands, closing her grip around the ring, and gave her a light kiss. "Of course. Take all the time you need. I'm not going anywhere. Not ever again."

Present Day

Roslyn lay in her bed in the psychiatric hospital. She was supposed to get up and join in the day's activities, but she couldn't make herself do it. Her head was foggy and numb from the medications.

"You clearly need something stronger than what we've been giving you, if you're still having delusions," the nice brown-eyed doctor had said. "Don't worry, Roslyn. We want to help you here." She looked so understanding that Roslyn wanted to believe her.

But it wasn't working. The memories—*delusions,* she corrected herself—were still coming, and she didn't know how to make them stop.

"Roslyn? Sweetie? It's time to get up." Roslyn's favorite orderly, the kind one with the smooth caramel skin, came in and opened her curtains. "You've got art therapy this morning. Don't you want to finish that lovely painting you started of your dog?"

Snookems isn't my dog, and it's not a lovely painting. For someone who knows as much as I do about art history, I can't draw for crap. That was what the old Roslyn would have said, the one from twenty years ago and the one from before the psychiatric hospital, but she didn't want to be either of those Roslyns anymore. One of those Roslyns was sick and delusional, and the other wasn't real. Maybe the good, healthy Roslyn liked painting pictures of dogs.

"Yes, okay." She got out of bed, ready to face another day.

CHAPTER 32

Present Day

JACK JUMPED OUT OF THE ship as soon as the gangway descended enough for him to slip through. He took a deep breath, inhaling the cold, stale air of Eurydice, and smiled. He had thought he would never leave Daedalus, and in the course of just a few weeks, he'd been to almost every moon in the system.

Every moon if you don't count Arachne, which is fair, because only government scientists go there. Once, he had thought his life would be the humdrum existence of a repair shop owner, and he had made it into a constant adventure. Stealing those diamonds was the best decision he had ever made.

Cobalt waited until the gangway descended all the way before walking down it. Jack still didn't know what was up with his brother. Cobalt was jumpy all the time lately. *Jumpy and grumpy, which isn't nearly as cute as it sounds.* He seemed to know the woman who was after them, and Jack thought they knew all the same people. He had hounded his brother for a bit but eventually decided if Cobalt wanted to keep his secrets, he could.

"Let's go buy some guns!" Jack practically skipped with excitement toward the settlement.

"Do I have to say again that this is a bad idea?" Cobalt followed along, carrying the remaining diamonds in a case.

"I mean, that's up to you," Jack said. "Personally, I think that would be a waste of time."

"This settlement is filled with people who trained as Bellerophon soldiers and munitions experts then chose to go rogue. They're lawless mercenaries. No sane person deals with them."

"Wouldn't it be cool to be a lawless mercenary?" Jack asked. "I wonder if they're recruiting."

"Jack!" Cobalt grabbed his brother's arm and turned him around. "Is this going to be our life from now on? Always on the run from people who want to kill or arrest us? I don't want that!"

Exasperated, Jack let out a breath. They were back to that again. "What do you want? Our boring old life on Daedalus?"

"Yes! Yes, that is exactly what I want!"

"But, Blue..." Jack trailed off. He almost launched in at his brother about how it was too late for a simple life since they were wanted criminals, but he realized he was being selfish. He had dragged Cobalt along on his theft because he wanted his brother with him—and because he needed Cobalt's expertise—but he shouldn't force him into a life he didn't want. "Okay."

"Okay, we can go home?"

"Okay, after we buy the guns, you can go home." Jack could find another partner. Maybe that Roslyn girl wanted a life of adventure. She was a server, but if he didn't buy the guns, he would have enough money to buy her freedom. "Or maybe we don't need to—"

Jack broke off when he heard the whirr of a laser rifle behind him. He looked over his shoulder and found that not one but three people had managed to sneak up on him and Cobalt. All three held the largest laser pistols Jack had ever seen. They must have aimed them in perfect sync. He didn't want to admit it, but he was impressed.

"Did I hear you say you were here to buy guns?" the man in front asked. He had spiky blond hair and a robotic eye that seemed to be trained on both twins at the same time.

Jack gave an easy smile that belied the riotous butterflies in his stomach. "That's right. Our ship could use some. I'm Jack, and this is Cobalt."

"His uniform says Blue," the only woman among the three, a tall, thin brunette with three piercings in her nose, said.

"Yeah, well..." Jack shrugged. "We were hiding out before. Did you want us to use code names?"

"The smart ones do," the man in back with tattoos covering his bald head muttered.

Jack pulled out every ounce of bravado he had ever mustered to keep his tone nonchalant. "I figured you would do your own version of background checks before selling us anything. Thought I'd save you some trouble."

"I've heard of these guys." The woman popped something she was chewing. It looked like gum, but it could have been one of those new designer chewing drugs. "They stole diamonds from ZimmerCorp and haven't been caught yet."

The yellow brow over the robotic eye rose. "Really? All right, you two can come in. But if the cops show up looking for you, we're turning you right over. We don't want trouble here."

Jack suspected the gunrunners of Eurydice sold out criminals on occasion to keep themselves in business. If they were enough of a boon to law enforcement, the cops wouldn't take them down. "Not a problem. The last police cruiser after us ended up with a giant hole in its hull. We rode in the wake of the train the whole way here, so no one could have followed us."

"You got that thing up to the pace of a train?" Tattoo nodded at the *Rose*. "All the way from Orpheus?"

"From Ariadne, actually," Jack said. The luxury moon was farther from Bellerophon that time of year.

Robot-eye nodded appreciatively. "I think we can do business."

Cobalt was worried about Jack, and not just because of the guns. Jack had wanted to turn the *Rose* into an arsenal, and Cobalt didn't know whether Jack thought they needed the protection or had a kid-in-a-candy-store desire to buy all the nifty toys the Eurydiceans showed them.

"I can only fire one, maybe two, guns at once," Cobalt had said. "And you can't fly and fire at the same time."

"My *Rose* needs thorns," Jack had said, but he had also allowed Cobalt to talk him down to a turret-mounted laser rifle and a front-mounted missile launcher.

What Cobalt was really worried about was Jack's memory—or rather, his *lack* of memory. After their encounter with Tegan, Cobalt had known he couldn't keep his weird dreams-slash-memories a secret anymore, so he had told Jack everything. Jack had laughed at first, until he had realized Cobalt was serious. He hadn't wanted to believe Cobalt's story, but he believed Cobalt believed it, and he hadn't had a better explanation for why Cobalt knew Tegan than reincarnation.

"And your girl, the one you're so sure exists," Cobalt had said. "She must be from one of these past lives."

"Then how come you remember and I don't?" Jack had asked.

Cobalt didn't have an explanation. And he really didn't have an explanation for why, after Jack had taken a nap on the trip over, he had forgotten the entire conversation.

"Blue, you've been acting weird since Ariadne. Are you ever going to tell me why?" Jack had asked.

Cobalt's body had gone cold. "I did tell you why."

Jack had huffed. "I know you're not just ticked about the robbery, so let me know when you feel like letting me in."

He didn't know what he was supposed to say to that.

Jack needed more help than Cobalt could provide, not that doctors or therapists were trained in past lives.

Cobalt shook his head. He needed to focus on the task at hand. Jack had said Cobalt could go home, but he wasn't going to leave his brother at the mercy of a killer like Tegan. They needed to find a way to neutralize her. Then they could both go home.

"Hey," Cobalt said to the man with the tattooed head, whose name turned out to be Ant. "Do you guys know this woman?" He brought up a picture of Tegan on his datapad and showed it to Ant. He figured since those guys dealt with a lot of lawless types, they might know her.

Ant studied the picture then turned his assessing gaze to Cobalt. "I might, and I might not. What'll it get me if I do?"

Cobalt considered offering the few diamonds left in the case but hesitated. He was loath to part with their remaining assets. "What do you want?"

Ant nodded toward the *Rose*. "You got that piece of junk to fly as fast as a train. I want to know how you did it."

Easy enough. "Sure. You know anything about ships?"

Ant grunted. "I do all the repair work around here, for all the different ships people bring in. But I'm self-taught, you know? Always happy to pick up a trade secret or two."

Cobalt shrugged. "If I tell you, you'll tell me about Tegan?"

"You tell me everything, I'll tell you everything."

He hoped that Ant didn't mean everything he knew about ships, because that could take some time. Cobalt launched into an explanation of how he reprogrammed the engine to give it that extra boost. "But you have to be careful not to let it overheat, which is why you have to add the extra coolant," he finished. "Do you need me to show you?"

"Naw, man, that's good," Ant said. "Where'd you learn that trick?"

Cobalt didn't answer, largely because he wasn't sure. He had thought he'd figured it out on his own, but he suspected he had learned it from someone else several lifetimes ago. "You promised to tell me about Tegan O'Leary."

"Sure thing. She comes by occasionally. She's got a real eye for guns, or knows someone who does. Always knows exactly what she wants, and she's willing to wait any amount of time to get it."

"But who is she?" Cobalt asked. "What does she do?"

"We've never been quite sure, and we don't ask too many questions here," Ant said. "But I think she does work for someone out of Arachne. She may be a high-level government spook or something. Only government folks have anything to do with that place."

Cobalt considered. He knew *he'd* had something to do with Arachne once upon a time, and he doubted he'd ever been a government spy. But Jack had a way of convincing people they were anything they needed to be. "Does she have any associates off Arachne?"

"Just one that I know of. His name's Detrick, and he lives on Orpheus, near Chora. I can get you his address if you want. We've had to ship stuff to him before."

"That would be great."

Ant nodded. "Watch yourselves, okay? Any associate of O'Leary's is bound to be dangerous."

Hm. Maybe we should pick up some handguns too.

CHAPTER 33

Present Day

GAVIN JUMPED AS THE SOUND of sirens filled the forest. *Surely they couldn't have just now figured out I escaped. I've been gone for hours.*

He wished he had grabbed one of the guard's laser pistols, but after Jesse's harebrained scheme, he'd needed to rush out for fresh air. At least he knew Jesse and Abe hadn't had time to grab lasers, either. If they had, they probably would have shot him, and he would be back in captivity.

"Attention all contestants!" a mechanical voice rang through the woods. "The Bellerophon Games have come to an end. Please report to the nearest camera drone, and it will lead you out of the woods."

Gavin didn't need to turn to see the camera drone in front of him. He was pretty sure at least two more were hovering over his shoulder. Their job was to record the games, which then got edited down into the footage the people across the system saw. Gavin wondered what people had seen of him and if they wanted him to win. *Funny I didn't think of that earlier, though the cameras have been hovering around me for two weeks.*

The walk to the exit took about half an hour, and more cameras joined Gavin on the way. He wondered if they were still watching him or if they had turned off recording when the games had ended. When the exit was in sight, he saw Abe and Jesse, as well as two other contestants, already waiting by the gate. The two competitors he didn't recognize looked as though they hadn't seen the inside of a bathroom in two weeks. *They didn't get caught at all. Surely one of them will win.*

An alarm sounded as he joined the other contestants, and the gate opened, letting them out. They stepped back out into the real world, though it didn't look much different from the forest.

"When do we find out who won?" *Trust Abe to be the first person to ask that question.*

A woman in military greens approached them. "The winner will be announced at a special ceremony that will air live across the system tonight. You will all get an opportunity to clean up before the event." She eyed Gavin, Abe, and Jesse. "Though some of you need less cleaning than others."

"I'd like to see Archon," Gavin said.

"Your friend is fine. He's in the care of the best doctors on Bellerophon." The woman turned and led them farther out of the woods. "You won't have time to see him before the ceremony, but I assure you, he will make a complete recovery."

"Can't have someone dying in the games, can we?" one of the scruffy competitors said. "Bad for publicity." Apparently this guy wasn't any more of a fan of the games than Gavin was, or at least two weeks of participation had soured his attitude toward them.

"Then they shouldn't have let a trimper on the grounds," Gavin muttered.

Scruffy's partner whistled. "Someone faced down a trimper? Was it you?"

Gavin gave a mute nod.

"You've got this in the bag, then," Scruffy said. "Too bad.

I figured if I had to run around in the woods for two weeks, I would at least try to win."

Gavin shrugged. "I got caught. I think the odds favor you."

As soon as they got clear of the woods, the woman loaded them onto a bus. Gavin couldn't remember the last time he'd ridden such a vehicle. After all, the general's children did not take the bus to school. It wasn't secure enough. Gavin had ridden a bus when he went to summer camp. He smiled at the idea of the woman leading them in patriotic camp songs as they headed to their destination.

Instead, she pressed a button, turning on vid screens all over the bus. "We thought you might want to watch some of the highlights of the games."

Not really. The last thing he wanted to think about—pretty much ever again—was the games. Glancing at the others, he suspected they felt the same way. The five men who were brave enough to take on the wild forests of Terpischore lacked the courage to tell one woman that they didn't want to watch their own feats.

The first part of the vid was easy enough for Gavin to watch, largely because it didn't feature him. He and Archon showed up on occasion in brief flashes of motion, but the early shots focused on Abe and Jesse and their attempts to trick other players into giving up the pass phrase. Gavin supposed that kind of drama appealed to viewers all over the system.

Footage from the first week lasted only a few minutes, and before Gavin knew it, the commandos entered the forest, searching for him and his fellows. He watched as the pair he'd seen in the prison took too much camouflage from a limited area, making themselves easy to track. Then Abe and Jesse chased the commandos around using animal sounds. *Those are terrible. No wonder they didn't work.* Abe and Jesse reddened in both the vid and in real life as the commandos laughed at them.

Gavin squirmed in his seat, knowing his big moment would be next. He didn't want to watch Archon get gutted again, so he leaned forward and asked their guide if there was a bathroom on the bus.

She gave him a puzzled glance but nodded and pointed toward the back. As Gavin walked down the narrow aisle, trying to keep steady over the bumps in the road, he heard the scream of a trimper behind him. He closed his eyes and moved faster. Once he got inside the bathroom, he clutched at the steel sink with trembling hands and stared at his reflection in the mirror. In his mind's eye, he could see the trimper running toward Archon, and he flashed back to the moment he realized his friend was going to die.

The bus jerked to a stop, and he nearly fell over. He took a deep breath and splashed some water on his face then headed back out to join his fellows.

"You killed that trimper with a utility knife!" Scruffy said as they piled off the bus. "How'd you do that?"

"It was a lucky shot," Gavin said. "I honestly thought I was dead." He hated not telling the whole truth, but he didn't think they would appreciate tales of sudden memories from past lives.

"And you saved your buddy. He was bleeding everywhere!" Scruffy's partner sounded even more impressed than Scruffy had, if that was possible. "I wish you'd been my partner!"

"Hey!" Scruffy said.

"Well, it's true. I didn't see you performing battlefield surgery after a trimper attack."

"If a trimper had attacked us, I totally would—"

"Ahem." The woman's stern voice called to the soldier in all of them, and they snapped to attention. She gestured to the building behind her, a sleek white three-story edifice that had to be the nicest building on Bellerophon. "Inside this building, you will meet with your personal fashion consultants for the closing ceremony. You are to do whatever they say, and after the winner is announced, four of you will be free to go home. The winner will accompany the Bellerophon Games staff to Orpheus for the first of a year's worth of public appearances representing our great moon."

As the five finalists filed into the building, winning took on a new meaning to Gavin. If he won, his life would not be his own for the next year. They would parade him all over the system like a show pony. He closed his eyes and prayed he would not win.

Praying again? But the same part of him who had once been a doctor and who knew how to slay a trimper with a utility knife also believed in a higher power. He had a hard time believing that part of him wasn't real.

A woman with coiffed black hair and an unfortunate nose that her makeup almost downplayed greeted Gavin when he entered the building. "My name is Endetta, and I'm here to help you get ready for the closing ceremony."

Gavin shook her hand, but he was too busy staring at his surroundings to pay much attention to her. The place was all white-and-gold marble with the occasional black accent stone. The foyer featured a sweeping staircase and a chandelier that might have been made of pure diamonds. He had seen lobbies like it before—on vids about Ariadne. But he'd had no idea such luxury existed on Bellerophon.

"Nice, isn't it?" Endetta gave him a wink. "Wait till you see the bathrooms."

She led Gavin to his personal suite, where, she told him, he could at least stay the night if he didn't win. A fluffy tan comforter lay atop what Gavin imagined to be the softest mattress he had ever felt, though he didn't get a chance to try it out. Endetta urged him into the bathroom, where she had already started a bath in the whirlpool tub.

Gavin had a long soak, during which time he allowed himself to think only of how nice the warm water felt after two weeks in the woods. He had gotten a shower in his cell, of course, but that had nothing on the tub's massage jets.

Though he could have stayed there forever, eventually,

Endetta came in, bearing fluffy towels and a robe the same tan color as the bed. She offered to give him a shave, but he confessed he didn't feel comfortable with the idea of other people holding sharp objects that close to him at the moment. After he had shaved his head and face, he put on the outfit she had left for him: a brown cadet's uniform from Calliope.

He barely had time to admire his appearance in the mirror before Endetta rushed him out the door. "Come on! We don't want to be late!"

Gavin, who had not seen a clock in two weeks, decided to take her at her word. He hurried after her until they came to a hallway with Abe, Jesse, and two men he barely recognized as Scruffy and his buddy.

"You two clean up nicely," Gavin said to them.

"Tell us about it!" Scruffy said. "The winner gets to live here for a year. If I'd known that, I would have tried harder to win."

Gavin clapped him on the back. "You've still got a good shot."

"I didn't take out a trimper."

The woman from the bus emerged from the door next to them, and Gavin heard the dull roar of an audience anticipating a show from the other side. He realized they were backstage from a massive auditorium, and his parents were probably in attendance. His palms began to sweat.

"Are you ready?" She looked each of them up and down in turn. "Good. Now, walk out when they call your name, and for Cronos's sake, *smile* at the crowd." She opened the door again so they could hear. Only a moment later, an announcer began calling their names: Abraham Lander of Euterpe, Jesse Engels of Terpischore, Sander Kyoto of Thalia, Martin Hernandez of Urania, and Gavin Ibori of Calliope. They paraded out on stage and stood at perfect attention. Gavin did his best to smile, but he worried his expression was more of a grimace.

He wanted to look out at the crowd to see if he could find his parents, but the lights shone too brightly in his eyes. A speaker droned on about the importance of the games and the glory and honor they brought, but Gavin couldn't hear very well over his pounding heart and heavy breathing.

Red and green lights blinked as vid stations from all over the system took his picture, and a deep voice chastised him in his head. "You must never, ever draw attention to yourself. Don't allow any public pictures to be taken of you, and above all, never become famous." His heart pumped so fast, he thought it might explode. *I have to get out of here.*

Before he could run off the stage, he heard the words that would doom him forever: "Ladies and gentlemen, I give you your champion, Gavin Ibori of Calliope!"

CHAPTER 34

Present Day

WILL WATCHED BLISS SLEEP AND wondered if he was being creepy. She was lying on his couch with an old orange heated blanket covering her. Her only pillow was the cylindrical throw pillow that matched the couch and was as hard as a rock. Nonetheless, she looked peaceful, especially considering the load of bombs he had dropped on her.

She had handled it all surprisingly well, then she had kissed him, something she'd never dared to do in all the years he had known her. Though he'd known she had something of a crush on him—he wasn't that dense—he was in love with Lexi. He figured someday Bliss would find the perfect person for her, and she would forget all about him. Given the limited Transient pool to pick from, he didn't know who that person could be, but he hadn't spent much time thinking about Bliss Bhanushali's love life.

The current Bliss, though, the one who had kissed him, seemed somehow different from all the Blisses who'd come before. She was bolder, somehow, and more in command of herself. She'd argued with him about megacorps, though she would probably regret her views once her memories came back. He'd never seen her argue with anyone in any of her past lives. The current Bliss had also done something to piss Roslyn off, so she wasn't the super-agreeable girl he'd known before.

She'd kissed him, and he had kissed her back. The kiss had only lasted a few seconds before Bliss pulled back and looked up at him, brown eyes glowing through black lashes, and he'd looked away. She'd let out a disappointed sigh, and he couldn't bear to look back at her and know what her expression was. He hadn't been able to explain that he'd enjoyed the kiss, but he didn't know how to process the well of emotions it had released in him.

He'd expected her to run out of the room, face afire, and refuse to talk to him for a few weeks or years, but again she'd surprised him with her boldness. "Can I stay here tonight? Just on the couch!" she'd hurried to add. "I can't go back and face Lexi, knowing everything I know. I have to tell her, and she won't understand, but tomorrow."

"Of course!" he had said. "Here, you can have the bed, and I'll take the couch." He'd glanced into his bedroom, at the stained sheets on his unmade bed, and realized she could see them as well.

"That's okay. I'll take the couch. Do you have a blanket?"

"Yes!" He'd rushed over to the closet and pulled out an orange blanket covered in dust. "I'm sorry. I don't have guests often."

Or ever. He'd been alone for so long. Six of his generation were essentially dead, and the other two had become his enemies. He hadn't spent time with anyone he trusted in so long.

Maybe that's why I'm watching her. I'm just grateful to have someone who knows me. A tightness gripped his heart as he watched her chest rise and fall, and he felt so much more than mere gratitude. He had never taken Bliss seriously before, but as her eyelids fluttered, he realized he wanted to grab hold of her and never let go.

Okay, now I'm definitely being creepy. He got up and went to the kitchen to make coffee. *I should go out and get tea. Bliss will want some. Will she disappear if she wakes to find me gone?* He needed to talk to her, and not just because he wanted to. They needed to discuss how they were going to break the news to Lexi.

He didn't have to decide, because Bliss was already awake and sitting up by the time the coffee was ready. Her eyes were surprisingly clear, given the amount of sleep she must not have gotten on the lumpy couch.

"Morning," he said, and he noticed a bit of shyness in his tone.

She looked him straight in the eye and smiled. "Morning."

He sat down across from her on the coffee table, steaming mug in hand. "I was going to get some tea for you, but—"

She waved off his excuse. "It doesn't matter. I can get some at the coffee shop. Lexi's got an early-morning performance. We should probably go catch the end of it then tell her about... everything."

Will cringed. "Do we have to? She never takes it well."

Bliss gave him a level look. "Yes, we have to. She deserves to know. But we've got a few minutes, and I have a question for you."

"Shoot."

"You said the engineer of Demitrius's ship died, so they couldn't repair it. But if he died, wouldn't he have been reborn like the others? Wouldn't they have been able to repair the ship in the next generation?"

"Well, I—huh. I never thought of that. I suppose they would have, unless... Demitrius always threatens us with permadeath when we get out of line, though he's never said how he could accomplish that. Maybe the engineer somehow ticked off Demitrius?"

Bliss pursed her lips. "Enough that he would give up his only ride home?" She shook her head. "I don't know. It seems like there's something Demitrius isn't telling us."

Will chuckled. "There's more than one thing Demitrius isn't telling us. He doesn't tell us anything about his planet, but it doesn't matter. For the nine of us, home is and always has been with humans, not with whatever race of people Demitrius and the others left."

"I suppose. But don't you want to know where we came from?"

Will took a sip of his coffee. "Not really. The desire to know who we are has driven my mother to some heinous acts. I would prefer to keep my ignorance and my soul."

"Do we have souls?"

"I wouldn't know. Certainly, the righteousness of our past behavior doesn't influence if and where we're reborn. I guess we have souls in the sense that our consciousnesses transfer to new bodies."

Bliss looked disappointed. She'd always been the most religious of them. After a moment, she gave him a small smile. "Shall we go then?"

He grimaced. "No?"

She laughed and grabbed his hand. "Come on! The sooner we tell Lexi, the sooner she'll get done ranting at us."

He didn't let go of her hand until they got out to her car.

"And the song goes, 'Baby, do you know who I am?

Cuz if I can't get no respect, then I'll be gone without a trace,'

But the cold, hard fact is we can never go home,

And so the only song I sing is 'Cronos, I hate this place.'"

Lexi's voice rang through the coffee shop, which was full of guests even at that early hour. *Sure, some of them are just coming in for their morning caffeine fix, but most of them are here to see* me. *I'm making a name for myself, and it's only up, up, up from here!*

As she strummed the last few chords of the song, she looked up to see two people entering the shop. She recognized both her roommate, Bliss, who had failed to come home the night before, and that traitor Will. *I can put two and two together. Looks like they've both betrayed me.* She didn't know what made her more angry—that Bliss had spent the night with the guy who'd called them aliens or that Bliss had spent the night with Lexi's boyfriend. *Sure, I don't want him anymore, but that doesn't make him any less mine.*

"Excuse me," Lexi said to the audience with a smile she didn't feel. "I need to take a fifteen-minute break."

As she strode past the bar, the barista on duty said, "Hey, you just took a break." Lexi let some of the wrath she had reserved for Bliss and Will pour out of her eyes, and the barista backed down.

When she caught up to them, Lexi crossed her arms and thrust her hip out in a defiant stance. "Neither of you is welcome here."

Lexi expected a humble "What did I do?" followed by endless groveling from her mousey roommate. Instead, Bliss met Lexi's gaze and said, "We need to talk to you."

"Well, I don't need to talk to you."

"Yes, you do, Lex," Will said, the soft way he said her name reminding her of how sweet he had been when they'd been together.

Lexi stuck out her lower lip, pretending not to be confused by Will's tone. She'd known what to expect of Bliss—though she hadn't gotten it—but she had no idea what to expect of Will. The man was clearly crazy if he thought she was an alien, but he had been showing up in her dreams like they were destined for each other for eternity.

"Fine. But outside." She stomped all the way out the door and almost missed Bliss rolling her eyes at Will. The autumn air was chilly, so Lexi hugged her arms around herself and leaned against the window. "What?"

"Have you been having weird dreams lately?" Bliss asked. "Ones where you're you and someone else all at the same time?"

A weird feeling crawled down Lexi's spine. *Maybe they're*

not just dreams. "You're describing every dream ever." *But no way am I admitting that to Bliss.*

"These are different," Will said. "These are real. I'm probably in some of them—"

"Oh, you wish!"

"And Bliss too. Maybe some other people. You have a brother named Gavin, perhaps?"

Lexi mustered all her self-control not to let her eyes bug out. She hadn't told anyone about Gavin. "Maybe I have been having some dreams, but they're just my self-doubt talking, telling me the best I can get out of life is wandering the galaxy with a conspiracy nut and a do-gooder brother. But they're *not real.*"

Bliss gently placed a hand on Lexi's arm. "That's what I thought, too, at first. But when you told me Will said we were aliens, it struck a chord. You know he was telling the truth."

"I am *not* an alien!" Lexi realized she'd said that louder than she'd intended, so she looked around to make sure no one had heard. One random passerby was giving her a weird look, and she gave him her most winning smile. Then she turned to glare at Will. "I am *not.* And I refuse to listen to this kind of talk any longer." She wrenched her arm away from Bliss and stormed back into the café.

"That could have gone better," Bliss said.

"Don't worry. She always takes it badly at fir—" The closing door cut off Will's words.

Lexi walked back over to her stool and picked up her guitar. "Sorry about that, folks. Just needed to have a quick conversation. Now, where was I?"

"Don't you go walking away.
Apparently, I'm not free to speak my mind.
Well, if you think I should just acquiesce,
Then, darling, think a little less,
Cuz you're falling behind."

CHAPTER 35

Twenty Years Ago

TEGAN WAS ALONE IN THE cockpit when the *Spirit* came into orbit around Arachne. The moon didn't look like much—a rugged black rock stuck out on the edge of the system. But Phedre was convinced the answers to their past lay on that moon, so Tegan mustered some hope that it was more than it seemed.

Speaking of Phedre, now that we're here, it's time to remove her voice from the system memory. With greater glee than was probably necessary, Tegan entered the sequence to remove Phedre's authorization.

The computer made a *blip-bloop* noise then flashed bright-red letters: ACCESS DENIED.

Wait, what? Tegan entered the code again and received the same response. She read the fine print under the big letters: "Only the system administrator has permissions to remove voice authentication authorization. Please check with your system administrator."

"I *am* the system administrator!" Something was clearly wrong with the computer, but she couldn't reboot while in orbit. She would have to wait until they landed, and if restarting it didn't work, maybe Jack or Cobalt could look at it.

A soft laugh rang out behind Tegan, and she whipped around to see Phedre standing in the doorway. "Tried to remove me from the system, did you?" Phedre asked. "I was wondering when you would do that."

Realization dawned on Tegan. "What did you do to my ship, you hag?"

Phedre chuckled again. "Don't you mean *my* ship, Tegan? It does answer to my commands now."

"It's not your ship! I never sold it to you! Put it back the way it was! Now!"

"Oh, don't worry, Tegan." Phedre slipped into the copilot's seat. "I have no interest in taking your little ship from you. After all, my new minion needs a mode of transportation."

"Pardon me?"

"I control your little ship now, which means I control you. Behave, and you can keep it. Act out, and you won't believe the information I've found on the hard drive."

Phedre had probably found some incriminating logs. Tegan had a habit of ranting at her ship about her fellow Transients when they annoyed her, but their secrecy wasn't worth losing her freedom over. "Do what you want to me. I'm not your puppet."

"Then there's your brother. He's nice and safe in that little apartment of his you know he'll never leave. Would you believe this ship has secondary controls for all the guns he likes to keep? It would be a shame if one of them misfired." Phedre's features morphed into an expression of mock sympathy. "Why, Tegan, whatever is the matter? You're looking quite pale."

"What do you want?" Tegan had planned for the words to come out tough and angry, but instead they sounded small.

"I told you, I want you to be my new minion. You're so good at running and doing favors for others without thinking for yourself. I think you'll find that working for me is the best of all possible options. Now, bring us down to the surface."

As Tegan followed Phedre's commands, she couldn't help

but think her new mistress was about to rain hell on the Transients on Arachne. *This is all Roslyn's fault, anyway. If she and Jack and Cobalt and Gavin had just told me about Arachne, I never would have had to turn to Phedre. They deserve whatever's coming to them.*

CHAPTER 36

Twenty Years Ago

"LET ME SHOW YOU WHAT we've found so far." Jack all but bounced up and down with excitement.

Two days had passed since he had proposed to Roslyn, and since then, she'd been on a strict recuperation schedule. Jack had spent as much time with her as he could, but he hadn't pressured her about marriage. He'd gone back to work with Hannah, but since he completely ignored her advances in public, Roslyn suspected that any illicit romance between them was over.

Roslyn hadn't given Jack a yes or no yet, but she kept the ring he'd offered her on a string around her neck and under her clothes. *Maybe he really has changed. Or maybe I'm a fool for believing that's possible.*

"You know I can't look at what you've discovered," she said, a hint of frustration in her tone. She felt better enough to be useful, but she couldn't do much if she couldn't analyze the artifacts. "My brain might explode."

Jack grabbed her hand and dragged her toward the dig site. "Nah, I talked to Gavin about it. He said if I tell you stuff, you should be fine. Just don't try to remember anything."

"Did you remind him that memory is automatic?" Sarcasm filled her tone, but she allowed him to lead her to the source of the artifacts. She didn't know what to say when she got there, except that she had expected something bigger. From the way Hannah had talked, Roslyn expected evidence of an alien settlement, but the space wasn't big enough for one person to live in, much less a colony. A circular indentation about twenty feet in diameter had been carved into the black rock. Large green sigils filled the circle, and similar script covered the walls of the circumference. At the north end, some kind of podium or control panel covered in the same symbols rose from the rock.

"I think I've figured out most of what it says," Jack said. "I didn't tell Hannah the truth, but I can tell you. Some of these indentations are the flaps for a giant box."

Roslyn looked at the circle again and realized he was right. A straight line through the middle and angled-out lines at each end looked like they might open.

"What's inside?" Roslyn asked. That seemed a wiser question than "How do we open it?"

"We don't know," Jack said. "There are instructions about opening it but nothing about what's inside."

"That seems short-sighted."

Jack tossed a rock back and forth in his hands. Roslyn hoped it wasn't one of the artifacts. "Well, if Demitrius and the others did leave this box here, they probably didn't think anyone would find it. They used some kind of tech to hide the moon from discovery for ages. Someone had to literally run into it to discover it."

"It still seems short-sighted."

"Well, I haven't told you how to open it yet." Jack held out the rock he had tossed around. It was an artifact, the one that had sent Roslyn into spasms her first day in camp. "We have to activate this device, which we have no idea how to do, then stick it in that"—he pointed at the control panel—"and 'pour the blood of three Ringati' into these sigils. Whatever a Ringati is."

Roslyn swiped the artifact from Jack's hand. "Does

Hannah know you have this? She wouldn't like you tossing it around like a toy."

"I don't really care what Hannah thinks."

She bit back the urge to say something sarcastic and instead focused on the device. Three of the symbols stood out to her. "Jack, you remember those words I said on the first day? The ones that made me pass out?"

"I remember you saying words that made you pass out. But honestly, I was more worried about the blood dripping from your nose than the nonsense you were spouting."

"It wasn't nonsense!" She thrust the device in his face. "I think it was the activation sequence. *Elleks. Tsufo. Kel.*" She pressed the symbols she somehow knew said *elleks,* and they blinked green. She pressed *tsufo* next, and the rock vibrated. Finally, *kel* made the top quarter of the device spin. Roslyn made her way over to the control panel and put the spinning rock in the indentation.

Jack ran over to her. "Rosie! You solved it!"

"Demitrius must have told me—" She looked at Jack. "Why hasn't Demitrius stopped us from exploring here? This is exactly the kind of stuff he doesn't want us to know."

Jack shrugged. "Dunno. Maybe he's decided it's time we found out. Maybe he wanted us to figure it out for ourselves."

Roslyn raised her eyebrows at him. "Does that sound anything like the Demitrius you know?"

"I guess not. Maybe he blocked his memories so he wouldn't remember the place. He likes blocking memories."

"He would have to have heard about the Arachne investigation. It's all over the news." Roslyn pulled the device from the control panel and turned the top piece the opposite of the way it was spinning. The lights stopped blinking, and it became an ordinary rock again. They weren't going to open the alien box that day unless they learned what a Ringati was. "Unless the memory blocks stop him from forming new memories too."

"Well, there's an easy way to test that theory," Jack said. "We'll see if you remember this conversation tomorrow."

"Fair enough." She looked around the room. "Do you think a Ringati is some kind of animal from Demitrius's native planet?"

"Animal sacrifice to open the box? That's pretty dark."

"Yeah." Roslyn tapped the stone against the control panel. She felt like she should know the answer, but if she forced the memory, she would risk an aneurysm. "Come on, let's go before Hannah finds us and pumps us for information."

Jack laughed. "She's going to try to get answers out of us no matter what we do. I've never met anyone more dogged about an archaeological investigation."

He put his arm around her waist, and she let him, and together, they strolled back to camp.

Present Day

Roslyn lay on her bed, her head too full of mush and clouds to process much that was going on around her.

The delusions still haven't stopped. Why haven't they stopped? A tear fell down her cheek. *I'm trying to get better. I am. I take my medicine. I remind myself every morning that they're just dreams. I'm using all the coping skills they're teaching me. Why are the memories still coming? No, not memories. Dreams, just dreams.*

She clutched her head and curled up in the fetal position. Her head felt so muddled, she could barely remember anything, anyway. *Except Jack.* She remembered Jack in her room on Ariadne and Jack in the camp on Arachne. She wanted to hold onto him as one solid thing to keep her sane, but her attachment to him prevented her from getting better. She scrunched her eyes shut. She was afraid to sleep but too disoriented to stay awake.

"Poor dear," someone said. *My favorite orderly.* "She's on so much Zyphonil she can't even get out of bed."

Another orderly spoke. "The doctor said everyone needed to get out of bed to—"

"Just let her sleep," the first said. "At least until she's adjusted to the new dosage."

Roslyn slept and tried not to dream.

CHAPTER 37

Present Day

"ORPHEUS!" JACK ALL BUT SANG as he pulled the ship into orbit. "Blue, do you realize we have visited every moon or planet in the system in the past month? This is amazing!"

Cobalt glowered at his brother. He couldn't believe Jack was still excited about their misadventures. *Well, yes, I can. It is Jack, after all.* Jack wanted a life of running from the law, while the trip from Bellerophon to Orpheus had only helped remind Cobalt that he didn't.

Jack hung his head at Cobalt's response, not bothering to hide the smirk on his face. "I'm sorry," Jack said. "We'll use this Detrick person to get Tegan off our backs, then you can go home."

"Then *we* can go home, right?" Cobalt asked. As crazy as his brother was, the thought of living without Jack left a hollow feeling in his gut.

Jack turned serious. "I'm not going home. I love it out here. I love knowing there's more to my life than fixing other people's spaceships so they can go off and have adventures."

"So you're just going to leave? Never come home again?"

"I'll visit, of course, but I can't stay there all the time, not now that I know what's out here. But I also can't make you come with me if you hate it. You're my best brother. I want you to be happy."

"I'm your *only* brother." Cobalt turned his gaze to the engine readouts and tried to look as if he were paying attention to them, but really, he wanted out of the conversation. He and Jack had been inseparable best friends their whole lives. *More than just these lives, if my dreams are anything to go by. And I'm not like other people. I can't find a nice boy or girl to settle down with. Without Jack, I'll be alone.* "Do you know where you're going to land this thing?"

"I've found a little docking station not too far from Detrick's address." Jack flipped a few switches, and they descended into the atmosphere. "They won't ask too many questions, but I wouldn't recommend leaving any valuables on board."

"The ship is a valuable thing," Cobalt said.

"Eh. By anyone's standards, our ship is a piece of commercial trash."

"That means they can sell it for parts."

Jack cruised through the atmosphere, and the viewscreen lit up. "Docking ships is their business. They wouldn't stay in business if they sold off their clients' ships for parts."

Cobalt sighed as he monitored the pressure gauges to make sure entry had gone smoothly. It had. "Sure, their properly disreputable clients with years of nefariousness. We're newcomers on the block, prime for scamming."

"Relax, Blue. We've got to start somewhere." Jack grinned. "Weren't the people at Eurydice nice enough?"

Almost too nice, Cobalt thought, but he didn't want to argue with Jack anymore. He kept his silence as they landed on Orpheus. The landing spot wasn't quite as sketchy as Jack had implied. The guy collecting the fee curled his lip in response to Jack's effusive smile, but no one pointed guns at them, which put them above Eurydice in Cobalt's estimation.

Jack seemed more effervescent than usual as they

walked down the streets of Daphne, the capitol of Orpheus and thus human civilization. No doubt he was reveling in walking through the biggest city in the system. Cobalt had to admit he enjoyed seeing the rush of gainfully employed citizens moving through clean streets. Daedalus always looked grimy, and jobs weren't easy to come by there.

"Do you know where we're going?" Cobalt asked after about ten blocks of hurrying to keep up with his brother. "You haven't looked at your datapad once."

"I'm taking in the sights!" Jack spread out his hands and spun around in a circle. "I'm not going to tell you again how amazing this is, because you'll scowl at me, but it totally, totally is!"

Cobalt took a deep breath and resolved not to prove Jack right. "So we're not going anywhere—is that what you're saying?"

"Don't be ridiculous. I memorized the route on the flight over. It was rather long, as you may remember, and you were in one of your grumpy, silent moods."

I wonder if I've become taciturn as a defense mechanism because talking to Jack is so useless. "Are we almost there?"

"As a matter of fact, we are!" Jack pulled Cobalt down a side street whose buildings looked more residential than the sleek white skyscrapers they'd passed. He pointed at a building with shiny mirrored-glass windows. "That's the place."

Cobalt pursed his lips. "Looks like they've got pretty tight security there."

Jack smirked. "I've got it covered."

Cobalt closed his eyes and counted to three then followed Jack into the building.

When they got inside, Jack grinned at the receptionist. She looked like a no-nonsense security type, with her platinum-blond hair tied back in a tight bun and at least two laser pistols on her waist. Cobalt didn't think Jack's flirting would get anywhere with her.

Jack just greeted her as he might a friend, though. "Hey, I'm wondering if you could help me out. It's my friend Detrick O'Leary's birthday, and I wanted to surprise him. I don't suppose you could let me up without letting him know."

The woman arched a sharp eyebrow. "Detrick O'Leary doesn't have friends."

"Aw, sure he does," Jack said. "We know him from school."

"Yet you have never visited him before, in all the years he's lived here." Her voice was very dry.

Cobalt knew he would have to step in. Jack was never going to bluff the woman into believing he knew Detrick, but Cobalt didn't have to bluff. Detrick's face had appeared in his dreams alongside the others'. "He doesn't like talking in person, so we mostly keep in touch via the datasphere," Cobalt said. "But we were in town today, and we thought he might like some company."

The woman still seemed a little skeptical, but she nodded. "I mean, you do seem to know him, and—" She swiped through a few pages on her datapad. "It *is* his birthday. I guess I can let you guys up."

Jack gave the woman a grin as bright as the one he'd worn in the streets. "Thank you so much! He's going to be so excited to see us!"

The woman shook her head but gave a small smile. "Somehow, I doubt that."

As soon as the doors to the elevator closed, Cobalt turned to Jack and asked, "How did you know his last name and birthday?"

At the same time, Jack asked, "How in Cronos's name did you know Detrick doesn't like interacting face-to-face?"

They blinked at each other. Jack answered first. "It was easy research. I did it on the ride over. It was good timing, his birthday being the day we landed, so I figured I would take advantage."

Cobalt pressed his palm to his forehead. "You didn't think

to mention his last name is the same as Tegan's? They're probably related! He's not going to side with us against her!"

Jack shrugged. "So we'll hold him hostage or something. Or just be friendly and pump him for information we can use against her. He's still the best lead we've got."

"Did you miss the part where he doesn't socialize?" Cobalt wanted to shake his brother but knew from experience it wouldn't do any good.

"Which brings us back to my question. How do you know about the social patterns of someone we've never met?"

Cobalt sighed, but the noise turned into an aggravated moan. "I told you. You don't remember."

"What? What do you mean, I 'don't remember'?"

"I told you on the *Rose*. You asked what was going on with me, and I gave you the full rundown. Then you went to sleep, and when you woke up, you didn't remember. I may be pissed at you, but I'm not keeping secrets."

"That doesn't make any—"

Ding. "Twenty-second floor," the soothing female voice of the elevator said.

"Okay, let's get this done," Jack said as the doors swooshed open. He strode with purpose down the hall to apartment 22F, and Cobalt followed, dragging his feet. Jack pressed the doorbell and placed his other hand over the laser pistol at his waist.

Motion sounded on the other side of the door, and a small peephole opened. "Who's there?" someone with a high-pitched male voice said.

Jack gave a friendly smile. "It's your old friends, Jack and Cobalt."

"Jack and Cobalt Zhao? Here?" Detrick muttered. "That wasn't in the plan."

"Are you going to let us in?" Jack sounded almost sweet in his suggestion. If the fact that Detrick knew their names fazed him, he didn't let on.

"Yes, I suppose that would be best," Detrick said. The door whooshed open. "Come in."

Jack and Cobalt stepped over the threshold almost in unison, and the door slid shut behind them. Cobalt knew that both because he heard it and because he stepped back against it, hoping he could get out. He had never seen such a pristine apartment in his life, and Jack constantly berated him for being a neat freak. The solid-white studio didn't contain a speck of dust, and the sheets on the bed looked so tight, Cobalt wondered if Detrick lifted them to sleep.

His gaze fell on the wall of screens to the left of the door. One was tuned to the Bellerophon Games, but the rest seemed to contain data research: a list of spaceships purchased on Ariadne, the train schedule into Bellerophon, and the registry of ships docking on Orpheus. Flashing on one screen in the upper-right-hand corner was a news story with the headline "Space Train Robbery Goes Unsolved."

In front of the screens sat a skinny man with hollowed-out cheeks, blond hair, and a smattering of freckles that reminded Cobalt a little too much of Tegan "Cuttlefish" O'Leary.

"Jack." Cobalt's mouth was dry. "We need to get out of here."

"Oh, no," Detrick said, his reedy voice surprisingly calm. He pushed a button on his datapad, and two of the largest laser canons Cobalt had ever seen descended from the ceiling and pointed at the twins. "You're not going anywhere."

CHAPTER 38

Present Day

GAVIN MARVELED THAT THE GIGANTIC ship he was riding in had the sole purpose of escorting him to Orpheus. The sleek silver vessel didn't resemble the military transports he usually saw, which solidified for him the fact that for the next year, he wasn't in the military at all. *Not that I was in the military before, but school was training for the military, and it was supposed to be my next step. Now maybe I'll get to do something else.*

He stifled a laugh at his idealism. He would get a year of fame and fortune before being sent back to the trenches. *I'm as trapped as ever, and fame and fortune weren't my dream, anyway. What I wanted was...*

Until he had saved Archon in the forest of Bellerophon, he had never known. Gavin wanted to be a doctor. Healing people was his calling. His father might go for it—after all, the military had doctors. He could go to Chora for medical training with the understanding that he would return to Bellerophon when he was done. It wasn't a perfect solution. Gavin got the impression that his past self, the one who knew how to slay a trimper with a survival knife and perform life-saving field surgery, wanted to do charity medicine. But he thought *that* Gavin had also seen war and come out of it stronger and more determined to make the world a better place. Gavin wanted to be *that* Gavin, but he would settle for being his people's champion. When his year was over, when the people had another games champion to fawn over, he would talk to his father.

The door to the lounge swished open, and Endetta walked in. Gavin stood up as she entered.

"Hello, Gavin," she said. The silky, false sincerity in her voice reminded him of someone, but he couldn't place whom. "We've got a bit of time before we reach Orpheus, and I would like to talk to you about what people expect from you for the next year."

"Okay," Gavin said. He sat down, and Endetta took the chair opposite him.

"Now, as you are aware, as a participant in the games, you would be contractually obligated to appear in public at a number of events if you were named the winner. We want to make this as easy on you as possible, so we've arranged a team of stylists and speechwriters for you."

"Oh," Gavin said. "I actually received top marks in school in my speech and debate curriculum, so I imagine I could—"

"That won't be necessary." Endetta smiled as she said it, but Gavin heard the command in her words. "Here is a list of questions you may be asked on Orpheus. We would like you to memorize the answers. Please try to make them appear extemporaneous. The reporters and presenters are under strict orders not to deviate from the approved question list, but if they do—" Her expression made it clear what she thought of people who dared ask a question she hadn't foreseen. "Try to answer in character."

In character? Gavin scanned the questions.

"Did you always know you were going to win the games?" appeared in bold print at the top of the list.

"Absolutely. I came to win and would have accepted no other alternative," the response read.

246

Okay, Gavin thought. *That's not so bad.* He skimmed farther down the page.

"How did you feel when you were assigned your partner?" jumped out at him.

The answer read, "Terrible. I couldn't believe they saddled me with a guy who hadn't even won his region. And it turns out I was right. He nearly lost me the competition."

Gavin lowered the datapad. "I can't say this. It's not nice, and it's not true."

Endetta sighed, as if to say she'd expected to have this conversation but had really hoped Gavin would be reasonable. "We do extensive studies on the type of image the public wants us to cultivate in our winners, and we have to give the public what they want. Bellerophon relies on the money we earn from the games, which in turn depends on their continued popularity. This year, the most popular contestants were Abraham Lander and Jesse Engels. People simply loved watching their underhanded tactics, and our intention was for one of them to win. However, you killed a trimper, saved your buddy's life, escaped from custody, and took your enemies with you. We simply could not choose another winner."

"If I won because of my actions, shouldn't these answers sound like me?"

"The datasphere is full of people unhappy about your victory. We think that if we can make you look more like Lander and Engels, the naysayers will come around. We can't have support of the military fading, not in an election year."

Gavin's face must have appeared intractable, because Endetta sighed again and pulled up a vid on her datapad. She thrust it in Gavin's face, and for the next few minutes, he had to watch the interview he'd given when he won the title for Calliope. Even he had to admit it was not very compelling. He looked like he was there out of obligation, not out of a sense of pride or accomplishment. *Which is true.*

"You can see that this is not the image of a winner." She gave him a smile he imagined she intended to be kind. "But that's okay, Gavin, because we're going to make you into one."

"Surely there's a compromise to be had here," Gavin said. "We can craft an image together, one that looks like both me and a winner."

Endetta gave yet another sigh. "Really, Gavin, I need you to be reasonable about this. The perception of the games affects all of Bellerophon. There is a machine of people working on their publicity, and you are one tiny cog."

Gavin couldn't quite believe what he was hearing. He had expected to serve in the military, and he knew that would mean following some orders he didn't like, but he never expected commands like this. "I won the games. Doesn't that make me at least a big cog?"

"We are rewarding you for your victory. Your name will be known across the system, and for the next year, you will be living in luxury that almost no one born and raised on Bellerophon will experience."

He thought back to the fluffy towels and plush mattress. Somehow, they didn't seem worth his self-respect.

"Oh, that brings me to one more thing." Endetta pressed a few buttons on her datapad. "You are not to leave the compound on Bellerophon without my express permission, and I guarantee I will only be offering that for sanctioned events."

Gavin blanched. "I'm a prisoner?"

"It's for your safety, of course," Endetta said. "And the safety of your image. Don't worry. The excursions I plan will be enjoyable. We need you seen with girls, fast cars, and the like."

Gavin felt heat rise to his face, though whether he was embarrassed or angered, he couldn't say. "I don't want fast cars, and I certainly don't want a lot of girls. I only want my girlfriend—" *Roslyn?* "Windla."

"Don't worry. We have plans for breaking the two of you up. Something rather public, I think. You'll be single in no time." Endetta laid a hand on Gavin's arm. Her cold fingers brought goose bumps to his previously warm arm. "We're not cruel, though. You can still see your family. They can visit whenever you want."

"Gee, thanks." The angry sarcasm rolled off Gavin's tongue. He didn't want to see his family. If he spent the next year pretending to be an asshole to the entire system, he doubted his dad would want to see him, either. He would be packed off to boot camp faster than he would be able to ask about medical training. Not that Chora would accept the playboy games winner just because he had performed one amateur surgery the year prior. "Now, if that's all, I apparently have some reading and memorizing to do."

Endetta ignored his tone. "Indeed, you do, and I have some preparations to make as well. I look forward to working with you, Gavin. I'm sure ours will be a memorable partnership."

CHAPTER 39

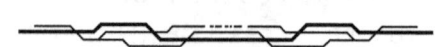

Present Day

"LEXI, I CAN'T HELP BUT feel you're keeping something from me." Her father had arranged for her transport to Daphne so they could have dinner together while he was in the city on business. The restaurant was beautiful, with crystal chandeliers and white tablecloths. Each table had five servers. The bread was baked to perfection, crispy on the outside and soft on the inside. The tangy house dressing tasted luscious, and her rare steak was seasoned with coffee and molasses. Her conversation with her father had focused on her, his beloved daughter, the apple of his eye. It was the life she wanted. But every clink of crystal, every bite of her chocolate torte, and every word of praise dripping from her father's mouth reminded her that she didn't belong there anymore.

Where to even start? she thought. *Should I tell you I met a boy? He's a conspiracy nut, and he may be sleeping with my roommate, but I think he loves me. Maybe I should say you're not really my father, at least not by our reckoning. My real father died thousands of years ago. You're just some kind of host whom I will long outlive.*

She didn't tell him any of that. Instead, she giggled. "Well, of course I can't tell you *everything*, Daddy. I'm at university now. I'm allowed to have some secrets."

"My little girl is growing up." Her father sniffed, fighting back the tear forming in the corner of his eye. "You are keeping your grades up, aren't you? I know you're pursuing your music performances, and I support you in that, but you need to have a university education to fall back on."

"Of course, Daddy!" *Not that it's hard.* She'd always assumed she was a natural at music history and theory, but it turned out her past lives provided all the answers.

She took another bite of her torte. The fudgy center was rich and delicious, and she didn't want to think she would have to walk away from the luxury her father lavished her with. In her past lives, she had apparently traveled the system with Will, sometimes in a crappy ship of their own, sometimes in a ship belonging to some blonde called Tegan. She didn't want that life anymore. She didn't want to strap herself to someone content with life as a poor wanderer, no matter how much he adored her. She'd had a taste of the truly divine, and she wouldn't settle for anything less. *I'm also pretty sure that Tegan girl is a murderer.*

Lexi's father stole a bite of her dessert. He closed his eyes, no doubt appreciating the exquisite flavor and texture as it rolled across his tongue. "There's not some boy I should know about, is there?"

"Of course not! You're the only man who matters to me!" Lexi said with a wink. *It's true. I am done with Will Turin.*

She glanced out the window at the passersby. The thoroughfare was largely empty, though that wasn't surprising for a Saturday evening. Only a few people strolled by—an olive-skinned girl walking her dog, a man with shockingly ugly yellow hair and sporting a silver shirt, and a blond-bobbed woman striding with purpose down the sidewalk.

As she passed the restaurant, the blonde looked in the window, and Lexi stared into her glass-green eyes. Lexi gasped as the woman stopped in her tracks. She knew that slim-yet-curvy figure and the dusting of freckles across her nose.

Tegan O'Leary smiled as if to say, "I'll be back for you," then continued on her way.

Lexi wiped her mouth with her napkin to cover her gulp. "Daddy, you don't mind if I take off a bit early, do you? Midterms are coming up, and I've just remembered something I need to do."

Bliss lay on her bed, staring up at the ceiling. She knew she should worry about her life as a Transient, her vengeful roommate's declaration of hatred, and the fact that she was sure to fail all her management midterms. Like some lovesick heroine in a romance novel, though, all she could think was *I can't believe I kissed Will. What kind of asshole kisses her roommate's boyfriend?*

Although Will and Lexi were on the outs, Bliss had no doubt they would get back together. Will had been Lexi's since before she had met either of them. Lexi had said in her last life that she didn't want Will to find her, but she had a penchant for the dramatic. She hadn't meant it. Will adored her, and Lexi loved to surround herself with adoring fans.

Before Bliss could contemplate all the horrible things Lexi would do to her as vengeance, the woman herself burst into the room. She didn't look angry, though. She looked terrified.

"I saw her!" were the first words out of her mouth.

Bliss sat up in one smooth motion. "You saw who?"

Lexi didn't hear Bliss, or at least didn't listen. "Oh Cronos, I saw her, and she saw me, and now she's going to kill us all!" Lexi paced in circles around the room.

"Who's going to kill whom?" Bliss wanted to make her roommate stop moving around, but she was too scared to touch Lexi. "Do we need to call the police?"

"Don't be ridiculous." Lexi stopped acting terrified enough to give Bliss a disgusted look. "I'm talking about Tegan O'Leary."

Bliss needed a moment to place the name. For all of Lexi's insistence that she was not a reincarnating alien, she seemed to have a better grasp on their histories than Bliss did. "The woman who killed Roslyn in our last lives?"

"The woman who tried to kill all of us in our past lives!"

Bliss's stomach sank. If Lexi acknowledged that she was a Transient, no doubt she would acknowledge her relationship with Will next. "So you admit you're one of us."

"Hardly," Lexi said. "Being one of you seems to involve lying low, staying off the radar, and not becoming famous. I say, 'No, thank you' to that. Besides, I still haven't forgiven you for sleeping with Will."

"I did not sleep with—"

"But I concede that Tegan O'Leary *thinks* I'm one of you, so our interests align for now."

I guess I'll take what I can get. "Where did you see Tegan?"

"On a street in Daphne."

"Lexi, we're a hundred miles away from Daphne. She's not going to track us here."

"She saw me," Lexi said. "She saw Daddy. She could use him to get to me!"

Bliss had a hard time believing Tegan would try the hostage route with Lexi, who was unlikely to sacrifice herself for others. *Of course, if Tegan knows Lexi and I are together, she might kidnap Lexi's father in hopes Lexi would exchange me for her meal ticket.* "What was she doing in Daphne?" Bliss asked.

"I don't know! Probably tracking down another Transient to murder for funsies!"

"Lexi, that's not very helpf—"

The door chimed. "Bliss, are you in there?" *Will.*

"'I didn't sleep with Will,'" Lexi mocked. "Yet he comes here looking for you and not me now."

"You told him you never wanted to talk to him again!" Bliss said, though she had to admit Lexi's temper tantrums had never driven Will away before. Maybe Bliss *had* changed something with that kiss. She pressed the button on the door to let Will in.

Will burst through the door and did a double take when he saw Lexi. "Oh, hey, Lex. You're going to want to hear this too. Do you watch the Bellerophon Games?"

Lexi studied her nails. "Do I look like someone who watches the Bellerophon Games?" she asked, her voice cool.

"Wait, did something happen to Gavin?" Bliss asked.

Will nodded. "He won the games. I figured he was safe on Bellerophon, but now he's coming to the far-less-secure Orpheus. Tegan will almost certainly make a move to capture him. She has to be aware of his location."

Bliss clutched her comforter. "Lexi just saw Tegan in Daphne."

"We've got to get over there! We have to stop her!" Will said.

Bliss turned to Lexi. "You in? This is your brother we're talking about."

Lexi pursed her lips, as if considering. Finally, she said, "Fine, but I'm driving."

CHAPTER 40

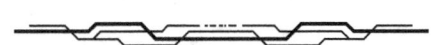

Present Day

D ETRICK'S FACE POPPED UP ON Tegan's datapad. She pressed the button to answer. "Tell me you've got good news."

"I have Jack and Cobalt Zhao locked in my bathroom. Does that constitute good news?"

"It does." Tegan smiled. Things were finally going according to plan. "I'm coming out of orbit. I'll be there in a few hours."

"Okay. Tegan?"

"Yeah?"

"Hurry, please. I have to pee."

Tegan still had a smile on her face as she took the elevator up to the twenty-second floor. She had no intention of going after Lexi—Phedre had forbidden it—but she liked to watch her squirm. Lexi had never been her favorite Transient—or *anyone's* favorite Transient, except Will's, of course. Even Gavin, noble until the end, had a hard time getting along with his self-absorbed sister.

Tegan rang her brother's doorbell and didn't have to wait five seconds before he let her in.

"Where have you been?" Detrick was shaking. "I told you to hurry."

"And I told you I would be a few hours." She swept inside, ignoring her brother's plight. "It takes a bit of time to land, park, and walk over here. They're in the bathroom?"

"Yup. I took these from them." He gestured at a pair of laser pistols.

Tegan picked one up and looked it over. "Not bad. Eurydice issue." She eyed the laser cannons that were still hanging out of the hatch in the ceiling. "Of course, there's no question as to which side is better armed."

"Can I please let them out now?" Detrick jumped out of his chair and bounced in place.

"Yes, fine, go."

As Detrick ran toward the bathroom, Tegan did a brief scan of his monitors. One was replaying the closing ceremonies of the Bellerophon Games. Gavin Ibori stared like a deer in the headlights as the announcer named him as the victor. She understood his fear. No doubt Demitrius was stewing, trying to find a way to solve the exposure problem. Little did he know, Tegan already had a solution.

Footsteps sounded softly behind her, and without looking away from the monitors, she aimed her pistol at Jack's head. "Don't even think about it." She pressed a few buttons on Detrick's datapad, and the laser cannons pivoted to back her up.

She turned to see Cobalt raising his hands. "We surrender."

"We do not surrender," Jack said.

Tegan pressed another button, and a purple pulse rocketed through the laser cannons as they powered on.

"Okay, so we surrender a little." Jack put his hands halfway up, looking more defensive than submissive. "Look, lady, who are you, and why do you want to kill us?"

She studied him for a minute then looked at Cobalt. "Does he really not remember anything?"

Cobalt shook his head. "Not a thing. I explained what was going on, and he forgot all of it by the next morning."

Tegan cocked her head. *That sounds like...* She laughed. "Wow. I guess old Demitrius decided you weren't good enough for his daughter after all."

Realization dawned on Cobalt's face. "You think Demitrius blocked his memories. It makes sense. He could have found us while we were babies. Not many Zhao twins are born in any given year."

Jack looked at Cobalt then Tegan then back at Cobalt again. "What are you guys talking about?"

Cobalt sighed. "If you still remember this conversation in the morning, I'll tell you." He glanced at Tegan. "Well, and if we're still alive."

"You'll still be alive tomorrow." Tegan made her voice as rock-hard as she could. "The plan's not quite in place yet, and we've got a bit of traveling to do."

Cobalt closed his eyes. "Arachne."

"That's right. I'm going to find out where we came from, with your support or without it. I'm—" She broke off when she saw Jack grinning like the fool he was. "What is so funny?"

Jack's face lit up like a police cruiser in space. "Arachne. Seriously. This is the best adventure ever! We get to go to Arachne!"

Tegan shoved the laser pistol in his face. "You're going to die on Arachne."

He threw back his head and laughed. "Lady, you have no idea who you're dealing with. My brother and I are the smartest people in the system, and we'll get out of any trap you set for us."

Tegan laughed that time. "Oh, Jack. Dear, sweet Jack. I do know you. I know every trick up your sleeve better than you do. You'd better start getting used to the fact that you're not going to make it out of this one alive."

CHAPTER 41

Present Day

"ROSLYN? ROSLYN!"

Someone shook her, and her head flopped in slow motion on her pillow. She squeezed her eyes shut. The world was too bright.

"Roslyn!"

She opened her eyes. The room was almost pitch-black except for the glow of a flashlight. A woman with sleek brown hair and strangely familiar features was sitting on the edge of Roslyn's bed, holding a glowing rock.

"Dr. Tanner?" Roslyn glanced at the stone. The strange sigils on it shone with an eerie green light. "That's the rock from my dreams!" She shook her head. *No. The dreams aren't important.* "I mean, from your office." The memory was fuzzy and vague, like everything around her. Her fingers felt thick as she rubbed them along the linen sheets, and her brain was stuffed full of cotton.

"I was wrong about everything," Dr. Tanner whispered. "I was wrong about you and your dreams. You knew this rock meant something, and I didn't listen."

"I don't understand." Roslyn tried to focus. Something was wrong. *Dr. Tanner shouldn't be here in the middle of the night.*

"I was working late at my office, and I knocked it on the floor. It lit up, and I realized you were right about it being an alien device. If you were right about that, who knows what else you were right about?" The light was dim, but Dr. Tanner's eyes were fervent, as if she had discovered a miracle.

I suppose she has. "You have to give that back," Roslyn said. "It belongs on Arachne."

Dr. Tanner grimaced. "I think you're right, but I need to shut it off first, and I don't know how."

Roslyn moved as if on autopilot, taking the device from Dr. Tanner. "You have to turn it all the way on first." She pressed the keys in sequence, her voice sounding distant. "*Elleks, tsufo, kel.*" The device whirred to life, and Roslyn turned the top the opposite way, reverting it to a dull stone. She handed the stone back to Dr. Tanner.

The psychologist smiled. "Thank you very much, Roslyn. You have been most incredibly helpful."

Something's wrong. I know that smile. Why do I know that smile? She lay back, unable to think anymore. She would worry about it in the morning.

"See you in the next life, dear," Dr. Tanner whispered as she turned off the flashlight.

Roslyn drifted back to sleep.

Twenty Years Ago

An Old Earth song blasted through the camp.

Roslyn smiled as she sorted through the "relics" in the trunk. Hannah was convinced every rock on the moon had the potential to be an alien artifact. *Evenings must be getting a bit dull here if I'm working through them, and Jack can't stand a dull moment.*

She wasn't surprised when, a few minutes later, Jack

wrapped his arms around her waist and whispered in her ear, "Dance with me, Rosie."

Roslyn stood and turned around, never leaving the circle of his arms. She kept her hands to herself for a moment, trying to gauge his expression. He'd been completely devoted to her the last few days, and devoted was not like Jack. Every look, every gesture, and every glance said, "You are the most precious thing in the world to me, and I am never losing you again."

She slipped her arms around his neck and swayed to the music. Though she was almost embarrassed to meet his eyes, so intently was he staring at her, she couldn't look away. She had never seen a look that full of desperate love on anyone, not even Gavin.

The thought made heat rise to her face, and she turned away and found they had an audience. "People are staring."

"Let them stare," Jack said, then a devil-may-care grin lit up his face. "Wanna give them something to stare at?" He snapped his fingers, and the music changed to a string quartet playing a waltz. He shifted his grip on her accordingly. "Ready?"

"Jack!" she whispered through clenched teeth. "What are you doing? You know I can't dance."

"Everyone can waltz." He led her in the steps.

She did her best to follow, but the best she could say was that she didn't step on his feet. She felt like she deserved some extra points for that, though, considering the rocky terrain. "Don't even think about trying to dip me."

He smirked and shook his head. "How can I love someone who doesn't even know how to waltz?"

She stumbled, and that time, she did step on his foot as she regained her balance. "You love me?" Jack had never said he loved her, not once in all the years they'd been together.

After looking at his feet for a moment, he met her gaze, and for once, his face betrayed no sign of mockery. "I love you more than anything, Rosie. I used to think the only thing that mattered to me was my freedom, but I've realized you're so much more important than that. I've been an idiot for my entire life, and I probably will continue to be, but I've finally figured out that I can't be free without you."

Roslyn opened her mouth to say something. She thought it might be "yes."

Before she could say anything, though, Gavin came up behind Jack and tapped him on the shoulder. "May I cut in?" he asked.

A look of irritation crossed Jack's face, but he bowed. "If it's all right with the lady."

"Yes," Roslyn said. "It's fine." She needed time to clear her head, anyway.

As Jack stepped away, he snapped his fingers, and the music switched to an elaborate samba.

"Very mature, Jack," Gavin said as he put his arms around Roslyn's waist. She twined her hands behind his neck, and they swayed to a different beat from the one Jack had provided. They stayed that way for a few minutes before Gavin asked, "So you and Jack are back together again?"

"Yes. No. I don't know." Roslyn sighed. Gavin was the last person with whom she should discuss her relationship with Jack, but he always listened to her, and she didn't have anyone else to talk to. "He asked me to marry him."

Gavin inhaled a sharp breath through his teeth. "He knows what that means, right?"

"Yes, of course he knows what it means. He's not a big fan of rules, but he's heard Demitrius's lectures as many times as the rest of us."

"What did you say?" Gavin's voice was quiet.

"That I didn't know." Roslyn closed her eyes. She wanted to lean into Gavin and lay her head against his strong chest, but that would hardly be appropriate. "And I *don't* know. I want to trust him, but—"

"But nothing. You love him. You've always loved him, since

the day he came speeding into our lives in that ridiculous red convertible and stole you away from me."

"Gavin..."

"I just want you to be happy. It's all I've ever wanted."

Roslyn stood on tiptoe and kissed his cheek. "You're too good for me. I hope you find someone twice as good as me someday."

He gave her a sad smile. "That seems unlikely."

"It's not. I know—"

Jack appeared behind Gavin and tugged on his arm. "Okay, you've had your turn. I want to dance with my girl now."

"She's not yours. She belongs to herself," Gavin said, rolling up his sleeves.

Jack took a step closer to Gavin. "That's not what I meant, and you know it."

Running footsteps came toward them, and Roslyn had never been so happy to see Cobalt as she was at that moment. "You guys had better come quickly! A ship has landed, and you're going to want to see it," he said.

Roslyn looked around as they followed him to the landing dock. Everyone had deserted camp, the new ship apparently being more interesting than Roslyn's relationship drama.

"Isn't that the *Transcendent Spirit*?" Gavin asked as they got closer.

"Yup," Cobalt said.

Jack frowned. "What's the *Spirit* doing here? Did you call Tegan, Rosie?"

Roslyn shook her head. "I didn't think she'd be interested in an archaeological dig."

"She might have been interested in learning about her heritage," Gavin said.

"I would have called her if we found anything interesting." Roslyn sounded defensive even to her ears. She went over to Hannah and asked what was going on. The two weren't on the friendliest terms, but they were still the highest-ranking archaeologists on the dig. But before Hannah could answer, Roslyn saw the woman who was descending the gangplank. She had shiny brown hair, perfectly tanned skin, and hazel eyes to match Roslyn's.

"Shit," Roslyn said. "Shit, shit, shit."

"What's Tegan doing with *her*?" Cobalt asked.

Hannah arched an eyebrow. "You know that woman?"

"That's Phedre Turin." Roslyn couldn't keep the bitterness out of her voice. "Also known as dear old Mom."

"Well, congratulations." Hannah tilted her datapad up so Roslyn could see it. "I just got the order. Phedre Turin is our new boss."

Present Day

Roslyn sat up straight in bed. "No, no, no, no, no." Her head was a muddle, full of fluff and medication, but she forced herself to think anyway. Dr. Tanner had just appeared in her dream, except she wasn't Dr. Tanner. She was Phedre Turin, her mother and the general plague of the Transient world.

She pretended to want to help me, got me locked up in here and all doped up, and tricked me into decoding the rock for her. She must want to open that vault. At least she still needs the blood of three Ringati.

Roslyn had no idea what a Ringati was. All she knew was that Phedre wanted to open the vault and would be willing to kill anyone or anything to do it. She needed to be stopped. *Roslyn* needed to stop her, because no one else could do it.

She lurched out of bed. *How am I going to get to Arachne? How am I even going to get out of this hospital?* Security at the institution wasn't great, but it was good enough to stop one hazy, over-medicated girl in her nightgown. *I have to try, though. I checked myself in. I should be able to check myself out.*

She wandered out of her room, surprised to find her door unlocked. *Keeping it locked is a fire hazard. Or maybe Phedre just forgot to lock it when she left.* Roslyn crept by the woman at the nurse's station, who was too engrossed in a vid to notice the wobbly girl sneaking past her, and made it all the way to the front door before anyone noticed she was out and about. She greeted the guard there as calmly and rationally as she could. "I need to leave now."

The guard chuckled, his full cheeks glowing red. "You know I can't let you do that, little miss. Why don't you head back to bed, and we can talk to your therapist in the morning."

"You don't understand," Roslyn said. "You know that woman you let in before?"

"Dr. Tanner, sure."

Roslyn took a deep breath. "She's not really Dr. Tanner. Her real name is Phedre Turin, and she's the chief researcher at the government base on Arachne. She's been using me to do research on the moon, and she wants to kill something to open an alien vault. I have to stop her!"

The guard crinkled his eyebrows in sympathy. "Sweetheart, you know what you're saying doesn't make any sense. How could a girl like you help research Arachne?"

Roslyn didn't have to fake the tears that spilled from her eyes. She realized how she must look, a girl dressed in a nightgown, unsteady on her feet from too much medication. *My story must sound like a paranoid delusion.* "Please don't tell my doctors," she said. "They've got me on so many drugs already."

The guard stepped around his station to help her, and she knew the few seconds his back was turned were going to be the only chance she got. She darted for the door, pushed it open, and ran out into the cool night air.

Roslyn hoped the guard decided to call for backup instead

of coming after her himself. She couldn't outrun him, but she could disappear before the police got there.

But she never found out what the guard would do because she glanced back at him in time to feel a rush of force hotter than anything she had ever felt. She stumbled then stared up at the building as all at once, it went up in flames.

PART III

CHAPTER 42

Present Day

COBALT SAT IN THE REAR cabin of the *Transcendent Spirit* with his back against the cylindrical force field surrounding him and Jack. The field created a rather pleasant buzz against his back, almost like a massage. He'd never thought to use a force field like that before, but the idea had merit. Maybe if he lived, he could go into business selling force field massages. *Or maybe I'm getting punchy in my desperation.*

Jack's desperation was more active. He was trying to figure out a way to disable the force field.

"It's no use," Cobalt said for the twentieth time. "You and I designed this thing to be impenetrable by common thieves like us."

"We are not common thieves." Jack's voice was muffled because he had one cheek mashed against the floor as he tried to reach any wiring in the lower part of the force field. "We are *un*common thieves, and I will figure out a way to break this thing."

"Let me know if he does, will you, Cobalt?" Tegan walked in from the front of the ship. "I'll need you to work out the kinks in the design."

"Somehow, I don't see myself doing much maintenance

work for you in the future," Cobalt said. "Especially since I doubt I have a future."

Tegan seemed offended by the suggestion. "Of course you have a future. We live forever, or at least reincarnate."

Cobalt flicked his finger at the force field, which made a *bzzt* sound. "You killed us in our last lives, and you seem determined to kill us again in this life, so you can see how I might be dubious."

"I still have no idea what you guys are talking about," came Jack's muffled voice.

Tegan crouched down next to Jack. "Speaking of..." She stuck a syringe through the force field and plunged it into Jack's neck. Cobalt lurched forward, and Jack tried to bat away the vial, but Tegan held steady, filling the syringe with blood. She withdrew it, her hand never passing through the force field. "I need to make sure you've got Transient blood markers. If you don't, I've got a bigger problem than I thought. Or rather, Lexi does."

Jack rubbed his neck. "Is this a bio-blocking force field? That's amazing! Who designed it?"

"You did, you moron." Tegan stood up. "Now, if you'll excuse me, I have to run some tests on this blood before I get dumber by proximity."

As Cobalt sank back against the force field, Jack sat up and joined him. "Do you think I could throw my shoe at the control and open it?"

Cobalt shook his head. "It's got a ten-digit pin we don't know, and we only have four shoes."

Jack seemed to still be thinking up ways to get out, so he surprised Cobalt when he asked, "Do you really think we're going to die?"

He considered the question. "She's killed us before, and we're not getting out of this force field until we get to Arachne. I'm not sure where we could escape to there. So I suppose, yes, I do think we're going to die."

Jack stood up and punched the force field, sending

purple sparks up his arm. Judging by the look on his face, Cobalt knew he regretted it. "I don't want to die! I'm not ready to die! I've just started to see the system, and I don't understand what's going on."

"I'm sorry," Cobalt said, and he was. He felt responsible for getting them into their predicament. Jack had insisted they rob the train and go after Tegan, but Cobalt was the one who knew Tegan's capabilities. He should have tried harder to keep Jack off the self-destructive path.

Jack collapsed next to Cobalt again. "I wish I knew what was going on, Blue. You say these crazy things about memories and reincarnation and immortal life, and none of them make any sense. If I have to die without meeting my girl, I want to at least know why."

"I explained it to you. I did. You don't remember, and I don't think telling you again will help. I think someone named Demitrius messed with your memory." He took a deep breath. "But you did meet your girl. It was Roslyn, the server girl on Ariadne. She was—*is*—your girl. Always has been."

Jack's brow furrowed. "She can't be. If she were, I would know, wouldn't I? Even if someone messed with my memory, I remember she exists, so I should remember her."

"I don't know. It will probably come as no surprise to you that you messed up with her, many times. I think you were so convinced you had to get it right this time that some part of her made it past your memory block."

Jack leaned back against the force field. "I didn't know I had that kind of conviction."

Cobalt chuckled. "To be honest, neither did I."

Jack closed his eyes, and for a moment, Cobalt thought he would let the soothing rhythm of the force field lull him to sleep. But then Jack spoke. "Blue, if you knew Roslyn was my girl back on Ariadne, why didn't you say something? I probably would have stayed. That's what you wanted, right? To stay on Ariadne?"

"I wanted to stay on Daedalus," Cobalt muttered. He considered giving Jack some cock-and-bull story about how he had told Jack, and he hadn't remembered, but their impending death made him feel honest. "I was jealous."

Jack's eyebrows shot up. "Blue—"

"I know, I know. We'll be twins and brothers forever, no matter what." Cobalt leaned his head far enough back into the force field that it hurt. "When she's around, you spend less time with me, and I resent it. I'm not like you, you know. I can't just find someone to be with. You're all I've got, and sometimes I'm scared you're going to leave me too."

"Not going to happen," Jack said.

"You say that, but—"

"Cobalt, I swear." Jack twisted around so he was looking Cobalt in the eyes. "You're my twin, my brother, my other half. My *better* half. I could never be with a girl who didn't understand that, okay?"

Cobalt opened his mouth to protest again, but Jack looked so serious, he had to trust him. "Okay."

Jack flashed his best grin. "Besides, bait-and-switch cons work so much better when you've got a lookalike on hand."

Cobalt laughed despite himself, and Jack slumped back against the force field. "I still don't want to die, Blue."

Cobalt felt his smile dim. "I know. Me neither."

CHAPTER 43

Present Day

"I GIVE YOU YOUR CHAMPION, GAVIN Ibori!" Gavin was getting tired of hearing those words, but he also accepted they were as much a part of his new life as pretending to be someone he wasn't. He walked onto the outdoor stage in Daphne's Central Garden, prepared to smile and wave at the gathered crowd.

When he saw the man sitting smack dab in the center of the first row, he froze. He knew those broad shoulders, that slicked-back brown hair, that wide nose, and those piercing gray eyes, and he feared them. Though he'd known Demitrius would kill him if he won the contest, he hadn't thought the Transient leader would do so in front of a crowd of Orpheus's elite press.

Demitrius nodded at Gavin, acknowledging that Gavin had recognized him, then nodded at the announcer. Gavin turned in the direction Demitrius indicated.

"So tell me, Gavin," the announcer said, "did you always know you were going to win the games?"

Gavin looked at his interviewer, then at Demitrius, then at Endetta, who was standing at the back of the crowd. He knew what he was supposed to say and had memorized all his answers on the way over. Though he had made the decision to play Endetta's game, Demitrius showing up changed everything. He was going to die, which meant he had nothing to lose. A startled laugh broke free from him.

"Honestly? No," Gavin said. "No, I did not expect to win the games. In fact, there were some moments—especially certain ones involving a trimper—where I didn't even expect to survive them."

The announcer looked startled for a moment—no doubt Endetta had provided him with the scripted answers as well—then gave a genuine smile. "Let's talk about that trimper. How did you know how to kill it? Forensic veterinarians have concluded you hit the beast in one of the few places where such a small weapon could have killed it."

"My father took me hunting a lot when I was younger," Gavin said. "Usually with weapons better than a utility knife. I must have absorbed more than I thought. Still, it was a lucky shot."

"Very lucky! Especially for your battle buddy, Archon. He was the public's best bet to lose the contest based on his performance in the preliminary games. How did you feel about being paired with him?"

"I couldn't have been happier," Gavin said. "Archon and I have trained together since we were children. I figured that gave us an edge up over the other pairs, who had only just met and needed to learn each other's methods."

The questions continued in a similar fashion. The interviewer asked Gavin's opinion on all aspects of the games, and Gavin answered with what was in his heart. He didn't quite have the courage to look into the audience and see Endetta fuming and Demitrius plotting, but he felt he was plenty brave for a walking dead man.

Eventually, the interviewer faced the audience. "All right, ladies and gentlemen, those are all the questions we have for our champion, but we have an additional surprise for him. Demitrius Allen of Chora University, would you please come up on stage?"

As Demitrius walked up the stairs to the stage, Gavin's heart rate increased. *Is he going to kill me in front of all these people?*

"Gavin Ibori." Demitrius smiled and held out a hand, which Gavin shook automatically. "It's an honor to meet you. I watched the games with great interest, and your performance impressed me."

"Thank you, sir," Gavin said, his head spinning.

"I work with the deans at Chora University, who were similarly affected by your performance on the battlefield. We feel it would be a crime to let such talent go to waste, and we would like to offer you a position at our university in the medical department. Would you like to train to be a doctor?"

"I..." Gavin blinked, not sure what was going on. "Of course, after my year of obligations."

"This is a one-time-only offer," Demitrius said. "Good for this year only."

"But... I... There are contracts, fees I have to pay if I break them..."

"We're prepared to pay those fees." Demitrius gave Gavin a look that suggested he was being an idiot.

The realization struck Gavin that Demitrius had found a way to get Gavin out of his year of fame and offer him the chance of a lifetime in the process. *Maybe I'm not going to die today.* "In that case, I accept."

"Excellent." Demitrius clapped Gavin on the back. "Let's get out of the limelight and go somewhere we can discuss the details."

Gavin gave one last wave and smile to the audience, a genuine smile that time, and let Demitrius lead him backstage.

"Is this for real?" Gavin asked as soon as he and Demitrius were in the quiet room behind the stage. "Are you really sending me to medical school?"

Demitrius raised an eyebrow. "Do you need to go to medical school?"

"If I want to practice medicine in this life, people are going to expect me to have degrees, so yes." Gavin ran his hands over his head. "I really thought you were going to kill me because of the fame thing. I didn't remember the rules until the games were over, and by then—"

Demitrius let out a full-bellied laugh. "Yes, well, I'm sure my daughter would never speak to me again if I killed you."

"Roslyn." Once the memories had started coming back, they had continued to return at a steady trickle. He knew who all his fellow Transients were and their relationships with each other.

"Indeed. I always did like you better than that miscreant she traipses around after."

Gavin sighed. "She loves Jack, not me. There's not much you or I can do about that, however much we want to."

Demitrius smiled as if at some inside joke Gavin didn't get. "Oh, I think you'll find you'll have your chance this time around. Speaking of, I haven't found Roslyn in this life. Have you seen her?"

"No. But then, since I started getting memories back, I've been trapped on a forest in Bellerophon. I haven't run into anyone except you."

"Fair enough." Demitrius patted Gavin on the arm. "All right, I guess I'd better go head off that shrew who's trying to manage your life. Don't worry. We'll sort everything out and ship you off to Chora tomorrow."

"Thanks, Demitrius."

Demitrius opened the door that led outside, in the opposite direction of the stage. "Why, hello, young lady," he said to the brown-haired girl who was standing outside.

"Windla!" Gavin rushed over to greet his girlfriend as Demitrius slipped past her. "I didn't know you were here!"

She looked beautiful, her blue dress the exact color of her eyes, and he tried to summon the love he had felt for her every day for the past few years. It was there but felt empty compared to the emotions of lives he had recalled.

"I know." Her voice sounded hollow. "I was sitting in the third row, and you didn't even glance my way. You kept staring at the man from Chora."

"I'm sorry. I—"

"Who's Roslyn?"

"Roslyn?" *Crap, she must have heard our conversation.* The fact that he was more concerned about her discovering he was a Transient than her knowing about Roslyn spoke volumes. "She's Demitrius's daughter. She—"

"You love her."

Though he opened his mouth to say, "No," the word wouldn't come. He couldn't lie to Windla. He cared too much about her. But he couldn't let her learn the truth, either, so he couldn't make her understand how much he had changed in the few weeks they'd been apart.

Windla's eyes filled with tears. "I'm such an idiot. I've been telling everyone the winner of the Bellerophon Games loves me, but apparently there's been some other girl all along. More fool me."

"Windla, I—"

"Please. Don't. Just leave me alone." She turned and fled.

It's for the best, Gavin thought as he heard the door click shut behind her. *It was never going to work out between us, and it's better to hurt her now rather than later.*

The door clicked open again, and he wondered who it was. *Has Windla come back? Has Endetta come to scream at me?* He turned around and saw that Windla had returned, but she wasn't alone. Tegan O'Leary was standing in the doorway, holding a laser pistol to Windla's head.

"Hello, Gavin. Good to see you again. I'm afraid you're going to have to come with me."

CHAPTER 44

Present Day

LEXI BROKE EVERY SPEEDING LAW on her way to Daphne, and Bliss didn't care. They had little chance of getting to Gavin before Tegan did, but they had to try.

About halfway through the ride, Will reached over and put his hand on Bliss's. "It's okay. We'll get to him, even if we need to go to Arachne to do it."

"I don't know why you're comforting her." Lexi took her eyes off the road for a second to glower at them in the rearview mirror. "It's my brother who's in danger."

"He's a Transient. He matters to all of us," Will said. He didn't talk after that, and he kept his hand on Bliss's for the rest of the ride.

When they got to the amphitheater, news crews were packing up their cameras, and cars were departing. No one looked panicked, so Bliss had to assume the interview had gone as planned. She breathed a sigh of relief. Maybe they were in time after all.

A man and a woman were arguing publicly among the seats. Bliss felt like she should recognize the man, and she realized why when Will hissed, "Demitrius."

"No business making him an offer like that," the woman said.

"And you, ma'am, have no business interfering in my business." Demitrius hadn't noticed them yet. "I'm paying you your money, so you have no reason to complain."

"You think I care about the money? This is about supporting Bellerophon! It's about the glory of the games!" The woman seemed genuinely offended. From the look of her designer suit and coiffed hair, appearances mattered to her, and whatever Demitrius had done had made her look bad.

"I know all about the glory of your games. You were prepared to turn a fine young man like Gavin into meat for your propaganda machine, and I simply won't have it." He looked up and saw Bliss, Lexi, and Will gaping at him. "Now, if you'll excuse me, I need to speak with these people."

As Demitrius made his way over to them, the woman looked them over and found them wanting. They'd spent over an hour in the car and hadn't taken time to freshen up before coming in, and their ordinary school clothes did look out of place at a formal press conference.

"What are you doing here?" Demitrius asked, his voice sounding as dark and harsh as it did in Bliss's memories. "Other than violating my rule that none of us spend too much time together."

Bliss cringed, but Will was not cowed. "The only rule we never follow."

"Indeed," Demitrius said. "I suppose that means you've come to lend support to your fellow, then."

Winding a strand of hair around her finger, Bliss said, "Not exactly."

"Oh, come off it, Demitrius," Will said. "You have to know what's going on with Arachne. I just don't know why you haven't put a stop to it yet."

Demitrius appeared puzzled. "Arachne?"

"The fourth moon in the system? The one controlled by a government branch run by Phedre Turin? The one where you buried something that is apparently coming back to bite us in the ass?" Only Will dared to talk to Demitrius like that.

"I don't have time for your conspiracy theories, young man." Demitrius's voice was harsh. "There is no such place."

"Come on," Lexi said. "Even I've heard of Arachne, and you know I don't study science if I can possibly help it."

Demitrius frowned. "I rather feel as though you are having me on."

Will rubbed his forehead. "Please, please, *please* do not tell me that you had Camarilla block all your memories of Arachne. I cannot tell you how insane and dangerous that would be."

Demitrius's lips turned down farther. "I can't believe I would do any such thing. It's far more likely this is some elaborate practical joke on your part. Or honestly, not that elaborate, now that I think about it."

"Think, Demitrius," Will said. "Do you remember why you came to this system from your home planet? You've always said you won't tell us why, and it's never occurred to me it's because you can't. You must have made yourself forget."

Demitrius inhaled and held his breath for several moments. His gaze became unfocused, as if he were searching his memory. "That does sound like something I would do."

"That's really, really bad." Will paced around in a circle. "Phedre—you remember her, right? The one obsessed with finding out why we're here—found some ancient box you left behind, and she's killing Transients to open it. She sent Tegan to kidnap Gavin, and we have to stop her."

"Tegan O'Leary? Working for Phedre? That can't be right. None of this can be right, but if it is..." Demitrius trailed off, and a hard look came into his eyes. "You three need to find Gavin now. He should be backstage. Keep him safe. I'll find Camarilla. We'll figure this out."

As the three jogged over to the stage, Will muttered, "Stupid Demitrius. So short-sighted."

"How is it that no one has talked to him about Arachne in the past twenty years?" Lexi asked.

"Well, let's see," Will said. "You were dead. Bliss was

dead. Jack, Cobalt, Roslyn, and Gavin were dead, and Tegan and Detrick were working for Phedre."

Lexi stuck out her chin. "What about you?"

"I was in hiding! I didn't want Tegan to kill me too! Someone needed to stick around to help you guys when you came back!" Will climbed the stairs to the stage, Lexi and Bliss on his heels.

"And the others?" Bliss asked. "Obseverus? Domina? Astrid?"

Will shook his head as he pressed the button to open the backstage door. "They must have forgotten, too, and Camarilla must have been too busy obeying Demitrius's commands to think about what they meant. She's always been kind of rigid that way."

Lexi darted past Will through the door, no doubt anticipating a reunion with her brother. "He's not here," she said as Will followed her in.

"What?" Will crossed to the back door. "Maybe he just stepped outside." He pressed the button to open that door and poked his head outside. "Gavin?"

Bliss scanned the amphitheater seating. Only a few people remained, and none of them were Gavin. Lexi and Will came out to stand on the stage with Bliss.

"He's not here," Lexi said. "Which means either he's gone to take a breather somewhere, or else—"

"Tegan's got him," Will said with certainty. "Looks like we're going to Arachne."

CHAPTER 45

Present Day

TEGAN SHOVED WINDLA INTO THE *Spirit's* hatch, though she didn't have to shove her. Windla and Gavin had cooperated with her all the way from the amphitheater, but the use of force was so satisfying. *Stupid girl Gavin loves. Stupid Gavin. So perfect all the time. I wonder what Roslyn's going to say when she meets Blue Eyes here.*

Jack and Cobalt jumped to their feet.

"What the—?" Jack started.

"Let her go, Tegan," Gavin said, his eyes locked on Windla. "I said I would go with you to the ship if you let her go. You don't have to hurt her."

Tegan nodded. "When you're in the force field circle, I'll let her go." Tegan had no intention of hurting Windla. She was just a means to an end. But Gavin didn't have to know that. She moved to the wall controls, keeping her pistol trained on Windla. "You two idiots inside had better not try to fight me, or I will shoot." She pushed the button.

Jack, of course, tried to rush her. She saw him coming a mile away and aimed the pistol shot straight at his chest. He collapsed face-first at her feet, his head hitting the steel floor with a solid, satisfying *thud.*

"He's going to have a nasty headache when he wakes up. Now, one of you help me get him back inside the force field."

"*Will* he wake up?" Gavin asked.

At the same time, Cobalt said, "I'm not helping you imprison my brother."

Tegan answered Gavin first. "Of course he'll wake up. I had it set to stun. I need you alive on Arachne. But don't think for a second I would hesitate to turn this force field on right now and slice Jack in half if you don't get him inside the cage. I'm not that desperate." She was bluffing. Tegan *was* that desperate. If she didn't have three Transients for Phedre, the bitch would sacrifice her or Detrick. *Probably me. I'll be closer.*

Gavin rushed to pick up Jack and put him inside the force field cage then stepped inside as well.

The fool. Always so honest and noble, he believes everyone else must be too. Tegan pushed the button, sealing them inside.

"Now let Windla go," Gavin said.

Tegan nodded at Windla. "You can go. But tell anyone what you saw or heard, and I will come back for you, and you will regret it."

Windla looked at Gavin, her terrified eyes full of tears.

Gavin said, "Go. I'll be fine. Just go."

Windla looked about to say something, but instead, she turned and ran out of the hatch.

Tegan looked Gavin up and down. "Was that a lie from our beloved hero? You won't be fine, you know."

"I know. But what was I supposed to tell her?"

Gavin's sad voice wrapped itself around Tegan's heart and squeezed. Part of her wanted to abandon the whole stupid plan.

"Cuttlefish..." Gavin said.

Tegan pushed her feelings away. Everything would be fine. Gavin would come back, like he had before, and she would find out where they came from. That was all that mattered.

Twenty Years Ago

"They're not going to tell us anything," Tegan told Phedre. "They don't trust you, and since I'm working for you, they don't trust me, either."

Phedre smiled, but Tegan could tell her new boss was annoyed. Phedre had spent the last two hours grilling Dr. Hannah Carriger about Arachne's secrets, and Tegan, at least, had concluded the woman didn't know anything. Either Roslyn and company had done a good job keeping anything they discovered secret, or they hadn't found anything. Tegan—and Phedre, it seemed—was betting on the former. Transients were, as a general rule, good secret keepers.

"Don't worry, Tegan, dear," Phedre said. "They'll tell us. I'm sure they'll need my help with something here."

As soon as her fellow Transients had seen Phedre emerge from questioning Dr. Carriger, they had disappeared into one of the camp's many tents. Phedre led Tegan over to it. When Tegan reached to open the tent flap, Phedre grabbed Tegan's arm and put a finger to her lips.

"I'm just saying she might have some insight that we don't," Jack said.

"Maybe so, but I still don't trust her," Roslyn answered.

"She's your mother," Gavin said.

"Yes, and I'm only alive because she wanted to manipulate Demitrius. When that didn't work, she had no further use for me. Excuse me for having trust issues."

"Okay, so she's evil," Jack said. "She might still have some useful information. Like what a Ringati is."

Having apparently heard what she'd been listening for,

Phedre pushed back the tent flap, stepped inside, and held the flap open until Tegan followed. Tegan was surprised by Phedre's courtesy until she realized Phedre was using her as leverage. *I've got one of you on my side,* the gesture said. *Think how many more I can lure in.*

"As a matter of fact, I do know what a Ringati is," Phedre said. "And I would be happy to tell you—for a price."

"You want money?" Cobalt asked.

Phedre glared at him. Apparently, she only tried to catch flies with honey where Tegan was concerned. "Of course not, you idiot. I want information. I want to know everything you know about this miserable rock and how it relates to us being stuck on this side of the galaxy."

Gavin and Jack raised their eyebrows at Roslyn, who threw her hands in the air. "Fine! Tell her! But when this all blows up in your faces, don't blame me."

"There's not much here," Jack said. "Just a giant sealed-up hole in the ground. To open it, we need a device and the blood of three Ringati. But we don't know how to activate the device or what a Ringati is."

"May I see the device?" Phedre asked.

Jack shrugged, pulled a black-and-green rock out of his pocket, and tossed it to Phedre, who caught it.

She turned the rock around in her hand, looking at the sigils scribed into it. "Elleks," she said, pressing one of the symbols. The rock glowed green, and Phedre smiled. "All it takes is a little proficiency of language, Jack. 'Elleks' means 'power.'"

"Great," Jack said. "Now fair's fair. What's a Ringati?"

He's hiding something, Tegan thought. Then she remembered she worked for Phedre, so she voiced the thought.

"Hm." Phedre pressed the green power button again, and the rock stopped glowing. "I'll tell you what, Jack. I'll happily tell you what a Ringati is—"

"Awesome."

"As soon as I verify your little story for myself."

Jack stood up straighter. "Are you kidding me? That wasn't the deal! I told you what I know!"

"Told you," Roslyn all but sang.

Phedre smiled. "Don't worry. I'm sure it will only take me a couple of days to verify your story, then you'll know everything I do." She snapped her fingers. "Tegan, come with me."

Tegan resented Phedre beckoning her like a dog, but she couldn't do anything about it. She followed Phedre to the other end of camp, watching, as Phedre was, to make sure no one followed them.

"So," Tegan said. "What's a Ringati?"

"My dear, *we* are Ringati," Phedre said. "Or rather, I am, and Roslyn is. You're only half, I'm afraid."

Tegan shrugged. No doubt Phedre meant to belittle her, but Tegan had always been a half blood, and knowing the name of her nonhuman race didn't change that. "So opening this vault requires human sacrifice? Doesn't seem worth it."

"Ringati sacrifice." Phedre examined the rock she had taken from Jack. "And it is absolutely worth it to find out why we are here. And that, my dear Tegan, is why you are going to kill the four of them."

Tegan blanched. "What? No! Absolutely not! I'll work for you, but I'm not killing anybody. Especially my friends."

Phedre's eyes narrowed. "Hm. I do see your point. Roslyn is a full Ringati, but the other three are only half. Three halves don't make two. Four halves, on the other hand, does, and I suppose four half bloods are on this moon."

Tegan glowered. She wasn't the brightest of the Transients, but she could put two halves and two halves together. "Fine. I'll do it." *It's not so bad. They'll come back.*

Phedre patted Tegan's cheek. "Good girl. Wait a couple of days until they're not suspecting anything, then knock them out and bring them to the vault. I can't wait to see what's inside."

CHAPTER 46

Present Day

ROSLYN RAN ALL THE WAY back to the Bhanushalis'. She needed to put on some normal clothes and figure out how to get to Arachne. As a server, she had very little spending money, but she'd hoarded it as if she'd known she would someday need to make an emergency trip. She should have enough to get her to Daedalus, and from there, she would find someone to take her to Arachne. Maybe she could hire onto a ship short-term, though what ship had need for a dog-walker-slash-archaeologist, she didn't know. *Worry about that when you get there. One step at a time.*

She hadn't stopped to think since she'd left the institution—or what was left of it. Phedre must have left a bomb, or perhaps many bombs, given how quickly the building went up in flames. She must have wanted to kill Roslyn and, in the process, had killed a hundred others, who wouldn't reincarnate.

Roslyn had stopped in her tracks, so she shook her head. *You can't think about that. Mourn your fellow patients later. For now, you have to get to Arachne.*

She didn't think waltzing through the Bhanushalis' front door in the middle of the night was her best bet, especially since her key had blown up along with the facility, so she rushed to the back of the house, where her room was. Though she didn't have Jack's rocket boots, she could climb the apple tree outside her window.

Roslyn hadn't climbed a tree since she was eight years old and had fallen and broken her arm, but she decided desperation might help her overcome her fear. The apple tree's coarse bark rubbed against her fingers as she pulled herself onto the lowest branch.

I can do this. She climbed a few more branches until she was level with her window then crept out to the edge of the branch. It dipped a bit as she got farther out, but she hoped it would hold. It did, long enough for her to wrest open the window and worm her way inside.

She changed her clothes as quickly as she could and grabbed her bank card. As she prepared for her return trip out the window, the sound of voices came from the corridor.

"Don't see how that's possible, Officer," Mrs. Bhanushali said. "Roslyn's always been such a good, obedient server. She was friends with our daughter, Bliss, but she always knew her place."

Roslyn froze. Mrs. Bhanushali's description didn't sound like Roslyn at all. *What's going on?*

"We have a report from Ms. Turin's psychologist that she was increasingly unstable and that she had threatened her fellow patients," a man said. *The police.* "She was also seen running away from the facility after the incident. We have no choice but to arrest her."

Roslyn gritted her teeth. *Of course Phedre pinned the explosion on me. I need to get out of here.* She hurried over to the still-open window and climbed back out onto the tree branch. She had just descended out of view when she heard the door *swish* open.

"See? No one's here," Mrs. Bhanushali said. "What did you say happened at the psychiatric hospital?"

"The window's open," the cop said. Roslyn heard the blip of his datapad as she dropped to the ground. "Check the ground outside my position. Suspect may still be present on site."

Shit. Roslyn ran. She was faster than the cops, or at least knew the grounds better, as she was able to slip through an opening in the fence as the policemen rounded the corner. Their lights focused on the house, not on the fence, so she was able to make a clean getaway.

When she got to the train station, she discovered the next train to Daedalus wasn't for another five hours. Since she didn't want to buy the ticket until the last minute in case they were tracking her credits, she plopped down in one of the chairs in the waiting area. For the first time, she didn't have to fall asleep for the memories to come.

Twenty Years Ago

Roslyn drifted toward consciousness. *I must be sick again.* Her head was pounding, and when she tried to sit up, her limbs wouldn't move. *I'm really going to die this time.*

"I'm afraid that looks likely." She hadn't realized she had spoken the words aloud until someone to her left answered her. *Jack.*

Roslyn opened her eyes. She was lying in the vault in Arachne, surrounded by green sigils. Her fellow Transients were in the room with her. Jack, Cobalt, and Gavin had black metal rope coiled around them, and Tegan was standing some distance away with a large knife in her hand. Roslyn tried to move again and discovered that rope, not illness, was restricting her movements.

"Cuttlefish turned on us," Jack said.

"What?" Roslyn stared dumbly around the room. "Why?"

"Well, I'm not one hundred percent sure. But my guess is we're the Ringati, and our blood is going to open the mystery box."

Roslyn laid her head back on the cold stone. "But Phedre doesn't know how to activate the device. Our blood isn't going to open anything."

"I know." Jack flashed a grin that didn't last. "It's my one consolation for not getting to see you for twenty years. But I'll find you, Rosie. As soon as the memories come back, I'll find you."

She shook her head. "There's got to be a way out of this. We're not going to die. Not now." *Not when we've finally found each other.* Roslyn looked away from Jack, and her gaze settled on Cobalt. He was talking to Tegan. Judging from the expression on her face, Roslyn thought the conversation was not going in their favor. Tears stung her eyes. They really were going to die.

Roslyn looked back at Jack. "Yes!" she said.

Jack's brow furrowed. "You're excited that we're going to die?"

"Yes. I mean, no. I mean..." She took a deep breath. "I mean, yes, I will marry you."

A smile crept over Jack's face until his grin was the brightest he had ever given her. "You picked a great time to tell me."

A goofy grin rose on her face too. "Well, there's no time like the present."

"Okay, everybody." Tegan burst their little bubble. "Time's up. Any last words?"

"The rocks say you only need three of us, right, Tegan?" Jack said. "So you could let one of us go."

"Trying to save yourself, Jack? Why am I not surprised?" Tegan stepped toward him. "Just for that, I'm happy to let you die first."

"I wasn't asking for me."

Tegan's eyebrows shot up. "You're willing to sacrifice yourself for your lady love? That's new."

Jack wore an expression of steadfast determination, and

Roslyn's heart tried to claw its way out of her chest to go to him. "Please," he said. "I'm begging you, Cuttlefish."

Tegan's face shut down. "Sorry, Night Thief. My orders are that she dies even if the rest of you don't. But I'll tell you what... you can die first so you don't have to watch her die."

Jack closed his eyes in defeat, but as Tegan approached, he looked up and laughed. "I love you. I'll find you," he said to Roslyn. He turned to Cobalt. "See you tomorrow, Blue."

Tegan grabbed Jack by the hair and pulled his head back, exposing his throat. As she brought the knife down, Roslyn couldn't bring herself to look away. She wanted to see Jack for as long as possible, even if that meant watching cold steel carve into his neck. As she watched, she screamed, unable to keep silent as blood gushed from the wound and the light went out of his eyes. Then Tegan turned to Roslyn, and she knew her time was up.

CHAPTER 47

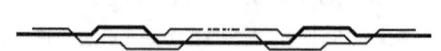

Present Day

"CRONOS, TRAINS ARE SO SLOW," Lexi said as the train left the station from Ariadne.

Will tried not to roll his eyes. As Lexi adjusted to life as a Transient, she was always the worst version of herself. She had complained the entire way from Orpheus to Ariadne. *Hopefully, she'll get tired and go to sleep on the trip to Daedalus.* "Trains are faster than individual spaceships," he said.

Lexi gave him a disgusted look. "Not the way I drive."

"Well, we couldn't afford an individual spaceship, and your father would only loan us one of his Daedalus vessels, so we're stuck with what we've got." Will looked at Bliss, expecting her to roll her eyes at Lexi's ridiculousness, but she was focused on a last-minute passenger looking for a seat.

"Roslyn?" Bliss said. "Cronos, it *is* you! Roslyn!"

Will jerked his head up. Bliss was right. The passenger making her way up the aisle toward them was his sister. Bliss stood up to go meet her friend, but Will was faster. He quickly stumbled down the narrow aisle to where Roslyn was standing and wrapped her in a hug.

"Will!" Roslyn returned the embrace. "What are you doing here?"

"I might ask you the same question." He glanced around at his fellow passengers, but those who were staring at them did so with affection rather than suspicion. "We should probably discuss this more quietly."

"Ugh, I'm starving." Lexi glared at Roslyn, so Will suspected hunger was not Lexi's actual problem. "I'm going to see if there's any food to be had on this miserable train." She stepped out into the aisle and made it past a few seats before turning back. "Bliss, are you coming?"

"I don't think *no* is an option." Bliss gave Roslyn a small smile. "We'll catch up later, okay? I'm sorry about everything."

"Oh, Lexi," Roslyn said as she sat next to Will. "I didn't miss you."

"Hey!" Will was about to say, "That's my girlfriend you're talking about," but he wasn't sure that was true. He wasn't sure it would ever be true again.

"Well, forgive me for not liking the woman who has treated my brother like shit for millennia," Roslyn said.

"I'm always nice to Jack!"

"To his face! You say nothing but trash about him behind his back!"

"Gavin loves you, Roslyn!"

"And Bliss loves you!" Roslyn sank farther down in her seat. "What a pair we are."

Will scrunched himself up so their shoulders were even. "Bliss kissed me," he said.

At the same time, Roslyn said, "He asked me to marry him."

"Wait, what?" Will asked. "Gavin asked you to marry him?"

Roslyn shook her head. "Jack did."

"What? *When?*"

"Last life. On Arachne. I nearly died, and it nearly killed

him, and—" She broke off and stared out the window into space. "I said yes. I love him."

"And I love Lexi," Will said, though he didn't sound convincing, even to his ears.

"Yet you're telling me that Bliss kissed you, which means something."

Will spread his fingers out in front of him, trying to grasp what he wanted to say. "She's different in this life. Bliss is. She's less... saintly."

"Tell me about it," Roslyn said. "You know she got me locked up in a psychiatric hospital?"

Will ignored her, promising himself that he would get back to Roslyn's problems in a minute. "Lexi is the same old Lexi, and maybe, just maybe, it's not working out for us this time."

Roslyn patted him on the shoulder. "With our mother, it's lucky we're capable of having emotional attachments at all, much less functional ones. You'll figure it out."

"Speaking of our mother," Will said. "I think she's up to her old tricks."

"Oh, I *know* she is." Roslyn sat up straighter. "She tried to blow me up."

"What?"

"We'd better fill each other in on why we're heading to Daedalus, or as I suspect is both of our final destinations, Arachne."

In hushed voices, Roslyn and Will filled each other in and formed a plan.

CHAPTER 48

Present Day

JACK WOKE UP WITH THE strangest feeling of déjà vu. He was tied up and lying on a black stone floor covered in green sigils, and he knew for a fact he had never been there before. Tegan O'Leary and a brown-haired woman he didn't recognize were standing behind a podium. His head ached like there was no tomorrow, and judging by the knife in Tegan's hand, he knew there wouldn't be.

Cobalt was sitting to his left, and a tall, dark-skinned man he didn't recognize was on his right.

Jack groaned. "Blue, what's going on? Do we know this guy?" He nodded at the man on his right.

To Jack's surprise, the stranger answered, or at least spoke to Cobalt over his head. "He really doesn't remember anything, does he?"

"Not a thing," Cobalt said. "It's getting kind of annoying. Our working theory is that Demitrius blocked his memories."

The man nodded. "That makes sense, given something Demitrius said to me." He turned to Jack. "My name is Gavin Ibori."

The name sounded familiar. "You were in the Bellerophon Games!"

Gavin inclined his head in acknowledgment. "You may

not remember it, but once upon a time, we were friends, of a sort. I once saved you from a rampaging trimper."

Jack wanted to kick his legs in frustration. "I wish everyone would stop telling me I don't remember things. My memory is fine, and even if it weren't, I'm pretty sure I would remember a live trimper."

Before Gavin had time to answer, a sickly green glow filled the room. The brown-haired woman lovingly set a spinning rock onto the podium.

"What's going on?" Jack asked.

Tegan didn't answer, just came around the podium, brandishing the knife.

"Are you really going to kill us again, Cuttlefish?" Gavin's voice was soft and sad.

"I don't have a choice!" She pointed the knife at Jack. "If he hadn't lied to us about the device last time around, none of this would be necessary. We would have opened the vault, and you could go on your merry ways in this life."

"I don't remember that," Jack said. "But it does sound like something I would do. I have zero problem lying to evil people to stop them from fulfilling their evil plans."

Tegan stepped toward him. "You have no idea—"

"Drop that knife!"

Everyone's heads turned toward the entrance, where a crowd of people led by Roslyn—*my Roslyn*, Jack thought—aimed any number of pistols at Tegan's head.

CHAPTER 49

Present Day

L EXI FLEW HER FATHER'S SPACESHIP to Arachne faster than
Roslyn would have thought possible. *She's always been
a reckless driver—skilled but reckless.*

"What are we going to do when we get there?" Bliss
asked, looking nervous. Roslyn couldn't tell whether Bliss
was concerned about the situation or afraid to talk because
Roslyn was still a bit miffed with her.

Knowing Bliss, probably both. "It's fine. Set up a
communication line with the moon as soon as we're within
range. I've got an in."

"Let's hope comm range is farther out than gun range,"
Will said, looking out the viewscreen at the metallic satellites
orbiting the black moon. "Did the place have those defenses
when you were last here?"

"Don't worry about it. I can dodge anything they throw at
us," Lexi said.

Bliss pressed the button to hail the moon. When nothing
happened, she pressed the button again. As the ship glided
closer to its destination, her finger jumped up and down on
the button like an Old Earth jackhammer. Roslyn wanted
to tell her to stop before she broke the thing, but before
she could, lights appeared on the defense satellites. Bliss

pushed the button even faster, which Roslyn hadn't thought possible.

Red lights appeared in the laser ports on the satellites, and six rays fired at the Transients' vessel. Lexi turned the ship almost sideways to avoid getting hit, and she was the only one to remain upright. In the few seconds it took Bliss to right herself, the comm station indicated a call was coming in. Bliss answered it.

A blond woman with crow's-feet around her piercing blue eyes appeared on the screen. "Incoming vessel, you are not expected. Please identify yourself."

Roslyn motioned for Bliss to move and took her vacated seat. "Well, well, well," she said to the woman on the screen. "If it isn't Hannah Carriger. Stolen anyone's boyfriend recently?"

Even over the poor connection, Hannah visibly paled. "Roslyn Turin? No, it can't be. You're dead. I buried you myself."

Demitrius is going to kill me. For some reason, the thought brought a smile to her face. With any luck, she would piss off both her parents that day. "Death is so passé, don't you think?"

The ship rocked as something struck it.

"What happened to 'I can dodge anything they throw at us,' Lexi?" Will yelled.

"They've got some kind of tracker on the lasers," she said. "I've dodged more of them than you could."

Roslyn decided she'd better get down to business before the ship exploded and she failed to stop Phedre in the current life as well as the last one. "Look, Hannah. Let us land. We can help you out with your Phedre problem."

Hannah gave a bitter laugh. "No one can help us with our Phedre problem. It's been a reign of terror down here since you... since you left. You think we haven't tried to get her out of here before? We've called in dozens of government investigation teams. Phedre plays nice with them for a few weeks, then they're gone, and things get even worse for us for reporting her."

Roslyn gripped the arms of her chair to stay upright as the ship rocked. "Didn't you show them our bodies? You said you buried them."

Tears formed in the corners of Hannah's eyes. "She moved them. I don't know where. She probably destroyed them."

"Hannah, Phedre wants to murder people tonight, the same way she murdered us twenty years ago. If you let us down, we can stop her, and we can get evidence that she did it. I've got a journalist with me who can help."

Hannah rubbed her face. "I'm losing my mind. I have to be. I'm finally cracking under the stress."

"Then you've got nothing to lose," Roslyn said. "Please. Turn off the lasers and let us land."

Hannah took a deep, shuddery breath then nodded. "Okay," she said. "Come on down. But know that some people here are still loyal to Phedre." She pushed a few buttons on her datapad. "I've rebooted the satellites. That should give you enough time to get down."

Roslyn nodded at Lexi, who steered the ship toward the surface.

"We should have brought someone who could fight," Will said. "We're a journalist, an archaeologist, a social worker, and a singer. What are we going to do against Phedre's bodyguards?"

"I'm a business student!" Bliss said in a small voice, but everyone ignored her.

"We'll just have to recruit some people down there," Roslyn said with certainty she didn't feel. "Hannah said Phedre's made everyone's life miserable. We'll have to persuade people to help us out."

Lexi landed the ship smoothly, and Roslyn headed for the hatch and jumped out before it had finished opening. By the time Bliss and Will followed her out, a small crowd of people had formed outside the ship. New arrivals were still a novelty on Arachne, it seemed, and most ships that came were government issue. The Transients had flown in on an electric-blue personal pleasure cruiser that stood out against the black Arachne backdrop like a sore thumb.

"Who are you?" a man in front asked. "I didn't know we were expecting visitors."

"My name is Roslyn Turin." Roslyn's voice rang strong and clear across the crowd. "I used to work here, oh, so many years ago."

"Wait, I know that name," a woman in the back of the crowd said. "Roslyn Turin is the name of one of the people who died in the accident on the site twenty years ago."

Accident? Is that how Phedre explained our deaths? I wonder what kind of accident results in four slit throats.

Another man pushed his way to the front of the crowd. Roslyn vaguely remembered him from her dreams. "I remember Roslyn and her team. That is her. But... she died. Or at least Phedre said she did."

"I've come back," Roslyn said, keeping her tone steady and confident. "I've come because Phedre Turin is a murderer, and if we don't stop her, she's going to kill more people."

A buzz went through the crowd, and Roslyn couldn't tell if they supported her or not. Eventually, the first man spoke again. "You can't stop Phedre."

"I can," Roslyn said. "*We* can. She left the moon for a while, right? She was gathering people she wanted to use as human sacrifices. She believes if she kills them on the ruin site, she can uncover alien secrets."

"She and her lackey, O'Leary, did drag some people to the dig site when she got back," someone spoke up.

"We were supposed to stay in our tents," another person hissed.

"So I peeked!"

"Why would she make you stay in your tents unless she was doing something she didn't want you to see?" Will came up and stood beside Roslyn. "Something that could get her in trouble."

"Who is this guy?"

He gave the crowd a bright smile and held up his camera for the people to see. "I'm Will Turin, journalist."

"Will you help us?" Roslyn asked.

The crowd murmured again, and eventually, a collective agreement rose among them. "Armed guards are standing watch outside the site, though," the first man said. "And we're not allowed to have weapons."

"Lucky for you all, this is my daddy's hunting vessel." Lexi appeared in the hatch, carrying two laser rifles. "Who among you is a decent shot?"

After a few more moments of murmuring from the crowd, Bliss raised a shaky hand. Will and Lexi looked at her, aghast.

Roslyn smacked her hand against her forehead. "Of course! Mr. Bhanushali takes Bliss to the rifle range all the time. It's his idea of father-daughter bonding time."

"I hate it," Bliss said. "But set a rifle to stun, and I can snipe the guards."

"I can help," another man said, coming forward. "I was born on Bellerophon, though I managed to escape to become an archaeologist."

"You got any more guns in there, Lex?" Will asked. "Somehow I doubt Phedre's going to stop just because we kill her guards."

"Daddy doesn't believe in handguns." Lexi tossed her beaded braids over her shoulder. "We'll have to steal pistols from the downed guards."

Roslyn nodded. "We have a plan. Bliss, you and... What's your name?" she asked the sniper volunteer.

"Ethan," he said. "Ethan Cameron."

"Bliss and Ethan will find a place where they can hide and still shoot the guards. Maybe that hill behind the mess tent?"

He nodded. "I know the spot. It's a good choice."

"The rest of us will move in when the guards get distracted," Roslyn said.

"Wait a minute." Will grabbed Bliss by the arms. "Are you sure you want to do this? You're basically acting as bait."

Bliss put a hand on one of his. "It's fine. I can do this. I'll just have to shoot them down before they get to me."

Will looked like he was about to protest further, but Lexi interrupted. "As loath as I am to disrupt this moment, my brother is likely going to die any minute now, so if we could speed things along?"

"Right." Bliss extracted herself from Will's grasp and nodded at Ethan, and the two of them headed off behind the tents.

Roslyn led the group around the tents on the other side of camp, moving as slowly and silently as she could. She expected the people behind her were attempting the same, but she was worried about the noise they were making. When the guards came into view, she stumbled to a halt. *Six of them. Enough for them to split if they see us, each of them with at least three pistols I can see.* She inhaled sharply when one glanced her way. *Please let me be enough in the shadows that he can't see me.*

The guard took a step toward Roslyn, but before he could take another, the guard next to him took a blue laser bolt to the chest and collapsed. The remaining guards' attention turned toward Bliss and Ethan as two more blasts took down two more guards. The three left standing ran toward the hill behind the mess tent, and Roslyn took a moment to hope for Bliss's safety.

As soon as the guards cleared the entrance to the dig site, Roslyn led her people, still as silently as possible, to the entrance. She stopped to pick up a laser pistol off the fallen guard and motioned that Will and Lexi should do the same. A few of the Arachneans followed suit. Then she led them through the opening into the dig site.

The ruins looked exactly as Roslyn remembered them from her dream, green sigils filling the rocky cavern with ghostly light. Phedre was standing behind the podium, placing the spinning Ringati device into its keyhole, Tegan was lurking in front of the podium, brandishing the same knife she had used to kill Roslyn all those years ago, and Gavin, Cobalt, and Jack were tied up in the same positions as before.

Roslyn wasn't there this time, though. She wasn't tied up and powerless. She aimed her pistol straight at Tegan. "Drop that knife!"

Tegan obeyed and held her hands up, a look akin to relief flashing across her face. Roslyn turned her attention to Phedre, who, upon seeing the crowd of people who had come to take her down, threw back her head and laughed.

"Oh, Roslyn," she said. "My dear, sweet Roslyn. My ever-brave daughter. Did you really think you could come here and best me?"

"I can. You'll never threaten me or these people again."

Phedre turned to the crowd. "Did she tell you who she is? Just a server girl from Ariadne, one who's spent the past several weeks in a psychiatric institution for her paranoid delusions. She thinks she lived here twenty years ago, when anyone can see by looking at her that she's not nearly old enough."

"She did live here!" the man who had remembered her called. "I knew her then!"

"Did you? But surely that's impossible. The girl who was here twenty years ago died. You all saw the body at the time. Dead people don't just come back to life."

Murmurs rose from the crowd again, and Roslyn could hear them turning against her. The doubt she had felt for the past few weeks at the institution crept into her brain. *Maybe this is all some elaborate delusion. Maybe I'm still dreaming.*

I'm not dreaming, and if I were, I'm in charge, not her. "It

303

doesn't matter who I am! It matters who you are and what you've done. You've got three people whom you plan to kill tied up on the ground."

"Well, I wasn't planning to kill anyone." She glowered at Tegan. "But it looks like my minion is scared of a few pistols."

"Give it up, Phedre," Tegan said. "We've lost."

"Have we?" Phedre scanned the crowd, as if looking for the right person to influence. "Zachariah." She took a few steps forward, seemingly unconcerned that nine laser pistols remained trained on her.

"Yes?" a man standing at Roslyn's shoulder asked.

"How is your lovely daughter? You would love to see her again, wouldn't you?"

"Of course." Zachariah sounded nervous. Roslyn didn't blame him. Phedre was clearly playing some game.

"Well, you're not going to." Phedre pressed a button on her datapad, and with a splatter of blood and bone against Roslyn's face, Zachariah's head exploded.

The crowd remained silent for a moment until the *thud* of Zachariah's body hitting the floor echoed through the cavern. Then everyone spoke or screamed at once.

"Silence!" Phedre yelled, and everyone obeyed. In a calmer voice, she continued. "You thought I didn't have a contingency for all of you turning on me? Those medical tracking chips you all wear? I had them rigged with explosives. So now all of you have a choice. You can tie up those three"—she pointed at Roslyn, Lexi, and Will—"or you can end up like Zachariah there. The choice is yours."

Before Roslyn could wipe the blood from her face or turn the pistol to defend herself, she was disarmed and dragged toward the center of the room. Metallic ropes wrapped around her limbs and torso, keeping her in place. *At least they put me by Jack,* she thought, looking over at him with tears in her eyes. He had been uncharacteristically silent through the argument. She wondered if he remembered her as more than the server girl from Ariadne.

"Now, Tegan," Phedre said. "Pick up that knife and kill them."

Tegan bent down and retrieved her knife. She stared at the blade for a long time, as if trying to see the bloodstains from the Transients she had killed long ago. "Did you put an explosive in my chip as well?" she asked, her voice distant and casual.

"Of course not," Phedre said, punching something into her datapad and not looking at Tegan. "Your blood is too valuable."

"Good." Tegan reached over the podium and stabbed Phedre in the gut.

"Wha—?" Phedre collapsed onto the ground, clutching the knife hilt. "Why, you miserable traitor! You—" A gurgle came from her throat.

"Get out of here," Tegan said to the crowd. They didn't need to be told twice. They all but ran out the door as Ethan and Bliss came rushing in.

"What happened here?" Bliss asked.

Roslyn was at a loss for words, and Tegan seemed disinclined to answer. She strode over to Gavin and untied his bonds. "Save her miserable life," she said, nodding at Phedre. "I don't want her being reborn to start over. I want her spending some serious time in jail for what she's done."

Gavin ran over to Phedre's side and pressed his hands to her wound. "Get a medic and a gurney," he said to Ethan, who nodded and left.

"You're going to jail, too, you know," Roslyn told Tegan.

Tegan gave a mirthless laugh. "Believe me... after the last two decades, jail sounds like a vacation."

Bliss untied Will first and gave him a tight hug. "I can't believe I shot those guards," she said.

"I'm a little surprised myself," Will said. "But I shouldn't be. You're the bravest person I know."

Lexi snorted, and for once, Roslyn was grateful to the girl for expressing what none of the rest of them dared. "You going to let the rest of us out, or what?"

Will and Bliss untied Roslyn and Cobalt then finally Jack.

"Hey, Roslyn," Jack said as he waited for his turn. "Not that I'm not thrilled to see you and your friends, but how in Cronos's name did you know to be here?"

"Don't explain it to him," Cobalt said. "He'll only forget, and it'll get super annoying."

When Jack was untied, Roslyn pulled him to her in a tight hug. Over his shoulder, she met Gavin's eyes. He had a sad smile on his face, then he turned away from her to lift Phedre onto the gurney Ethan had brought.

They all headed out of the ruins. Roslyn expected the crowd of people to still be hovering outside the entrance, but the only figure there was a thin white-clad figure with graying blond hair.

Roslyn approached Hannah. "I suppose I owe you an explanation for... everything."

"No. Well, yes, you do, and I want it more than I can say, but that's not why I came over here." She took a deep breath. "You were murdered here twenty years ago. I knew it, and I said nothing. Phedre claimed it was an accident, but I saw the bodies. Your throats were slit."

The memory of Tegan's blade cutting through her neck overwhelmed Roslyn for a moment. "Yes."

"Yeah." Hannah reached into her pocket and pulled something out. It glittered in the dim light. "I found this on your body. I tried to clean it up as best I could, and I've held onto it for all these years for reasons I couldn't even begin to tell you. But it's yours."

Hannah held out what looked like a necklace, and Roslyn started as she recognized the engagement ring Jack had given her twenty years ago. Tears welled in her eyes as she took it from Hannah. "Thank you."

"I've called the authorities, and they're going to come

pick up Tegan and Phedre," Hannah said. "I'm going to recommend this research facility be shut down. You guys clearly have secrets, big ones, and you deserve to keep them."

"I will tell you, if you want to know," Roslyn said.

"No," Hannah said. "I've spent the last twenty years living in fear of what Phedre would do to me if I stepped out of line. Now I don't have to fear anymore. That's worth more to me than your secrets. It'll remain a mystery to me. I could use some mysteries in my old age."

Roslyn slipped the chain around her neck and hid the ring under her shirt. "Thank you, Hannah."

CHAPTER 50

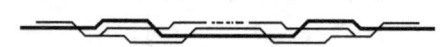

Present Day

"WELL, Ms. TURIN, YOU ARE a very lucky young lady."
Roslyn didn't feel particularly lucky, but she figured if the man at the police station in a very expensive suit thought she was lucky, she had better at least pretend to agree. "How so, sir?"

The man sat opposite her in the police interrogation room on Ariadne. "The cops called me in to investigate your case. It seems that one Phedre Turin—she's not any relation, is she?"

"*No.*"

"Well, it seems that she targeted you specifically. She came here all the way from Arachne, took you on as a psychiatric patient—her only patient, I may add—and sent you to an institution. She called the police, insisting you were dangerous and planned to hurt people at the facility."

"That's crazy," Roslyn said. "Why would she do all that to get to me? I'm just an ordinary server."

The man folded his hands. "If you don't know, Ms. Turin, I'm certain I don't. Fortunately for you, we have video evidence of her purchasing the explosives detonated at the institution. She's also been arrested on several charges related to her time on Arachne, which are so confidential even I can't get my hands on them."

Roslyn didn't have to feign her relief. "I suppose it's back to the Bhanushalis for me."

"Actually, that's something else." The man pulled something up on his datapad. "When I looked over your record, I discovered Dr. Turin was instrumental in keeping you out of university. The case was predicated on your scoring above expectations on art history and archaeology, but your scores in the basic subjects were sufficient to win you a scholarship as well."

"What are you saying? I can go to Chora?"

"You'll be starting school three weeks behind schedule," the man said. "You will have to work very hard to catch up, or else you will be back with the Bhanushalis."

Roslyn couldn't keep the smile off her face. "I can work hard, and believe me, sir, I will!"

"Let me get this straight," Detective Polanski said. "You're telling me you didn't steal those diamonds. They were the payment for extensive repairs you made to Tegan O'Leary's ship."

Jack and Cobalt were back in an interrogation room on Ariadne, but at least they were together that time.

"That's correct," Jack said. "We had no idea they were the stolen diamonds you had come after us for."

"Yet you ran away."

Jack spread out his hands. "What did you expect us to do? You insisted we had stolen those diamonds, and we hadn't. We didn't want to go to jail for nothing. O'Leary was the one who blasted a hole in your cruiser. We were just trying to get away from her. She clearly wanted to kill us to prevent us from ratting her out."

Polanski tapped his finger on the table. "Do you have any proof whatsoever of your claim? We have no record of Tegan

O'Leary on the train that was robbed. Both of you, however, were there."

Cobalt spoke up, surprising Jack. "The wires in her navigation computer are braided. Red, orange, and white. You'll see they're the same as on the *Rose*. Nobody does that but me."

Polanski narrowed his eyes and nodded. "I'll check it out." He left the room.

Jack wanted to ask how Cobalt knew about the wires, but not in full view of the cameras, so they waited in silence for a few hours until Polanski returned.

"Your story checks out," the detective said. "It helps that Tegan O'Leary is wanted for some secret crimes on Arachne and blew a hole in our police cruiser. I'm willing to let you go with a fine."

"Let me guess," Cobalt said. "The *Rose* and whatever diamonds we have remaining."

Polanski smiled.

Bliss waited for Will outside his office in Chora. Lexi and Gavin had driven into town with her, but they decided to go off and have brother-sister bonding time. Bliss wished Gavin luck. Lexi had been absolutely miserable since she couldn't become a famous singer.

Eventually, Will came down the stairs, looking rather serious.

"So?" Bliss asked. "How did it go?"

"Well enough, all things considered," Will said. "George likes the story of aliens on Arachne better than aliens on the university campus. More plausible, he says. He's still a little pissed about the university tuition, but I get to keep my job, and Demitrius won't remember I told anyone about us."

Bliss grinned. "Sounds like you've got everything covered."

Will's face remained serious. "Not everything. You kissed me, Bliss."

Her smile fell. She'd prepared herself for an "I like you, but I'm eternally devoted to Lexi" conversation, but she'd hoped Will would be too cowardly to have it. "Yeah, I did."

"That's all you have to say about it?"

Bliss held out her hands. "What else is there to say?"

"You're right," Will said. "I can't think of a thing." He grabbed her arms and pulled her closer to him, and suddenly, his lips were on hers.

Happiness bubbled up in her as she returned the kiss. Will's change of heart might not last forever, but she planned to embrace it as long as she could.

Roslyn slipped into one of the few empty chairs in her first art history class. The professor hadn't seemed thrilled about a new student joining three weeks into the semester, but Roslyn had answered all his pre-test questions, so she could stay.

As soon as Roslyn got out her datapad and set it to record, the door swished open, and Jack walked in. He showed his datapad to the professor, who rolled his eyes and muttered something about "another new student" then gestured for him to take a seat.

He chose the spot immediately in front of Roslyn.

"What are you doing here?" she whispered.

Jack stretched his legs out into the aisle. "I'm an art history student now."

"What? You don't know anything about art!" She had tried to interest him in any number of pieces over the years, and he had shown little to no appreciation for it.

"Well, that's why I'm here. To learn." He nodded toward a student in the front row with a striped shirt and a red beret. "I figure if that schlub can understand art, I can too. Besides, if I'm an utter failure, you'll just have to help me." Jack winked at her.

She wanted to question him further, but the professor

started class. Roslyn's smile remained in place for the entirety of the lecture. He was still her Jack, and he would remember her someday.